"Was Nietzsche right? Does the abyss truly gaze into us? St. Jarre has penned a haunting tale of one man's quest to circumvent an incomprehensible and unstoppable evil. Far too believable, and absolutely terrifying, the cost of this pursuit may be beyond imagining. Cinematic, timeless, and well-executed, *Absence of Grace* will stick with you long after reading the final page."

—**Bruce Robert Coffin**, award-winning author of the Detective Byron Mysteries

"Part *Jacob's Ladder*, part Dan Brown's *Inferno*, St. Jarre's *Absence of Grace* is a dizzying, full-tilt ride into the origins of evil and those who pull the strings behind it. I couldn't put it down."

—**Katherine Silva**, award-winning author of *The Wild Dark*

Novels by Kevin St. Jarre

Aliens, Drywall, and a Unicycle

Celestine

The Twin

ABSENCE OF GRACE

KEVIN ST. JARRE

Encircle Publications
Farmington, Maine, U.S.A.

Paperback ISBN 13: 978-1-64599-316-2
Hardcover ISBN 13: 978-1-64599-317-9
E-book ISBN 13: 978-1-64599-318-6
Kindle ISBN 13: 978-1-64599-319-3

Library of Congress Control Number (LCCN): 2022930992

Cover design by Christopher Wait
Cover photographs © Getty Images

Published by:

Encircle Publications
PO Box 187
Farmington, ME 04938

info@encirclepub.com
http://encirclepub.com

For my son, Dmitri,
who I will always think of as my Meetch.
I love you.

I

"Whoever fights monsters should see to it that in the process, he does not become a monster."
—Friedrich Nietzsche

Ch: 1

Morning
Coford Brook
Goodwin, Maine

Her skin was pale; it gave but didn't bounce back. It sort of stayed indented. The impression of his stick remained, whiter than the grey around it. He never knew her—the girl from the posters. He didn't know she'd be there, and he hadn't been looking for anything more than something to do. He was only looking for crayfish to catch. Going through the culvert made much more sense than climbing the bank, crossing the street, and then sliding down the gravel on the other side.

When Jack Killarney and his friends came to the corrugated steel culverts, they always went through them. Their hands would stick to the spots of pitch on the inside and the air would change from fresh brook-side breeze to a stale, petroleum-based stench. With their hair shorn by fathers with barber's clippers, nothing really got in it. They would waddle through the pipe, watching the stream pass between their plaid shorts and tan, bony legs. The water would darken as they went, seem to swirl more, and they wondered at the creatures that must live under the few rocks they saw. It would be dicey to lift those slick stones, because stopping forward progress might lead to falling into the water, so widely set were their feet.

But it was in there, beneath the undeveloped end of 22nd Avenue, where he found her. In the distance, backlit by the opposite end of the culvert, she could have been a clutch of branches cluttered with plastic Zayre bags.

Lying there, her body caught on a discarded car wheel, the cold rushing water pushing up her floral dress. She was bloated and, despite the current, nothing else moved but her hair. Her mouth was open, and there were bruises on her throat—purplish-brown against the grey. Marks left by the danger that so many mothers have long warned their children about. The bruises were left behind by the evil hidden in every dark basement, under every bed, and inside every windowless van. However, Jack wasn't scared—instead, he was curious.

He had picked up the stick, with half of the bark missing, and about the diameter of his mom's hair curlers, it was as long as his leg. It was pinned beneath the girl's right arm. He pulled and she held onto it. With a yank it came free, but the arm didn't move. Maybe it tore free.

Why didn't she smell, he wondered? Was the water washing that away? Just the odor of the pipe, and water too rich with life. Except for her.

He used the stick to stay away and yet touch her. Her skin caved, like mud under soft cloth. He wasn't nauseated. He was fascinated. The way a child might be interested in anything odd found beneath a rock or log.

Everyone knew she was missing, but she wasn't from town. She wasn't much younger than he was. He poked again—poke, poke. Why the hell was he poking her? He knew she wouldn't wake. Was he trying to push her out of his way? He was three-quarters of the way to the end. Was he poking her because he didn't want to have to walk upstream? He duck-walked closer. Her dress moved a bit on the downstream side of her. He tried to move her hand with the stick and it did lift a little, but it required more effort than he expected.

He looked at both sides of the pipe to see how he might get past her. He couldn't have both feet on either side of the brook. The water was too high on the walls of the pipe. He moved closer. Could he duck-walk over her? It felt a dangerous and disrespectful thing to do, but he decided to try it anyway. Slowly, he went slowly, his steps small and echoing, mingling with the gurgling. He passed over her—her feet, her legs, her thighs. He straddled her, above her, looking down. There was a glimpse of underwear. Were they on backwards? He lifted his gaze so as not to see. Looking at her chest and throat, he could see she was ashen. As he stood over her face, he could see her eyes were not completely shut. They were like those of the many fish he'd caught in the same brook, when they came out of the freezer, when his mom would fry up five or six of the little trout to make a respectable lunch for one young boy—filled with tiny bones.

Her hair framed her face, but it had given up long ago. He passed completely over her, and then realized she was behind him.

He braced his hands against the ceiling of the pipe, panicked. For the first time since he'd found her, she was looking at him, but he couldn't see her. Committing to turning around, he quickly brought both feet to one side, and then threw one foot back to where the other had been. It slipped. He fell to his knees onto the girl's left arm, and it flattened sickeningly beneath him. Putting his hands out to catch himself, he lifted his knees off her, and he sank into her middle. He reflexively let his elbows bend so the pressure on his hands would be lessened, and he came down with a crash into the water. There was a burning in his arm as it ran down the edge of the rusting wheel that anchored her. His face went into the water. Downstream of her. He drank her—in his mouth, nose, and eyes.

He leapt to his feet, horrified. She was shifted now, and shaped differently. Her dress was up higher. His fault, he did that, he thought. The water, the girl-tea, ran off him mixing with his blood, and dripped from his arm and hand. Stepping backward and stumbling on a rock, he fell to one knee. He looked at her, looked down, and rose again. Turning all but his head, he felt his way out of the pipe. He stepped out into the open stream and looked up at the sky.

What was she doing there? Why did she do this to us? He looked at his wet clothing, the blood, and he stood there in the calf-deep brook. The water ran past him and into a wall of granite before turning right and heading downstream, north, beneath the tracks, through another culvert, to the river. When he turned back to her, the tears came. She wasn't right now. She looked horribly wronged. He had found her, and knew nothing of her, and he had fucked her up.

"I'm so sorry," he wept. "I'll get someone, I'll get someone." He almost added a plea for patience, but he thought she'd been patient enough. He scampered up the gravel embankment, with the sand beneath the larger pebbles sticking to his wet and bloody clothing and skin. It lodged beneath his nails. Reaching the weeds, and stepping out into an empty lot near where the avenue transitioned from pavement to dirt, he staggered a bit, and then broke into a run. He was drying. She was drying on him. She'd never come off.

Ch: 2

Decades later
June 1
Morning
Williamsburg
Brooklyn, NY

The windshield wipers swept away the light rain, but not the grey. Jack looked left, past his partner Ben, as Keely's Lounge went by. Its blood-red exterior, rain-soaked, looked more than a little sinister. The radio chirped again, the voice excited, competing with the dragging sound of the wipers. Jack lay back in his seat and folded his arms.

Up ahead, where Metropolitan met North 6th before it passed beneath the Brooklyn-Queens Expressway, sat a burning dumpster. Thick black smoke billowed from beneath its lid. Jack saw the patrol cars and a firetruck parked around it, their flashing lights painting the gloom.

As soon as Jack stepped from the vehicle, a uniformed officer approached.

"Detective. Sergeant Wells," he said. "You're not going to believe this one."

Jack buttoned his coat. "I remember you, from that thing over on Meeker," Jack said, nodding north. "What have you got?"

"Victims," Wells answered. "We don't know how many, but from the smell, there's a few in there. Looks like someone threw them in and set fire to them. Smells like burning bodies and diesel."

Jack walked past Wells, and Ben and the sergeant followed.

"Nobody saw anything?" Ben asked. "It's broad fucking daylight. I mean, who dumps bodies in a dumpster, at a crowded intersection, beneath a busy overpass, in the middle of the day?"

"I know, right?" Sergeant Wells answered. "We're knocking on doors now. We got one witness says he saw a guy with a dark coat and a limp."

"Are you kidding me?" Ben asked. "A limp? That's our description?"

"Thanks, Sergeant," Jack said, just dismissively enough.

Wells left, and walked over to a cluster of other uniformed officers. Firefighters approached with a pike and pushed the dumpster open, allowing the steel lid to flip over the back with a clang. Flames rolled up and out, and acrid smoke rose to meet the rain.

"Whoever it was, wasn't afraid," Jack said. Jack ran his fingers through his short hair and water ran down his neck. Scattered around the base of the dumpster were lifeless forms of dead pigeons, maybe a dozen of them.

Ben saw them, too, and asked, "What's with the birds?"

The firefighters stepped back. Jack and Ben approached and looked into the dumpster. Through intermittent gaps in the smoke they could see six adults, sitting up in the bottom of the dumpster as friends might around a card table. Hair, eyes, and lips gone; sitting and grinning at each other in a whirl of red-orange flames. Clothing spent or melting, with the skin bubbling. It wasn't the sight, however, but the smell.

Jack suddenly felt dizzy, and nauseated. He put his hand out to steady himself and would have grabbed the edge of the dumpster had Ben not grabbed his arm.

"Whoa, Jack-buddy," Ben said. "Easy. That's hot, man."

Jack said, "Get me away from here."

Ben grabbed Jack by one elbow and led him back to the car. The uniforms watched. Jack knew they'd all heard the story, how last year a detective had watched his wife burn alive in a car wreck. It had been one more tale of heartbreak, but now Jack felt them watching him.

"All right," Jack said to Ben. "I'll be all right. It's the smell, man." He sat back against the car.

"Just take it easy," Ben said.

"I'm good," Jack said. "Go on, get to work. I'm good." Jack put his hands on his knees. Ben studied him for a moment, briefly touched Jack's shoulder, and then walked back to the dumpster. The firefighters were spraying foam into it, burying the dead in white.

The smell of burning meat and rendering fat, and the sickly-sweet perfume of evaporating spinal fluid, eyes, and brain mixed with the metallic, coppery smell of boiling blood. The stink of crisping skin, and the hair, Jack thought, that damned sulfurous stench of burning hair.

In truth, Jack was not all right, and not good. This was deeply personal. It was the smell of Beth dying. The day she died, that odor had replaced her screams in a frontier of horrific possibilities; the force of her screams trading off for the power of the smell.

Jack slid down to the ground and sat. Dreading this day, he hadn't known how he was going to face it, and he had known it was inevitable. Jack was a detective with the 90th Squad—the homicide unit—and when he came back to work, he knew he'd see death. It was his first week back. On the first day, there'd been a stabbing, and he had come through no sweat. Still, he'd worried how he would handle a burned body, and he'd been right to doubt himself. Jack rocked forward, trying to maintain his balance. Suddenly, Sergeant Wells was pulling him to his feet, and Ben was jogging over.

"Detective," Wells said softly, "this isn't going to work for you. You've got to go."

"Give me a sec," Jack said.

"Jack," Ben said, "I got this, go on home. I'll call the lieutenant. Go on home."

Ch: 3

June 1
Evening
Jack's Apartment
Centereach, NY

Dream

I'm driving the car. It's the White Mountains, and we're in Franconia Notch. There's snow. Vacation. Beth is beside me. She's talking, smiling, and I'm pretending to listen, while nodding. The highway is a bit slick, and I want to get through the Notch. The weather can turn so quickly here. Walls of rock rise a mile high on both sides, covered in trees. So, I take out my gun. No, wait, no I don't. Profile Lake is ahead. There's a truck coming up from behind. It's carrying wood, timber. Probably going to exit at Route 3. It's coming quick. It doesn't change lanes, comes right up on my ass. Beth looks back, and asks what he's doing. He switches lanes, he passes me, and the huge load comes within a couple feet of my mirror. I grip the wheel tighter. He swerves into my lane. He hits us. He clips our front end. Our car spins, goes off the shoulder, and then rolls. Beth is screaming. The world is colors. A camera hits me in the teeth. Beth is screaming. The car comes to rest on its roof. Beth is screaming. I smell gasoline. I say we have to get out. She screams that she can't. I get out. I go to her side. Her arm is out the missing window, there's blood in the snow. Her arm is pinned between the car and a lone, flat boulder. I try to lift the car off her arm. It's in the ditch. I can't lift it out. Beth is screaming. I smell gasoline. I look both ways. No one. Not the wood truck. No one. An on-ramp for a closed scenic turnout. No one. Beth is screaming. Flames. I lift again, I tell her to pull her arm out. Beth is screaming. Beth is screaming. Flames reach for me through the back windows. I lift with everything I have. My hands burn. Beth is shrieking. Beth is burning. I can smell it. Her.

Jack woke with the first ring of the phone. Sitting in his armchair, soaked with sweat, he answered it.

"Hello," Jack said, and then, "What? When? Where is he? Be there as soon as I can."

Stunned, he swung his legs off the bed and pulled on his rumpled clothes.

* * *

Arriving at the trauma center at Lutheran Medical, Jack saw them sitting, huddled together, and he headed straight for them. Deb, Ben's wife, rose to meet him.

Jack opened his arms for her. Her hair was disheveled, and her face streaked with makeup.

"How is he?" Jack asked.

Deb looked up at him. "It's not good, Jack."

Marissa, Ben's daughter, came around her mother and hugged Jack as well. She wasn't a teenager yet, but her face looked older with worry, trying to process what was happening.

"Let's sit," Jack said, and they moved to red-orange chairs upholstered in a rough and durable weave.

"He came home, and everything seemed normal," Deb said. "He went into the bedroom. About an hour later, he came out, and..."

Deb had to stop, and Marissa leaned against her mother and cried. Jack put one hand on her arm.

"Did he say anything?" Jack asked.

Deb stared, and didn't speak. Marissa answered instead.

"He came out and said, 'It's the goddamnedest thing.' And then he put the gun," she said, and fought to get the last few words out, "to his head."

Both Deb and Marissa were crying hard, but Jack asked anyway, "Any idea what he was referring to?"

Both shook their heads. Jack pulled them both in close, felt their bodies rising and falling with the sobs. A doctor approached them, Jack saw him first, and rose to meet him. Deb and Marissa did not follow.

"I'm Dr. Kimball," he said. "Are you a member of the family?"

Jack replied, "I'm his partner. Jack Killarney."

"Mr. Killarney, the news isn't good," Kimball said. He was holding a folder, probably results on Ben, but he never opened it.

"He's not going to make it?" Jack asked, trying to maintain his cop voice.

The doctor's face grew grim. "Detective, he's already gone. He's only breathing because of our assistance. The man you knew isn't in there anymore. I'm sorry."

Ch: 4

Nearly a year later
May 4
7:00 a.m.
Home
Goodwin, Maine

Jack stood naked beside the bed that had once belonged to his parents. He was back in Maine, in Goodwin, and in the house where he grew up. He stared at the dresser, and the sweat on his body and in his hair began to cool.

He sighed as he rubbed his face, and then hung his head and closed his eyes.

The dreams—the night terrors—they hadn't faded. It'd been almost a year since leaving the NYPD, and two since Beth died, but the images were as clear, the stink as strong, and the screams as loud. He was lean, appeared fit, but he was also hungover, with a headache and cottonmouth.

Grabbing a towel off a hook on the door, he walked out of his room. There was movement downstairs. Someone was in the house. Jack rose up on the balls of his feet; adrenaline ran through him. He moved quickly, deliberately, scanning down the stairs for any sign of the intruder. Whoever it was would surely hear Jack coming down if he tried. The house was almost one hundred years old.

Jack owned guns, but he kept them locked in the basement. He cursed himself for it now, but he had always thought if someone came into the house, he wouldn't want a gun for fear he'd use it. Better they take want they want and leave, he thought, than kill someone over the silverware. At this point, however, Jack wished he'd not been so high-minded.

Jack could hear the intruder approaching across the dining room floor. He watched down the stairs, with only part of his head exposed. It was then that an elderly woman appeared, and when she looked up the stairs, she screamed. Jack stepped back into his room, and with both his hands on the wall, he waited for his heart to slow.

"Mr. Killarney! I'm so sorry! I let myself in, it's Tuesday, I thought you'd gone! I'm so sorry!" She was shouting from the dining room.

Tuesday, Jack thought, the cleaning lady. He normally would've gone out for his coffee by now, but he'd overdone the drinking last night. Now he had old Mrs. Martin downstairs, and had scared her half to death.

"Mr. Killarney? Should I come back later?"

"No, Mrs. Martin, it's alright. Sorry to have startled you. I'll shower and be out of your way," Jack called back.

Only silence from below. Jack thought Mrs. Martin was probably trying to decide what to do next.

"Would you like me to make you some breakfast?" she called up half-heartedly.

"Just clean the house," Jack hissed to himself.

"Mr. Killarney?" she called again.

"No, thank you, Mrs. Martin, I'll eat later," Jack replied, trying to sound at least somewhat grateful.

After a pause, she said, "Suit yourself."

Jack chose clothes based on what was least wrinkled. He grabbed a pair of Levi's, a white shirt, some socks, underwear, T-shirt, and a belt and walked straight to the upstairs bathroom.

He figured if she looked up again, it would only be his bare ass whipping by, but she was nowhere near the stairs. Jack doubted she'd approach them again until he left.

Between his dreams and his encounter with Mrs. Martin, Jack was strung out. The headache wasn't helping, and the hot shower only made him dizzy and nauseated. He stepped out and toweled off. The steam felt oppressive. When he bent over to pull on his socks, the blood pounded in his ears. The toothpaste had only temporarily beaten back the taste in his mouth. He washed down a handful of Advil and then looked over the prescription bottles, considering each of them in turn as one might when selecting a necktie. He picked only one, deciding he'd take his chances and pass on the others, but this was one of those meds, Jack thought, where you don't feel much of anything until you start skipping it. He hated being dependent on it, but didn't want to go without, and was relieved whenever a delivery arrived.

As dry as he felt, he knew he'd have to drink a shitload of water to rehydrate himself. He wondered what his liver looked like, with his daily drinking and meds. Some mornings he ran, and he still practiced martial arts on his own, but more for his head than his body. Frankly, he didn't care much about physical fitness anymore.

He had left the NYPD soon after Ben's suicide. He knew that between the emotional scars he'd suffered losing Beth, and then Ben a year later, he wasn't up to the job anymore. He simply didn't have the emotional bandwidth, and the department psychiatrist had agreed.

Jack was world-weary. He was tired of being a widower, tired of remembering, tired of hurting, tired of thinking too much, tired of people, and their needs and questions. Jack was tired of forcing himself to be polite when he actually wanted to tell someone to shut up.

He had come back to Maine, returning to the house that his parents had left them, not far from the farm where his brother

Keenan was raising his own family. Jack had returned to wait out his life. Only 40 years old, he knew that most of his family members had lived well into old age, but he hoped the drinking might speed things along.

Jack came down the stairs in his stocking feet and stepped out into the dining room where Mrs. Martin was vacuuming the same spot again and again, apparently hoping to be too busy to speak with him. Jack's mood shifted, he chuckled and walked over. She stopped, stood upright facing him, but left the vacuum cleaner howling. Jack tilted his head, and her shoulders slumped. She turned it off. It wound down to silence.

"I'm leaving now, Mrs. Martin," Jack said. "Sorry about startling you."

"No, it was my fault," she answered. "I should've called out louder when I came in."

Jack turned and walked away, and he heard old Mrs. Martin sigh. Slipping into his shoes, he grabbed a light jacket and his keys, and went out to the truck.

Dents and spots of rust stood out against the 1998 Jeep Cherokee's black paint. His small monthly disability check, along with his savings, was enough to keep the lights on, and to have Mrs. Martin over one morning every other week. He might have also afforded a newer vehicle, but he loved the old Jeep. He even loved that they had stopped making the model. The vehicle was as obsolete as its owner, he thought, and both with high mileage.

He drove into town, with his medication producing only the faintest mental fog, but enough to make Jack wonder if he'd actually seen the man. He wore a long black coat—weird for Goodwin—and crossed quiet Main Street almost a hundred feet ahead. Jack couldn't make out the man's face, but he somehow looked familiar. Just a black coat and dark, shaggy hair, but there was something in his gait. Something about how he carried himself. Sure, calm, practiced, but with a slight limp. The man crossed the road, stepped between Benton's Barbershop and Cup 'n' Time, and was gone. Jack craned his neck around to see as he passed, saw no one in the alleyway, and then had to slam on his brakes to avoid running over three kids coming out from behind a parked car. They waved as if they had played a prank on Jack, and he half-waved back as they ran off.

He turned into the Agway parking lot. Jack was determined to grow a good portion of his food, in part to save money and in part to depend less on others. He wasn't attempting to "get off the grid" as so many had, and he still had power from the local utility, along with high-speed internet, but he had hoped to retreat from face-to-face society a bit. Walking into the store, he approached the counter.

"Mr. Killarney," said the clerk. The name tag read only, "Avery" and was as red as the old man's face.

Jack said, "Hey. I came to talk about tomatoes."

"I remember," Avery said.

"Well, I planted rows of those seeds and I haven't seen a single sprout. How will I know if I have bad seeds?" Jack asked.

Avery said, "I'm sure the seed is good, but if you're in a hurry, I've got plenty of tomato plants you could put right into the ground."

"Would that help the seeds germinate, too? If I mixed in plants in the rows among the seed?" Jack asked.

Avery smiled, "Couldn't hurt."

"I wouldn't put plants in the ground just yet," said a voice behind Jack. Avery's smile fell. Keenan, Jack's brother, stepped forward and nodded at Avery.

"Why not?" Jack asked. The brothers shook hands and smiled at the chance meeting.

"Early May in Maine," Keenan said. "You put them plants in the ground now, almost sure a frost will kill 'em. Been nice the past couple weeks, but I've seen a Memorial Day frost kill entire hobby gardens."

"It's not a hobby for me. I'm trying to grow my food," Jack said.

Keenan smiled. "Mostly what folks are trying to grow in gardens, Jack."

Jack paused and then asked, "Should I get cold frames then?"

Avery perked up.

"Time for cold frames is pretty much passed now," Keenan said. "What you need is some patience. Those tomato seeds are probably just waiting for the soil to warm up. They'll come up in time."

"Alright," Jack said. "You're the pro."

"Come on up to the house. I'll feed you in the meantime. Carol's got a bunch of canned stuff we'll never get to, you can have your pick," Keenan said. "Besides, I want you to come see something up at my place. It's weird."

"The point is to grow the food myself," Jack said. "What's weird?"

"Taking things in stride, in their time, that's part of farming," Keenan said. "You aren't a big-city cop any more, big brother. You can't kick the doors in on this."

Avery couldn't remain quiet any longer. "Could take this time to throw some fertilizer down."

Keenan put a rubber belt, Jack had no idea what its purpose might be, on the counter and Avery rang it up. Keenan turned and walked toward the door, pushed it open, but then stopped and turned to face them both. "Jack, if you get a chance, you swing by the farm today. I want to show you what I found. It's the goddamnedest thing." Keenan stepped out and was gone.

Jack's back straightened, muscles tight. Those had been Ben's last words, and that night at Lutheran came rushing back. Then, he remembered the six burning bodies in the dumpster, and then his thoughts went to Beth. He tried to shake it off, turned to Avery, and said, "Hey, I saw some strange guy downtown, long black coat, messy hair. Heard any talk of someone new in town, or someone passing through?"

"Not yet. Where'd you see him?"

"Down by Benton's."

Avery grinned. "Well, Shelly over to Cup 'n' Time will know the whole run down on the guy soon enough."

Jack smiled back. "Okay, let me know if you hear anything."

* * *

After getting home, he double-checked the time for his appointment with a local shrink. Before lunch, he'd spread some fertilizer and, after lunch and the appointment, he'd ride up to the farm and see Keenan.

First though, he thought he'd quickly check his email. Sitting at his laptop, he skimmed through the spam and friends trying to stay in touch. However, he found one odd email.

From: Augustine@freemail.com

"Hey Jack-buddy… He who created us without our help will not save us without our consent."

"What the fuck?" Jack whispered. No one but Ben had ever called him that. He replied with, "Who is this?"

Within seconds, a response kicked back.

"No such account exists on server. Permanent fatal error."

Jack's brow furrowed. He stared at the email address and then reread the message. Is someone fucking with me? He deleted the email, and hit refresh. A part of him expected it to reappear or something equally bizarre but, instead, it was gone. He lay back into his chair. It had already been a strange morning. Things would get stranger.

Ch: 5

May 4
12:20 p.m.
Dr. Havel's Office
Goodwin, Maine

The white-noise machine whirred, the volume low, knocking the sound of their voices down and ensuring confidentiality. A luxury rarely found, or at least expected, in Goodwin.

"You know, you dreaming about Beth, it's perfectly normal. You're attempting to process it; you're subconsciously dealing with the loss. And the guilt," Dr. Havel said. He was middle-aged, with spare hair neatly trimmed. His necktie was expertly tied, his shirt a perfect fit, and his pants neatly pressed.

"Guilt? It wasn't my fault," Jack said.

"I know that, Jack," Havel said, "but maybe you're not as sure of it as you think you are. Not to mention, you are almost sure to be feeling some survivor's guilt."

"I don't feel any guilt. We were both victims of some asshole with a truck," Jack said.

"Right," Havel said. "You were completely blameless in the accident."

For a moment, Jack felt a flash of anger, but then realized Havel was not speaking sarcastically. "And I did everything I could to get her out."

"I know you did," Havel said softly. "But she didn't get out, so maybe you have some guilt there? Most people would question whether or not there might have been some more that could have been done. That would produce self-doubt and then guilt."

"Why are you searching for guilt?" Jack asked.

"I'm only trying to help you search your feelings, and search for the source of the nightmares."

"You're pushing for guilt though." Jack's face grew hot, he could feel his jaw working, grinding his back teeth. "You didn't go looking for random feelings; you pushed for guilt. You weren't there. There was nothing else I could do."

"If you truly believed that, without a shadow of a doubt, do you think you'd be having these difficulties?"

"Hey, let's move on. I didn't come here to have you make me—or worse yet, make myself—feel guilty for Beth," Jack said.

Havel sat with professional patience, looking at the floor and then at Jack. He cleared his throat and spoke. "Let's talk about the previous dream. The one you said is recurring."

Jack said, "Okay. It was a car crash, but not *the* car crash. I was driving a woman to the hospital. Something flew by the windshield and caused me to swerve, and the car went into the ditch. Not a bad wreck, but when I looked at her, she had a rock lodged in the middle of her face. I looked down at myself and there was blood all over me."

"Your own blood?"

"It was her blood."

"Was this a dream about something that happened to you?" Havel asked softly.

"I've had this dream before. Like I've told you, I've never met this woman," Jack replied, frustrated. They had discussed this dream before and Jack believed Havel should remember this stuff, or at least look down at his legal pad and read notes from the last session.

Havel frowned. "Dreams are often reliving previous traumas,

previous ordeals. This is something different. Interesting."

Havel jotted something down. Jack waited and wondered if Havel was actually doodling, and not really paying attention.

"How does the dream make you feel?" Havel asked.

Jack's mouth drew tight. "Well, I felt like it was my fault. But I'm not sure why."

Havel inhaled deeply, paused, then asked, "And what do you think it means?"

Jack could feel the anger building within him. Why was he even here?

"I have no idea what it means," Jack said. "That's why I come see you."

"Hmmm," Havel replied, and then scribbled on his pad. "So, tell me how you think this recurring dream is connected to your night terrors about your wife."

Jack could feel something stir in his chest. It was faint, but it felt empowering. A defensive switch coming on; an edge usually held suppressed.

"You remember," Jack asked softly, "when I told you about how we moved all those children out of that apartment building before the perps inside set fire to it?"

Havel paused, and then replied, "I remember."

Jack's face twisted into a smirk. "I never told you about that day."

Havel blanched, "Wait, I thought you did, I'm sorry, go on. What do you think the connection is to this recurring dream? What do you think it means?"

Jack thought that this was a waste of money, even if it wasn't his. "It means you could be replaced by a doll with a pull-string," Jack said, standing.

"Sit down, Jack."

"Naw, fuck this," Jack replied. "I know your heart's in the right place, Doc, but seriously, I wonder... do you ever have regrets? All those years of school, all those college loans. For this? 'Tell me more, and how do you feel'?"

Havel said, "You're lashing out—a defense mechanism. Sit, let's work."

Jack's voice remained steady and controlled. "Think about it. When you were a kid, on a bike, whizzing down a hill, the wind in your hair, and you felt like you could do anything, *be* anything… is this what you pictured? That this would be the sum total of your potential realized?"

Havel's face darkened. "Fine, Jack, we'll end it here. We'll see you next month. Maybe then you'll be ready to work."

"Have a good day, Doc," Jack said, and walked out to the parking lot. The breeze was cool and rich with salt.

* * *

He hopped into the Jeep and drove around Pelletier Mountain, more of a hill really, and up Dalton Road to Keenan's place. Jack drove around the long curve of the driveway, parked, and saw Keenan approaching with that tired but purposeful farmer-walk.

Jack's feet weren't on the ground before Keenan called out, "Hey, Jack, did you buy those cold frames?"

"Keenan," Jack said. "What do you have to show me?"

Keenan's two daughters came slamming out the front door, flying off the porch, and into the drive, the younger chasing the older.

"Mariah! Taylor! Slow down, and leave the door on the house, will you?" Keenan called. It wasn't harsh, only loud enough to be heard over two laughing girls. The spring-loaded door clapped again and Keenan's small son, Kenny, tried to catch up with his sisters.

Jack smiled. "Why aren't they in school?"

Keenan smiled back. "Couldn't make myself do it. We were getting a couple sheep in today and the girls wanted to be here, and if they stay home, there's no way Kenny's going anywhere."

"You spoil them," Jack said, teasing.

A woman's voice called out. "You're right about that."

Jack looked over at the porch. Keenan's wife, Carol, barely five feet, and pretty, stood there grinning at them. "How you doin', Jack?"

"Nothin' wrong with a father doting on his girls," Keenan replied. "Especially when he works them as hard as these two."

"Just fine, Carol," Jack said.

Carol smiled, and then asked Keenan, "You going to show him?"

"Yeah, why am I here?" Jack asked.

Keenan paused, his smile came down a notch, and he said, "You know, I feel sort of silly about it now, but I found something yesterday morning, in the barn. Come on."

Carol didn't follow, and instead, went back into the house.

The men went to the barn, through the big open door, with the smell of animals growing stronger with each step. Cavernous inside, the lofts were nearly empty. Cows moaned in scattered harmonies throughout. Cats played in a corner.

Jack and Keenan walked between the rows of dairy cows, and the twin conveyor belts of manure that lay in tracks behind the animals. Keenan stopped and pointed up at the far loft. Up on a timber, a cross-tie, lay small brown lumps.

"Birds?" Jack asked.

"Barn swallows," Keenan said, the smile gone. "They're dead, Jack."

Jack looked again. All along the thick, rough-hewn timber lay swallows, evenly spaced, as if neatly placed there in a row.

"Eighteen of them," Keenan said. "All facing the same way, I've been up there."

"How'd they die?"

"Not a thing wrong with them that I can see," Keenan replied. "Necks aren't broke."

Jack squinted. "Poison?"

"Okay, Jack, but why would eighteen poisoned birds fly up there, line themselves up, and die?"

Jack said, "Someone put them there."

Keenan shook his head. "The ladders weren't touched. Timber neither, except where the birds landed. Wing marks in the dust too; they were alive when they got there."

Jack stared up at the birds, dumbfounded. "This isn't silly."

"Damned if I know what did it," Keenan said. "Called the state to send a vet out here, make sure it's not that bird flu or something."

"Let's go up," Jack said.

"Already been," Keenan said. "Help yourself."

Jack climbed the ladder. When he reached the timber, it was just as Keenan had described. Little birds, all laying on their sides, each tan breast facing Jack, with their dark backs facing away from him. Marks from little wings in the dust, but no other sign of anything. The birds were evenly spaced, and the bird farthest from Jack had to be at least nine feet away. A man placing that farthest bird would have had to walk across the timber, and would have left footprints. He would also be a man without a fear of heights. It was easily thirty feet to the barn floor below.

Jack suddenly remembered Ben's voice asking, "What's with the birds?" when they had seen the dead birds at the dumpster, the one that had contained the burning bodies. A wave of nausea came over him, and he wanted off the ladder. Climbing down more carefully than he climbed up, Jack walked over to Keenan.

"Any ideas?" Keenan asked.

"Never saw anything like this on the farm before?" Jack asked.

"It's a farm. I find dead animals now and then, but nothing like this," Keenan said.

Both men were looking up at the dead birds when a shrill scream behind them made Jack jump.

Mariah, Kenny, and Taylor all ran up and grabbed their father's legs with both arms, laughing.

One said, "Hi, Uncle Jack."

"Hi, Mariah." Jack smiled down at her. "How old are you now?"

"I'm six now, first grade." She smiled at him, top two teeth missing.

"I'm five!" Taylor offered.

Then, of course, it was Kenny's turn, but he said nothing, he just stared at Jack. Jack looked at the boy, their eyes locked. A thought filled Jack's mind—*I am I.*

Mariah rolled her eyes. "He's three."

Keenan laughed. "Okay, okay, let me go, run along, stay out of trouble." The kids ran off.

Jack was still shaken about the birds. There couldn't be a connection—between this and Brooklyn—but something was seriously wrong.

Jack said, "Let me know what the state says about those birds."

Keenan extended his hand. "Sounds good. We'll see you around."

Jack took it, and said, "My best to Carol."

He left the barn and headed for his Jeep. He got in, pulled away, and in the rearview mirror, he could see the girls chasing each other, with Keenan watching them play. And then, little Kenny was in his mirror, standing stiff and motionless, hands at his sides, staring at Jack's departing vehicle. Jack stared back at his nephew, only snapping his attention back to the road when an oncoming vehicle honked to let him know he'd strayed into the wrong lane.

Ch: 6

May 5
11:37 a.m.
Cup 'n' Time
Goodwin, Maine

Jack sat waiting for his chowder, drinking coffee, and reading *The Portland Press Herald*. They covered hard news, which Jack usually liked to avoid, but he was feeling a bit disconnected. He had begun to feel like he was being stalked, as if the world was tracking him down. By reading the *Herald*, he sort of felt like he was looking over his shoulder.

The Cup 'n' Time was small, and smelled like the diner it was. It was a touch too warm, the air was a bit stale, and a quiet place to read, it wasn't. Locals sat laughing too hard at jokes told too loudly. The customers called Shelly by name far more frequently than one would in a normal social setting, as if only to keep proving they knew her on a first name basis. The place closed at 2:00 p.m. every day, but served breakfast until then. Jack came by once a week to treat himself to someone else's cooking.

He put a bit more Equal in his coffee. The paper had a story about an arsonist in Gorham who said he'd set a dozen fires as stress relief. One of the fires resulted in the death of an elderly woman. The dirt bag burned up an old lady because he couldn't relieve his stress any other way.

"Here you go, hon," Shelly said. She set a large bowl of clam chowder in front of him, the oyster crackers still in a plastic bag on the saucer beneath.

He folded the paper, gave her a smile. "Thanks, Shel."

He took a large spoonful and tasted the fresh clams. White instead of pink. The locals used to tease him, asking if he, having moved back from New York, wanted some tomato juice for his chowder. It didn't seem to matter to them that he'd grown up here.

Looking out the window, he stopped eating. The man in the black coat was there, across the street and looking at him. Jack stared, trying to make out his face. The man turned and walked a few steps before disappearing behind a beer truck being off-loaded in front of Vogler's Pub and Grill.

Jack looked back down at his chowder. It was writhing with blind, naked, newborn mice, scalding in the hot soup. The bowl was filled with them, squirming. Voiceless mouths were screaming. Tiny toes splayed as they struggled. Jack jumped up, and the chair groaned loudly.

"Holy shit!" Jack said, spitting clams and potatoes onto the floor.

Everyone in the place stopped and looked, but Jack's eyes met Shelly's.

"What is it, Jack?" Shelly called, coming out from behind the bar.

Jack pointed at his chowder as Shelly arrived. It was perfectly fine. The mice were gone.

"Jack, what's the matter?"

Jack's eyes shot back outside. He couldn't see any trace of the man in the black coat.

"Nothing," Jack said. "Shit sorry, burned my tongue. Sorry, what do I owe you?"

"For one spoonful of chowder?" Shelly asked. "Nothing."

Jack insisted. "No, what do I owe you?"

"Nothing, Jack. Come back tomorrow, and I'll make you another bowl," Shelly replied.

Jack paused for a moment, realized she was worried and being kind, and he softened. "Thanks, Shel, see you tomorrow."

Turning, he left the diner, jogged across the street, and looked as far down the way as he could see. No sign of him. A deep feeling of dread swept through Jack, a feeling he'd experienced now and then since, as a boy, he had found the girl in the culvert. The image of her misshapen body flashed through his mind, and he remembered the bloody water dripping into the brook from his fingertips. He hadn't had that feeling since leaving the NYPD.

His cell phone rang.

"Jack, it's Lem." Lem Holt was the local police chief, and he might have been the first one to know they had a retired NYPD homicide detective living in town. The local police had asked for Jack's cell number his first week in the area.

"What's up?"

"Jack, I'm on my way up to Keenan's place. A neighbor called in, reported a woman screaming, glass breaking."

"Carol?" Jack asked.

Lem said, "It sounded bad."

Jack said, "I'm on my way."

* * *

As Jack drove back up to the farm, the large red barn nearly obscured the police cruiser from view. Jack pulled into the horseshoe drive and could see the car parked between the shingled garage and the white farmhouse. The driver's door was open, up against an antique gasoline pump.

Jack put the Jeep in park and stepped out. Running up the steps, Jack could hear a woman wailing inside the house. There was a cast iron pan lying on the porch, surrounded by the broken bits of the window it had come out through. Jack looked inside through the kitchen window as he passed it, and he could see Lem had Carol in a bear hug, off the floor. Her arms were pinned at her sides and she was thrashing and screaming. Rushing to the door, Jack pulled it open, and his shoulder smacked against the doorjamb as he went in.

Jack shouted, "Jesus, Carol!"

"Jack, help me get her to the ground!"

The two men wrestled the tiny woman to the floor. Even with their combined law enforcement training and experience, they were barely able to handle her. Once she was pinned down, Lem handcuffed her. She struggled to kick her legs free of Jack's grip and pulled ferociously at the cuffs.

"Lem, what the hell did she do?"

"Nothing!" Lem shouted over Carol's continued screaming. "Hold her down while I get the leg hobbles!"

"Got her," Jack said, and Lem ran out the door. Carol became suddenly calm, and the room was absolutely silent. Lying on her belly, she turned her head back to look at Jack. Her mouth was twisted, as if in pain, and her eyes were wild. Slowly, she bent backwards, and nearly in half. She looked as if she had broken her own back, folding the wrong way. He was on her legs, pinning them down, but her upper body was off the floor.

Jack said, "Carol, lie down."

Carol smiled, broad and cruel, and swiftly slammed her body and head into the floor with such force it made Jack jump.

"What the fuck?" Jack stared, as Carol lay unmoving.

Coming back in with the leg irons, Lem saw Carol, and asked, "What the hell did you do?"

"Not a damn thing!" Jack said, standing and backing away. "She drove her own face into the floor and knocked herself clean out."

Lem checked her pulse. "You were supposed to be protecting her from accidentally hurting herself."

"Lem, I know damn well how to manage someone in custody.

That was no accident!" Jack shouted. "She smiled at me, man! She smiled and then did that!"

Lem rolled Carol only an inch or two, exposing a growing puddle of blood under her face.

"Shit."

Jack said, "Call an ambulance."

"One's on the way." Lem went to the sink and grabbed a dishcloth, returned to Carol, and applied pressure to Carol's broken nose.

Jack was thoroughly shaken. "What the hell is going on here?"

Lem looked up at Jack. "She was crying, hard, I was comforting her, trying find out what was wrong, and then she went berserk."

"Crying why?"

Lem's mouth set hard. "I don't know yet, but she went nuts when I reached for that door."

Lem pointed toward the basement, and Jack looked that way. He felt emotional tumblers in his head slowly clicking, like a lock being picked. A voice in his head screamed for him not to go down there, to instead return to the Jeep, that he'd seen enough horror in his lifetime. He should go flirt with Shelly, or to go see Dr. Havel and make up. The feeling of dread swept through him again and again.

Jack's feet felt like lead, but they took him to the door, to the steep wooden steps. He looked down and couldn't see anything but the dirt floor.

Into his radio, Lem said, "Listen, Dan, speed up the EMS." Jack looked back at Lem, then down the stairs once more.

Lem said, "Wait for me."

Jack said nothing, and went through the door. With each step, he expected to see something, anything, but all he saw was furnace, buckets, and a windshield for an old snowmobile. He stepped onto the dirt floor. The air was musty, thick, with the odor of soil and heating oil, and of drying wood. Jack turned, scanning. He saw shadows first—odd shadows, flying.

He stepped around the stairs. There they were. The children, all three of them, dressed as if ready for school, hanging from ropes. Hanging by their necks from the floor joists above. The two little girls facing each other. Little Kenny was hanging directly above his father. Claw marks from little fingers on their throats, little nails that had torn at the rough ropes around their necks. Urine glistening on the dirt floor beneath them. Keenan lay, not moving, as his son hung above him.

Jack knelt by Keenan's side. He had a bullet hole in the side of his head. Like Ben's, he thought, although Jack had never seen Ben's injury. Doctors had wrapped Ben's head, but Jack had easily imagined the hole in his temple. Jack had seen enough gunshot wounds to know the same raised and bruised skin, the same peppered look caused by burning powder, the same neat hole, and the blood.

Keenan was still gripping the gun in his dead hand. Jack tried to stand, but one knee gave way. He tried again, and rose. His sobs fought for sound, but found none. He was dizzy, and his vision blurred. He turned and collided with little Mariah, and she swung away and then back. She was still warm. Jack felt his knees sag again for a moment, but he caught himself. He staggered, without looking back, to the stairs.

It had followed him, he thought. Jack paused at the bottom of the stairs and gripped the two-by-four railing. He had seen more of the evil that men perpetrate on other men than anyone should see—certainly more than anyone he knew. He had fled back to this quiet corner of nowhere in order to leave it behind, and to hide at home, but it had followed him here. He wondered what could make a father do such a wicked thing? Keenan had always been the normal one, the stable one, the family man. What was this evil, Jack wondered, this madness that could make a man do this?

Lem came down rushing down the stairs, and leaned over the railing.

"Oh God, no," he said.

Jack climbed the stairs past him. He was slowly becoming steadier, his vision clearing, but he was also slipping mentally. Defensive barriers were flying up; Jack could feel them setting in place. He could feel himself slip a bit deeper into himself, a bit safer, and becoming more the NYPD detective again. But then right past that point, and safer still.

He stepped out into the dining area where paramedics were wheeling Carol out on a gurney. A ridiculously large pressure bandage was affixed to her forehead, even though most of the blood had come from her nose.

Lem came up behind him, and as he passed, Jack wrapped his fingers around Lem's upper arm. The police chief stopped, looking down, apparently surprised at the force of the grip.

Jack said, "It doesn't make any sense."

Lem shook his head. "It doesn't."

"What did Carol say?"

"She was shrieking, again and again, something like, 'He did it!'"

"That's it?"

Lem looked down. "Let go of my arm, Jack."

Lem met Jack's gaze for a moment and then looked away. Jack released Lem's arm, and walked out to the Jeep.

Lem called, "Jack!"

Ignoring him, he climbed behind the wheel, and sped away. He felt something inside him awaken for the first time in a long while. Jack was badly shaken, horrified, heart-sick, confused, but he was also pissed off. Tears streamed down his face—he had lost his brother, the kids—and he ground his teeth together.

He decided he would chase this. Something, some power—some *evil*—had taken Beth from him, and Ben, and now Keenan and the kids. It killed singularly, in pairs, in small groups. It let, or caused, little children to be murdered at the hands of their own father. It came to schools and picnics, church congregations, and shopping malls. It could even wipe out tribes, ethnicities, and whole nations. It appeared arbitrary, but Jack didn't believe in random. He had once believed in bad luck, but not anymore. This had gone on long enough. Jack was going to find out what this was all about. He was going to track it down. For Ben and Beth and his brother. A howl, at first seemingly from the backseat, moved forward and through his abdomen, up through his chest, and erupted from his mouth. A howl of pain and rage, punctuated by his beating fists on the steering wheel. He was going to hunt this thing down. *Enough.*

Ch: 7

May 6
7:00 a.m.
Home
Goodwin, Maine

Dream

I'm inside the car. It's on its roof. I look to my right. Beth is not there. I release my seatbelt and drop. On hands and knees, I turn. The backseat of the car is cavernous. I crawl between the front seats onto a sand floor. I stand. I walk into the dark and find a door. I open it and step inside. I can see. I slowly turn to my right and there, hanging from a floating steel I-beam, are Ben and Beth and Keenan and the kids. Hanging from nooses around their necks. Beth in flames, being consumed, hair gone. Ben and Keenan with holes in their temples, the wounds badly bruised and swollen. Beth smiles and waves, skin blistering, eyeless. Ben's mouth opens as if he is about to speak. Wider and wider. There's an odd beeping sound. His face is contorted, stretching. I look at Beth, flames consuming her, lips missing, charring, she waves again. I look at Keenan and then Ben. I can barely make out facial features any longer. There is more mouth than face.

Suddenly, streaming out of Ben's mouth, comes a flock of small black birds. A voice bellows, "I am I."

Jack woke, with the alarm clock beeping, and sat up in bed. "What the fuck?" he whispered. "They're hanging now."

* * *

The Maesteg Morris Public Library was small, redbrick atop a grey, granite foundation. Two columns rose up to an ornamental gable end, above wooden double doors, and were the same grey as the trim around the windows. The corners of the library were accented with large blocks of sandstone tan. A maple stood out front, centered in front of the bank of windows.

When Jack entered, the lights were on, but Dotty was nowhere in sight; she was probably down in the basement, or in the office. It was not that surprising that Jack had the library temporarily to himself. Who would steal these old books?

Dotty Turnbull had worked there since Jack's childhood. She was sweet, and loved being the librarian. Like most, she took the job seriously. She had asked Jack once what he thought of a new collection she'd purchased, and he was careful to appear impressed. He couldn't bear to let her know what the rest of the world already knew, that the Internet had made whole tracts of her role in town obsolete. She wasn't the primary source of information anymore. She was more an anachronistic leftover from the pre-Internet age, Jack thought. Wikipedia entries might change day-to-day, but unlike the encyclopedia shelved near the bank of the library's yellowing computers, Wikipedia knew that Prince Philip had passed away.

Dotty walked into view, with a thick oversized cardigan over her shoulders. It flashed through Jack's head that in small New England towns, the librarian's job must come with a kit—a costume complete with wire-rimmed glasses and cardigan sweaters.

"Oh, Jack," Dotty said. "Just terrible. I'm sick about it. Such a nice family. Who would ever have thought?" Dotty had whispered the last sentence.

Jack said, "It was bad."

"And you were out there, I heard?" Dotty asked.

"I was."

"A shame, a crying shame. I'm so sorry for your loss," she said.

"Dot, I need some help," Jack said. "I'm looking for these books." He handed her a list on a slip of paper.

"*On Evil* by Thomas Aquinas, *God and Evil* by William Madore, *Evil and the Deeds of Men* by Vivian Rueil..." Dotty's voice trailed off. Her eyes darted nervously from title to title.

"Do you have them here?" Jack asked, knowing Dotty was a walking card catalog for the little library.

She looked up. "We have two for sure. I remember the Rueil book. The cover always gave me a bit of the willies." Dotty walked toward the stacks and Jack followed. She pulled the books down and handed them to Jack.

Jack took them. "Can you order the others, please, through the library loan whatever? And throw in any books you can find linking murder and suicide." He didn't mention the birds.

She whispered again. "Jack, you think the devil did it?"

Jack was surprised by the question. He had never consciously considered a theological basis for the evil, mostly because Jack didn't believe in God. He had thought there must be psychological explanations for what Ben and Keenan did. With Beth, he had entertained a fatalistic explanation, maybe. But to hear Dotty whisper, hear her articulate that she believed it possible that the devil made them do it? It was outside the box he normally lived in.

Jack said, "I want to understand why these things happen."

Dotty straightened and seemed a bit dissatisfied with Jack's answer. She parted her thin librarian's lips, placed her hand on the books Jack was holding, and said, "Keep yourself from the ways of the violent."

Jack held her gaze for a moment, and then turned away.

"I'll get you these others," Dotty said. "The university will have them, they always seem more intent on collecting bad news than good." She walked around her counter still looking at the list.

"Thanks," Jack said. Dotty never looked up; she had moved onto the keyboard and focused on the monitor.

Jack walked into a small room with a couple of bookracks, a large wooden table, and two donated armchairs. The shelves contained row after row of sets, such as *Who's Who in America.* He sat down in one of the overstuffed and worn armchairs, with his back to Britannica's *Great Books of the Western World.* As he sat, the back of his head struck some of the volumes, pushing them in on the shelf. Jack twisted in his chair and pulled those volumes forward and flush with the others. Volumes 18, 19, 20. Augustine and Thomas Aquinas.

Jack said, "He who created us without our help will not save us without our consent." Augustine. The mysterious email he had received two days before. He pulled Volume 18 out of the set. Putting the other two books aside, he opened the volume to a random page. Dotty came around the corner.

Jack read aloud, "There is great need of God's mercy to preserve us from making friends of demons in disguise, while we fancy we have good angels for our friends."

Dotty stopped and stared. Jack looked up at her.

She said, "I didn't take you for a religious man."

"I'd like to sign this book out also," Jack replied.

"I'm sorry, that's a reference book," she said. "We don't lend them out."

Jack paused, and then said, "I'll buy it, then."

Dotty blinked. "But it's part of a set, Jack."

"Then how much for the goddamn set?" Jack asked, frustrated. Dotty's face hardened as she composed herself. He had never even burped in the same room as this woman before.

"First, I know you've suffered a terrible tragedy, but don't speak to me that way," she said, her voice low. "Second, if you promise to return it, we can make an exception."

"I'm sorry, Dot, of course I will."

"You understand that without that volume, the entire set is incomplete and therefore ruined."

"I understand," Jack said. "I promise to be careful with it."

Dotty turned toward the counter, Jack followed. She found his card and added the Augustine volume.

"Two weeks," she said.

"Thank you, and sorry again."

She only stared at the monitor screen, tapping keys with long fingers. Jack returned to the chair, collected the other books, tucked them all under one arm, and made for the door.

"Take care, now. Again, I'm sorry for your loss," Dotty said, without looking up.

"Thank you," Jack replied, without looking back.

Ch: 8

May 7
Canada

He watched. His hands were in the pockets of his black coat, and while his hair moved in the wind, his face was completely impassive. Through the windows he watched and no one noticed him. Inside, three-dozen people calmly fell to their knees, with their children beside them. Most were dressed in green robes. They simultaneously interlaced their fingers and began to pray. Three men, also in robes, walked behind them, carrying plastic bags and duct-tape. Methodically, purposefully, the three men began to place the plastic bags over the heads of those kneeling in prayer. Each bag was then sealed with a collar of duct-tape. Translucent plastic, fogging, soon blurred the facial features of every kneeling person.

Still standing outside, the watcher watched. Inside, two children stood and moved as if to remove their bags, but their parents restrained them until any sign of struggle faded and was gone. As those kneeling in prayer began collapsing, two of the three standing men knelt as well. The third man, with small eyes and hair dyed jet-black, sealed bags over their heads. The two men prayed until they, too, fell.

The watcher stood unmoving, continuing to observe from outside as the black-haired man feverishly stripped off the green robe exposing a navy polo shirt and blue jeans. He stepped into a closet, grabbed a leather bag, and walked out the door. He strode to the garage, never noticing the watcher. He pulled the cover from a red Ford Mustang, climbed inside, and drove away.

The watcher watched him go.

Ch: 9

May 7
Noon
Home
Goodwin, Maine

Jack made himself a sandwich. CNN was on as background noise, repeating the same tired stories again and again. He had been up all night with the library books, but his reading hadn't been limited to what he'd gotten from Dottie.

It had started small. A few newspaper clippings and some Stephen King novels, and then the Internet. At first, he had searched and read articles online, but then found himself wanting to see an article from hours before, so he began printing everything. He laid them out, printed essays, news articles, grad student papers, and blogs. The printouts had spread from his small den, into the living room, and across the dining room table. Murder-suicide, mothers who had killed their children by shooting or drowning them, a teenager who had shot his parents and younger siblings to death, an act of arson that had killed a sleeping family of seven, and on and on. He'd also printed references he'd found to dead birds and evil, and he was trying to cross-reference all this with Augustine.

Still chewing his lunch, Jack walked to the center of printouts, his growing record of madness. Even with all this, there were no answers. Plenty of explanations, but not a shadow of an answer. How does a human being transition from being a nursing infant to a serial killer? Were the answers to be found in the mountain of psychological theories? Was Freud right, with his cocaine, and prostitute test subjects? Were the answers contained in the philosophy of Aquinas or Augustine, or maybe Dennett? Perhaps evil was a parasite invading our brains, a meme, driving us to murder and suicide? Was it Satan by whatever name, pulling strings, making bets with God against our better natures? Was there a difference?

Jack cleared a space on the sofa and sat with the remainder of his sandwich in hand. He scanned the room once more, and the television caught his eye.

The CNN camera feed came from a helicopter circling a sprawling house, surrounded by trees. The caption read, "Prévost, outside Montreal, Quebec."

Jack turned up the volume. "…are preliminary, but sources tell CNN that authorities have counted at least forty dead, some of them children, by all appearances a ritual suicide, among members of a secretive cult here known as Stellar Light. Some of the dead were reportedly found in a position of prayer, fingers still interlocked. Locals say the cult members kept to themselves, and many of them lived on this large estate here in Prévost."

Jack stared at the television, then looked around the room again.

The report continued. "Meanwhile, a search has begun for this man, known as Brother Luc to cult members. His real name is Alphonse Basileau. It is believed he is not among the dead and that he has escaped with more than a million dollars in cult members' money."

Jack looked at the photo of Brother Luc as it filled the screen. A man perhaps in his early fifties, hair dyed jet black, small eyes.

"We have, joining us now, Serge Levesque. Serge, you live here in Prévost, and you work for Postes Canada. I understand that today you were up near the estate. What were you able to see?"

Serge wore a light jacket and cap. He cleared his throat and then spoke directly to the camera. "I don't see too much. I go near… *la maison*." Serge gestures toward the house and then continues speaking. "*Quand c'est faire beau*, usually de kids run outside. I stop at *des boîtes*… mailboxes, I don't go right up, *tu comprends tu*? So, while I look, I see in de driveway, somet'ing is dere."

"Can you explain what it was?" the reporter asked, hoping to help Serge along.

Serge paused and then replied, "*Les oiseaux morts*."

"The dead?" the reporter asked. "You saw the dead?"

Serge was shaking his head and then called off camera to a friend, "*Comment tu dit ça, les oiseaux morts*?"

Jack sat watching as Serge and the reporter both looked somewhere Jack could not see, not until the camera swung around. There stood a plain-looking man, wearing jeans, a white T-shirt, and a leather jacket. The man said, "Dead birds."

Jack leapt to his feet.

"*Oui*, dead birds," Serge said. "I see many dead birds across the driveway. So, I call police because it must be somet'ing like poison or disease, eh?"

"Dead birds?" the reporter asked, but didn't follow up. He touched his earpiece, trying to hear, and then he wrapped up his report, "Obviously, the facts are still being sorted out here, the scene of what appears to be yet another terrible tragedy. This is Glenn Hart, for CNN, in Prévost, Quebec, Canada."

Jack ran into his office and brought up Google maps, searching for Prévost. It looked like it was about an hour northwest of Montreal. Birds. How were birds a part of all this? He switched to Google News and ran searches on "birds suicide," "birds crime," and "birds evil."

Google found hundreds and hundreds of stories, many of them written by melodramatic environmentalists. Jack tried "birds tragedy" and the first ten stories were about bird-strike causing plane crashes. Jack paused and thought for a moment, and then tried "dead birds" and "suicide."

The first story was a few months old, about Palestinian refugees under white flags and also under the guns of the Israeli Defense Forces, being forced to leave their homes. Many Palestinian children were killed in the IDF incursion when a supposedly errant bomb struck a school. HAMAS suicide bombers were involved as well, striking and murdering Israeli civilians. The article briefly mentioned the unexplained death of dozens of chickens—dead, without a mark on them.

The second story was only six days old. In Fortaleza, Brazil, a group of Chilean and Columbian terrorists had violently taken control of a resort hotel filled with foreign tourists and businesspeople. When authorities attempted to take the hotel and free the hostages, the terrorists began executing their bound and gagged captives. Fifty-three hostages were killed. The thirteen terrorists were also killed. The odd thing was that witnesses reported they thought the rescuers were using some sort of chemical weapon, because a dozen birds tumbled from the rooftop like rain. One woman was quoted as saying, "They fell dead, without any attempt to fly."

Jack jotted down "Fortaleza." He brought up Google Maps again. He attempted to get directions from Fortaleza to Prévost, only so he could learn the distance between the two, but the attempt failed. Apparently, someone at Google didn't believe one would drive the distance nor need directions. Jack got up and went to his closet. From the bottom, he pulled out two boxes. He opened the first, and as quickly closed it and pushed it back into the closet. From the second, he pulled out a world map. Out of date, but exactly what he needed. He grabbed the yardstick leaning up against one bookshelf, and laid it across the map. He did a bit of quick math in his head—about 4,000 miles. Birds dying at scenes of horror, thousands of miles but only days apart.

He grabbed a pen from the cup and attempted to mark a line between the two. It didn't write. He tossed the pen into a corner of the room and grabbed a mechanical pencil. Jack tried to extend the lead, and then gave it a shake. It was empty. This too, he tossed.

"Doesn't anything work?"

He grabbed a standard No. 2 pencil, with its lead intact. He quickly drew a line from Fortaleza's approximate location in eastern Brazil to Montreal. He stopped. After thousands of miles of ocean, the line crossed into Maine. Just south of pricey and touristy York Harbor. And right through Goodwin.

He dropped the pencil and sat back. Jack's mind reeled. The cop in him started working the facts, skeptically. Skepticism is the heart of sanity, he'd said many times. A terror attack with dead birds on May 1. Keenan and the kids, murder-suicide, on May 5. The cult suicide on May 7. All along the same line. There must be an explanation. A natural phenomenon? A hole in the ozone? Sun spots? Stupid.

He stood. The three library books sat on the desk, and he picked up the first book and scanned the index for any mention of birds. Nothing. Jack had checked it before, but he checked it again. Nothing listed between "Bedlam" and "Blood."

He picked up *Evil and the Deeds of Men* by Vivian Rueil. The back cover included a large photograph of the author. She had dark brown hair, short, not even shoulder-length. Her eyes were a bit too large for her face, bright blue. Her cheekbones were high, her mouth full, and she was wearing no make-up. Jack had found her book accessible and yet still informative, what he'd read of it anyway. He pulled the back cover open, and flipped a few pages until he found the entry he wanted.

"Birds, symbolism and meaning," read the index entry. He flipped to the pages indicated. Jack had read these entries also, but he felt like he must have missed something.

"Birds are symbolic of the spirit," he read, "They represent the spirit or soul free of the earthly body, set loose to find the afterlife."

Same shit, as if the entry might have changed since he read it last. What about *dead* birds? Jack flipped the back cover open and read, "Prof. Vivian Rueil is a professor of Philosophy at Boston College. Her research areas include Metaphysics, Phenomenology and Psychoanalysis, and Philosophy of Religion. She is the author of three critically acclaimed books…"

Boston College. A couple hours' drive. Jack checked his watch. Could he simply head down there? And what if she wasn't at the school today? What if she thought he was a nut? What if she were right? Jack moved back to the computer, and ran a Google search for Rueil at Boston College. He found her page. Jack expected an email address at best and maybe a general phone number for the Philosophy Department. Instead, she had listed her email address, fax, and office number. The photo was the same one from the book jacket. He jotted down the number and picked up the phone, but then Jack stopped. What would he say? "Professor you don't know me, but there was a murder in New York with dead birds, and a murder-suicide here in Maine had dead birds, too, just like the Montreal cult-thing with dead birds, and Brazil, and maybe Palestine, too… is it a sign of evil?"

Jack looked around at his mess and knew he was exhausted. Maybe he should wait, take a shower, and script out what he would say to her. He looked at the phone, and then looked at the photo of Vivian Rueil. Sighing, Jack dialed.

The phone on the other end rang once, twice, and then a voice answered; it was soft but confident. "Professor Rueil."

Jack hesitated, scanning his mess one more time.

"Professor, my name is Jack Killarney."

"Yes?"

"Professor, we've had a tragedy here, a murder-suicide. I've been reading your book."

A moment passed, then Rueil asked, "Which one?"

"The Deeds of Men book," Jack said.

Another pause.

"Do you have a question about the book, Mr. Killarney?"

"Professor, I really think this would work better in person. I can be there in a couple hours. Are you free for dinner?" *Damn,* Jack thought, *she's a prof and an author, and I just asked her on a date. She must get propositioned by wackos twice a day.*

A longer break.

"Mr. Killarney, who do you work for again?"

"I'm a retired cop, living in Maine now."

"I see," she said. "Maybe you could email me your questions."

"Professor," Jack said, "I used to be a New York homicide detective. I'm not crazy. I've stumbled onto something here, a pattern around several tragic occurrences, and I'm feeling a bit over my head. I'll meet you in the most public of places; you pick the spot. I'll share what I've got, listen to what you have to say, and I'll be gone."

"Mr. Killarney…"

"I'll even pick up the tab," Jack said, hoping a little humor might alleviate some of the unease.

Another pause but then she said, "Alright. Meet me at Montzura on Union Street in Newton at six o'clock. How will I know you?"

"It's okay, I know what you look like," Jack said, then winced. What the hell was wrong with him? Was he trying to be creepy? He quickly said, "I'll be wearing a light blue oxford shirt with khaki pants." He didn't add that he was currently in pajama bottoms and a T-shirt covered in crumbs from lunch.

Jack held his breath, thinking she might have changed her mind.

"That outfit ought to narrow it down to half the men in Boston."

He heard a smile in her voice and he relaxed.

"See you at six o'clock, Mr. Killarney," she said.

"Six," Jack answered. "Thank you, Professor."

Ch: 10

May 7
Evening
Newton, Massachusetts

Jack arrived at Montzura's before six o'clock and parked a short distance from the entrance. The building had a long bank of windows, with a dramatic white entranceway and ornate molding surrounding the door. Painted letters ran vertically down the right side, spelling out the name of the restaurant. Jack went in and, looking left, spotted her sitting alone at a table near the wall of windows. She was looking his way. As the hostess approached, he pointed toward Vivian Rueil. The hostess nodded and walked that way with him.

The wonderful aroma of garlic permeated the room along with the sounds of low music, clicking flatware, and hushed conversation. The walls were painted in a charming, muted, and mottled gold pattern. Structural load-bearing posts were painted in a contrasting blue, probably both for aesthetic and safety reasons, making them visible to customers to avoid broken noses.

"Vivian Rueil," she said, holding out her hand as Jack arrived at the table.

"Jack Killarney," he said. "Thanks for meeting with me."

He sat, and the hostess said, "Your server will be right with you." A warm smile and then she was gone. Jack noticed the professor was already halfway through a glass of red wine.

"Been waiting long?" he asked.

"Only a few minutes," she replied.

"Well," Jack said again, "thanks for meeting me."

"Instead of repeatedly thanking me, Mr. Killarney," she said, "why don't you let me know why we're here?" She didn't sound irritated, only business-like. Jack thought she was even more striking in person. Her hair was down now, but it showed signs of having been up most of the day. Her clothes were business-casual, and slightly wrinkled. Her shoulders were narrow, as were her long fingers.

"First, professor, please call me Jack," he said. "Okay, I have a lot to tell you, and any single piece of it means little, but if I could lay it all out, maybe you'll see what I'm seeing."

She nodded as he pulled out a small notepad and flipped it open. The music playing softly in the background had Italian vocals.

Just as Jack inhaled to begin his explanation, a young woman appeared. "Hi sir, my name is Jamie, I'll be your server tonight. Would you like a drink?"

He leaned back. "Sure, I'll have a glass of Pinot."

"Noir? Or Grigio?" Jamie asked.

Jack's brow furrowed. "Noir, please."

"Would you like another, ma'am?"

The professor nodded.

"Great. I'll be right back with those." With a smile, she was gone.

"Okay, Professor, I've found something interesting." He took out a pen and began drawing a rough map of the Americas.

He drew a dot on what some might have recognized as the east coast of Brazil, and then another in the neighborhood of Montreal. "There was a terror attack in Fortaleza, in Brazil, on the first of May."

"Here you go, sir." Jamie the server was back. Jack leaned back once more and she moved two glasses of wine from her tray onto the table. She removed the professor's empty glass. "Would you like a little more time to decide before you order dinner?"

Jack hadn't even considered food. They hadn't touched the menus. Professor Rueil smiled and said, "We'll start with the bruschetta and then we'll both have the merluzzo."

"Very good," and with another smile, she left them alone.

"Thanks, professor," Jack said. "What am I having?"

"It's Vivian, and I hope you're okay with haddock and mussels."

Jack smiled. "Sounds good." He felt himself relax a bit.

"Back to what you were saying about Brazil," Vivian said.

"Right," Jack said. "There was this terror attack here, six days ago, then the cult suicide today in Montreal." He pointed at his dots as Vivian leaned forward to see. Jack noticed her eyes were so blue, he wondered if they were real or if she were wearing colored contacts. He drew a line connecting the dots. Along the line, he made another dot.

"Here is Goodwin, Maine," Jack said, "where a man killed his three small children and himself."

"So," Vivian asked, "you think it interesting that they all died along that line?"

"Well, along the line in chronological order," Jack said.

"Jack, I bet there was a murder in London and another in Chicago that same day, and those would line up with Maine, too."

"I'm sorry, I forgot to ask, would you like cheese on your bruschetta?" Jamie was back. Jack sat back hard, getting frustrated with the interruptions.

"Yes, thank you," Vivian said. She gave Jack a look; he flashed an irritated smile, and then abruptly dropped it. Jamie left.

"Jack, I'm listening."

"Okay, sorry. So, the birds."

Vivian shook her head. "What birds?"

"At the scene of the terror attack," Jack said, "witnesses reported dead birds falling from atop the building. At the farm in Maine, the scene of the murder-suicide, I saw twenty dead birds, strangely and neatly dead. And in Montreal, a witness on CNN today reported seeing many dead birds in the driveway."

"Environmental? Some sort of disease?" Vivian asked, guessing where Jack was going.

"The birds on that farm were lined up neatly in a row, not a mark on them. As if they'd lined up, lay down, and died." Jack said.

Vivian considered this. "There must be an explanation."

"I can't explain it, that's why I wanted to talk to you."

"Why me?"

"Well, you wrote the book, about evil, and I wondered…"

"Did you read the book, Jack?" she asked.

Jack squirmed a bit. "Some of it. Skimmed some of the rest. I haven't had it very long"

"I'm not a witch doctor," Vivian said. "I'm not an exorcist. I dispassionately study the ideas surrounding what we humans label as evil."

"I'm not looking for hocus-pocus. I was hoping there was something in history, something like this, that you would know about."

"Something like what? A pattern of human and avian deaths caused by some unseen evil force?"

"Look, I don't believe in this shit either. But this is weird enough to make me drive two hours to ask you about it," Jack said. "I'm a cop by training. I want answers. Some sort of resolution. I'm not someone who goes in for ghost stories or UFO sightings. You have to admit it's weird."

Vivian glanced at his scribbled map. "There's not enough here, Jack. You could draw a straight line on any map and you could find human tragedy along that line. I admit the birds are weird, but that's all it is so far. Weird coincidence."

"In my experience, there's no such thing as coincidence," Jack said.

"I study the phenomena of evil; in fact, I study reactions like yours. I'm not an expert on evil as a supernatural force, I'm someone who studies how we as human beings have created the idea of evil to explain coincidences we find too terrible to live with, or to motivate our fellow countrymen to kill others. Pure evil is a myth."

"What do you mean, pure evil is…"

"Is everything alright here?" Jamie was back, looking their glasses over.

"Lady, please," Jack said.

"I'm sorry, I didn't mean to interrupt."

"No, it's okay, been a long day," Vivian said, as Jack leaned back in his chair once again. Jamie nodded and left.

"Jack…"

"Sorry. I'm sorry."

Vivian looked at him for a moment and then said, "Pure evil is a myth because in order for pure evil to exist, the actor must acknowledge that he is evil. His actions must be intentional, must be directed against what we perceive as the harmless and innocent, and the actor must know that all his actions—every thought, every deed—are evil. Hitler and Stalin, with all their atrocities, are considered evil in every corner of civilized society. However, history does not record them as considering themselves evil, and thus even those monsters were not what a philosopher would categorize as *pure* evil."

"So, in history," Jack asked, "there's never been pure evil?"

"There might have been this psychopath or that serial killer who thought of himself as an agent of evil while committing evil acts, but even those crimes, society explains away with psychology. We say they were sick, ergo too sick to be trusted when they referred to themselves as evil. We say they were sick, and did terrible things. When we consider the ugliest acts of horror humans have committed against other humans, such as the Cherokee Trail of Tears, the Vendée women and children, the Herero, the Armenian genocide in Turkey, the Holocaust in Europe, the mass slaughter resulting from the orders of both Stalin and Mao, the Cambodian Killing Fields, Sabra and Shatila in Lebanon, dead Kurds in Halabja, the Tiananmen Square massacre, the nightmares of Rwanda, Bosnia, Darfur, Syria… the list goes on and on… the perpetrators never pronounced that they were acting on behalf of evil. In each case, someone explained it away, rationalized it, as either an act of insanity or revenge or self-preservation or even an accident of history. Bad luck. Whatever, but pure evil? No. Did you read Roy Baumeister's book?"

"I've got that, too," Jack said.

"Read his chapter on the myth of pure evil."

Jack thought for a moment. "Even if pure evil is a myth, and human atrocities can be viewed through the social sciences, that doesn't explain the birds."

Jamie arrived with the bruschetta. She set the tray on an adjacent table, and then set plates before each of them. She never said a word, turned, and took her tray away. Vivian shot a look at Jack.

Jack lifted his hands. "Sorry."

They began to eat, and both remained silent for a few moments.

"Birds have been symbols of the spiritual since antiquity. From ancient peoples like the Egyptians right through Judeo-Christianity to today, people have associated birds with souls set free from the body. There are stories of birds accompanying souls on the way to Heaven or on the way to Earth."

"Wait," Jack asked. "Why would souls be coming to Earth?"

"To be born," Vivian answered. "From the 'Body of Souls,' or the 'Guf,' or wherever. But the point is, birds and souls have long been linked, or the birds were said to actually *be* the souls, as in an albatross supposedly being the soul of a sailor lost at sea."

"Let's say these stories are true," Jack said. "Why would the birds be dead?"

"The stories are *not* true," Vivian said. "That's my point. Listen to what you're suggesting. That birds, the shepherds of souls, are somehow dying or being killed along with people at the scenes of various tragedies. The truth is there is some unknown correlation here, some coincidental connection between the birds and what has happened, but why are you insisting it be mystical? As a cop, does that make sense to you?"

Jack's eyes focused on her. "You know what makes no sense? A perfectly sane man—my brother, in fact—who doted on his kids, hanged them in the basement before blowing his own brains out. I stood there, with little feet dangling about waist-high around me, their father with a hole in his head." This Jack said with one hand held flat at the height of his ribs, and the other in the shape of a gun to his temple. His eyes filled with tears, he tried to blink them away, but they fell. "You'll have to forgive me if I'm willing to bend a little on this." His tone had been harsh, and other diners looked over.

Vivian put her fork down. "You know what? I've had enough. I've listened, I've told you what I think. I'm very sorry for your loss, but if you'll excuse me, good luck with your search for evil." She stood.

"No, I'm sorry, please sit," Jack said, standing.

"I'm going Jack," she said, her voice not angry, but resolute. She dropped a fifty-dollar bill on the table.

"I said I'd pay," Jack said.

Vivian paused, and said, "You know, you can go nuts on something like this. You might want to consider that you are trying to solve the insoluble. It's a moving intellectual target. If you don't treat it like a thought exercise instead of a puzzle with a definitive solution, you can lose your grip. You've obviously been traumatized by this, losing your brother and his children, and you should consider seeing someone."

Jack closed his eyes and clenched his teeth as Dr. Havel came to mind.

"Vivian," Jack said, as she walked away.

"Goodnight."

As she went out the door, Jamie appeared. "Here's your entrée," she said, and then spun on one heel and quickly walked away.

Ch: 11

May 10
10:00 a.m.
Home
Goodwin, Maine

Jack dialed. "Ah yes, this is Jack Killarney, returning Dr. Glickman's call." In fact, Dr. Robert Glickman had never called. Instead, Jack had called Glickman once before and was told he was in a meeting. Jack had left a message but it had not been returned.

Glickman was the State Public Health Veterinarian at the Maine Center for Disease Control and Prevention. It was Glickman who had ended up with Keenan's dead barn swallows.

"Please hold."

"Thank you," Jack said. Claiming to be returning a call at least forced the secretary to check with the actual person, overriding whatever instructions had been given regarding unexpected phone calls. It could also piss off the person you were trying to reach.

"This is Dr. Glickman." The voice was tired.

"Dr. Glickman," Jack said, "this is Jack Killarney. I'm calling to follow up on the dead birds from the Killarney farm. Have you determined a cause of death?"

Glickman sighed audibly before he answered. Never a good sign. "Mr. Killarney, the investigation is ongoing."

"But doctor, I'm not asking for a detailed analysis," Jack said. "I only need to know what killed those birds."

Glickman fell silent. This was a good sign; it meant he was considering it.

"Doctor, please. It's important."

"Mr Killarney," Glickman said, "I can't explain what caused it, but these birds all suffered a very peculiar brain injury."

Jack said, "What brain injury?" He scribbled notes as quickly as he could.

Glickman said, "In each of these birds, the pineal gland has…"

Jack waited, heard nothing, and then asked, "Dr. Glickman? There's a problem with a gland?"

Silence.

"Dr. Glickman?"

"The pineal glands in these birds are destroyed," Glickman said. "As if the gland ruptured violently."

Jack's brow furrowed. "Could a tumor cause that? Or something environmental?"

"As I said," Glickman answered, "I can't explain what caused it yet, but there is no sign of tumor. In each of these birds, the gland simply burst."

Jack thought for a moment. "Do people have this gland?"

"Yes," Glickman said. "It produces melatonin. The pineal gland regulates your sleep cycles by producing melatonin when it's dark. Cells in our retinas signal parts of the pineal gland, and let it know that it's night and that you should be sleeping."

"So, could something have been wrong with the birds' eyes?"

"Oh no," Glickman said. "In humans, the pineal gland is deep in the center of the brain. In birds, the pineal gland is on the surface and light reaches it directly, without depending on the birds' eyes."

A pause.

"I really must go," Glickman said. "If there's nothing else?"

Jack said, "Thank you very much for your time."

A click and Glickman was gone. The pineal gland? Jack had never heard of it. Normally, he would have simply Googled it, but this gave him a reason to make another phone call.

"Professor Rueil," she answered.

"Vivian, it's Jack Killarney."

Nothing.

"I'm sorry about the other night," Jack said. "I had no right to behave that way."

"I agree."

Jack bristled momentarily. He had expected her to accept the apology and move on. He rubbed his forehead with his hand. "I'm hoping we can get past it. I could still use your help."

"I am sorry about your brother, but I'm not sure I can help you."

"I've learned something about those birds, the dead birds."

Silence, but then she spoke. "Well?"

Jack straightened. "According to Dr. Robert Glickman, the state vet here in Maine, each bird had a ruptured penile gland."

Laughter erupted from the phone. Not what Jack had expected.

"A what?" Vivian asked, still laughing. Jack realized what he had said, his face went hot, but then she abruptly went quiet.

"Wait, do you mean the pineal gland?" she asked. "In the brain?"

"Yes," Jack said. "A ruptured pineal gland."

"What the hell could do that?" Vivian asked.

"You know what a pineal gland is?" Jack asked.

"An endocrine gland," Vivian answered. "But Jack, it's got a philosophical history as well."

"What do you mean?"

"Since the second century, people have been writing about the pineal as the focal point of consciousness," she said. "The connection between body and soul. More than a few brilliant people, like Descartes for instance, have believed that the soul was located inside this tiny gland."

The room began to spin, and Jack sat down on the arm of a chair. "You mean, the souls of these birds exploded?"

Vivian said, "Well, first, most people who believe in the existence of a soul believe that animals do not have souls, that having a soul is a human-animal differentiator. Second, most of these people, including Descartes, have been proven wrong on countless points when it comes to human physiology."

"But don't you think it's quite a coincidence?" Jack asked. "That birds are dying at scenes of tragedy, of evil? And that in these birds, this particular gland is destroyed?"

"Yes, it's odd," Vivian said. "But even a correlation wouldn't mean it's evil or that it involves the 'soul.' It could still be environmental. Maybe you're onto something, something environmental occurs, it kills birds and it affects humans, causing them to behave in unthinkable ways. I remember something about low radio frequency radiation affecting the pineal gland in rodents, impacting melatonin levels in the animals."

"Causing what? Did it make them violent or was it an insomnia thing?"

Vivian said, "It's been a while, but I only remember it lowered the pineal melatonin. My point is that there are environmental anomalies that can impact our physiology and our behavior. Sometimes it's chemicals, an environmental poisoning, or maybe high-tension power lines."

"Along a line on the map from Brazil to Canada," Jack said.

"We don't know that your line has anything to do with anything yet," Vivian said. Still, Jack could hear in her voice that she no longer seemed as firmly rooted in her skepticism.

And then Jack realized what she had said. "We?"

After a moment, Vivian went on. "Maybe there's something here worth looking into that supercedes your behavior in a restaurant."

Jack smiled. "Thank you."

"Just keep in mind that I have no interest in illusions of a supernatural or paranormal basis for these phenomena, but you have raised enough questions that I'm professionally curious."

Jack said, "Fine with me. I'm not looking to prove anything either, I only want answers."

"Should we meet with this Dr. Glickman, and follow the pineal gland lead then?"

"Glickman has told me everything he's going to," Jack said. "But the local police chief and I have arranged a meeting with Carol, my sister-in-law, to ask her a few questions. She's my brother's widow and the mother of the victims of the murder-suicide we had here."

"Why are the police meeting with her? Aren't they sure about what happened? Are you helping in the investigation somehow?" Vivian asked.

"It's a small town," Jack said. "They'll never be sure about what happened. She's my sister-in-law, and he knows I was a detective. I think Lem wants to try to understand this as much as I do."

Vivian asked, "Where are you meeting?"

"She's a patient at Winter Harbor, a mental health hospital up in Westbrook."

Vivian asked, "What would you ask a woman who's been through what she's been through? And hospitalized at that?"

"I was hoping you'd help with that," Jack said. "Come with me."

Another pause.

"I don't know, Jack," Vivian said.

"What's the matter?"

No answer.

"Drive up here tomorrow, to Goodwin," Jack said. "I'll drive the rest of the way."

"I don't think I can," Vivian said.

"I'll ask all the questions," Jack said. "You observe, take notes.

We'll go over it after. If I go alone, I can capture what she says and relay it, but I might miss something I didn't know was important. We can't bring in a recorder of any kind."

Vivian was quiet.

"What time?" Vivian asked. Her voice was soft.

"Are you okay?"

"What time tomorrow?"

"Can you meet me downtown?" Jack asked. "At the Cup 'n' Time, say around 10:00 a.m.?"

"Do I need directions to find it?"

"The downtown is only one road," Jack said. "You'll find it. There's a huge sign, past a bunch of shops decorated with lobster buoys."

"Alright, Jack, see you tomorrow." She hung up.

A tone sounded from the laptop, indicating received email.

From: Augustine@freemail.com

"Hey Jack-buddy… nothing else can make the mind the companion of evil except its own will and free choice."

Jack immediately hit reply and typed only, "Ben?"

Within seconds, as before, his response kicked back.

"No such account exists on server. Permanent fatal errors."

"Someone is fucking with me," Jack said to himself.

Ch: 12

May 11
10:00 a.m.
Outside the Cup 'n' Time
Goodwin, Maine

Vivian pulled into the parking lot. Jack was surprised. He had expected an old Volvo sedan or maybe a battered Subaru Forrester, forest green. Instead it was a silver Mercedes CLK350, top down.

Jack walked up to the passenger door. "Nice car."

"Where's yours?"

"Vivian, would you mind driving?" Jack asked. The side-effects of his meds had him feeling sluggish this morning.

"Are we hungover, Jack?" she asked.

Jack bristled. "No, we're not. I'll navigate."

Vivian motioned for Jack to get in.

After he closed the door, Jack said, "You look like a tourist driving a Mercedes in Goodwin."

"It's just a car," Vivian replied.

Jack scanned the leather interior. It was impeccably maintained. He said, "It must have been tough to swing it on a professor's salary, with book sales included."

"My parents left me some money."

"Oh," Jack said. The word wasn't much, but there was the slightest bit of tone, and Vivian picked up on it. She hadn't even pulled out of the lot yet, hit the brakes hard, and said, "You don't know anything about me, Jack."

"What? What did I say?"

"Well, ask me straight out, and spare me your ham-handed NYPD information gathering," Vivian said. She wasn't simply irritated; her face was pained.

"Sorry," Jack said.

She didn't pull out. "Maybe coming along was a mistake."

"My meds," Jack said.

"What?"

"I can't drive because I take meds, and the side-effects have me feeling a bit off today," Jack said. It was an offer of some private mental real estate, to make up for obnoxiously stepping into hers.

She looked at him, understood, and pulled out of the lot. "So, I guess I'll drive then."

"Thanks," Jack said.

They headed north on Route 103. As they crossed over the York River, a cool crosswind blew through the interior of the car. Jack glanced over at Vivian. Her hair whipped around her face in the wind, and she didn't bother to pull it away. Jack looked down to his right, out over the L-shaped dock, the small skiffs tied to it, most of them white. Further downriver, anchored fishing boats lolled and rolled, alongside pleasure craft. Around the bend, the river would empty into York Harbor. Along the banks were large houses the locals could no longer afford. The sights of a working fishing community at once picturesque and unfair. The smell filled the air with the reality of what the place had always been about, long before outsiders started building summer homes here.

Soon they were on Route 1A. Then historic gave way to convenient, and they were headed north on Interstate 95.

"Aren't you cold?" Jack shouted, trying to be heard over the wind.

"What?" She leaned his way without taking her eyes off the road. Her hair at times seemingly hanging in mid-air.

He waved her off, and said, "Nothing." He watched her a bit too long. In his chest, he could sense alternating waves of appreciation and apprehension, and Jack knew it made him seem moody and unapproachable. He looked out at the highway.

Vivian thumbed a button on the steering wheel and music began competing with the howling wind around them. Jack listened and leaned back into the leather. He hadn't heard Jeff Buckley sing "Hallelujah" since before Beth died. After a minute or two, it was clear even the anti-depressants weren't going to help with this kind of stimulation.

"Hey!" Jack shouted over the wind.

Vivian looked over. Jack made a slashing motion once across his throat, and then pointed at the radio. She frowned, but with another quick flick of the thumb, the speakers went silent. The song, however, was still loud in Jack's head.

Not long after, he was relieved to see their exit. He pointed, and she nodded. They left the highway, passed beneath it, and then came to an intersection.

"We're going straight through," Jack said, a bit too loudly. They waited on the traffic light. A low-slung red brick building sat off to their left.

"Is that it?" Vivian asked.

Jack said, "It's a little way down that road."

The light changed and they went through.

"Take the next left," Jack said.

"Have you been here before?" she asked. She sounded almost hopeful.

Jack said, "Lem gave me directions."

A mud-colored building appeared, new and modular, as if someone had attached houses and barns together. The roof was complex, with gables, valleys, a variety of pitches, and covered in brown asphalt shingles. They pulled into the lot. Lem was in uniform, leaning against his cruiser, and waiting for them. When the Mercedes came to a stop, the wind was gone, and the sun immediately began warming them. Lem walked over as they got out.

"Thanks for coming, Jack," Lem said, extending his hand.

Jack took it. "Have you been in yet?"

"I was waiting for you."

"Lem, this is Professor Vivian Rueil."

"Vivian," she said.

"Jack said you'd be coming along," Lem said. "Ever interview someone in one of these places before?"

She looked up at the banks of windows. "Not exactly."

They headed for the doors. "Well, prepare yourself, it can be a bit upsetting inside," Lem said.

Vivian said nothing, but pushed her hands into the pockets of her pants.

"They're expecting us?" Jack asked.

"I called ahead and spoke with Carol's doctor," Lem said. "He says not to get our hopes up."

"What is it you two are hoping for, exactly?" Vivian asked.

"I just want answers," Jack said.

As they reached the doors, Vivian said, "I bet she does, too."

* * *

A large reception area, well-lit and appointed, greeted them. A nurse volunteered to take them up to see Carol, and led the way upstairs to the second floor. The nurse paused and glanced back before punching in the key code to unlock the door to the corridor. With a metallic clunk, it opened an inch. The nurse pulled the door wide. Lem went through, but Jack had to wait for Vivian, who hesitated, trading a look with the nurse. Jack couldn't see Vivian's face, but the nurse's expression seemed to soften a bit in the moment before Vivian looked away and went through. Jack followed. The nurse walked quickly past them in order to lead the way.

The interior was painted in soft yellow and tan, with white trim. It felt like a new college dorm. The hallways had burnt-orange colored carpeting and not the wide tiles Jack had expected. Jack slid a foot on the carpet, testing the texture.

Vivian said, "It absorbs sound."

He looked at her, but she didn't make eye contact.

Despite how new the building appeared, this floor for adult patients smelled of urine and strong disinfectant. Natural light streamed in through large hallway windows. That, at least, was different from the countless Eisenhower-era facilities, whether hospitals, schools, or post offices, that seemed to exist in every city and town from coast to coast. Here, no bars on the windows and no two-tone green paint covering cinder-block walls.

The nurse pointed at a room as they went by and said, "This is her room, but she's down in the lounge area." Inside the open doorway were a neatly made bed and a simple chair. The room was an array of greens and blues.

They passed a nurses' station. Some of the staff wore scrubs, some street clothes. Jack assumed a tall man in the white coat was the sole doctor among them. A patient sat biting her nails, furtively listening to someone on the phone, while another walked slowly down the hallway. The staff seemed to have the patients outnumbered on this floor.

Stepping into the lounge area, they saw Carol. She looked calm, with her hair clean and brushed. The little makeup she normally wore was not present. The bruises around her mending nose had begun to fade into an array of greens and blues. She wore a pair of nylon track pants, a baggy T-shirt, and flip-flops. She didn't rise to greet them, but she did attempt a weary smile.

Lem, Jack, and Vivian tentatively took seats around her. The chairs looked like they had come straight from IKEA. Wood-grain frame, too smooth to be actual varnished wood, and dark brown pleather upholstery. New, but inexpensive. The nurse remained standing, and said, "Carol, I'll be right at the station if you need me."

Carol managed a bit more of a smile in acknowledgment, but then it fell completely away as the nurse left. Carol turned to look at Lem. Her head movement was slow enough to suggest medication.

"Hi Carol," Lem said. "We're here."

"Hi," Carol said to all three of them. "Jack, did you take care of everything?"

"I did," Jack said.

Carol looked at the floor for a moment and then said, "You can call me in here, Jack. They let us take phone calls."

Jack nodded. "I'll do that, Carol."

Lem looked at Jack, as if hoping Jack would continue his exchange with Carol and move right into the questions they came to ask, but Jack did not.

Lem shifted in his seat and asked, "Carol, we were wondering if you might be willing to answer a question or two."

Silence.

"At the house," Lem said, more to fill the pause than to help her.

"I don't know," Carol said.

"Why would…" Lem began, but Jack touched his arm.

"Do you remember what you had for breakfast that morning?" Jack asked. Start small, build from there, and construct a timeline. Jack never expected to be using these skills on Keenan's wife. Widow.

She just sat, silent.

"I looked out in the dooryard," Carol said. "I saw someone."

The three exchanged quick glances.

"Who was it?" Lem asked. Jack double-tapped Lem's arm. Lem slid back in his chair.

"What did the person look like?" Jack asked.

"Never saw his face," Carol said. "I was up in the bedroom, looking down. I saw him. From up there."

"What was he doing?" Jack asked.

"Walking. Slow. He was lame."

Jack was taken aback. "You mean he had a limp?"

Carol nodded and turned to look right at him.

"What was he wearing, Carol?"

She said nothing.

"Carol, what did he have on?" Jack asked.

"A long, black coat."

Jack felt his mouth go dry, and he paused.

"What happened next?" Lem asked.

"I went down into the kitchen. I looked out again. I was looking for him." Her voice was rising.

"Where was he?" Lem asked.

She paused, turned her head slowly toward Lem and said, "On top of the barn."

Lem looked at Jack and rolled his eyes. Keenan's barn was high. Getting up there would take a series of ladders, time, serious effort, and no fear of heights.

"Squatting, like a monkey, on the peak of the roof," Carol said. "I didn't know where Keenan was."

Lem sat all the way back.

Jack looked at Vivian who sat motionless, watching Carol.

"What happened next?" Jack asked.

"This feeling came over me," Carol said.

Silence.

"What feeling?"

No answer.

"What happened after the feeling?" Vivian asked.

Carol's head turned surprisingly quickly to Vivian, as if she were suddenly aware of her presence. "I heard the gunshot."

"Before the gunshot, you never heard the children?" Lem asked.

Carol did not turn to him. Her eyes began searching, the wall, the ceiling, and then her face screwed up in anguish and she began to cry.

Vivian left her chair and went to one knee in front of Carol, wrapping her arms around Carol, consoling her. Jack shot an angry look at Lem. It wasn't his fault; as police chief in Goodwin, the worst Lem had to deal with was vandalism at the middle school or the occasional minor drug bust. Last week, his department actually received a call on a chicken running loose in the road. Still, Jack wished Lem would shut up.

It seemed the interview was over, but then, unexpectedly, Vivian asked, "What feeling came over you?" It was scarcely more than a whisper.

Carol cried more loudly.

"What feeling, Carol?" Vivian asked.

"Vivian," Jack said.

Vivian continued to hold Carol, and asked again, "What feeling?"

Carol gripped Vivian tightly and said, "I felt… I grabbed a knife off the counter." She sobbed, gasping the words out.

"What feeling?" Vivian asked again.

Jack watched, and Lem slid forward in his seat.

"Tell me," Vivian said. "What feeling?"

"I grabbed the knife. With the long blade. So sharp!" Carol wailed. "I grabbed the knife! I had it!" Carol came out of the chair now and slid down to her knees. The two women holding each other, Carol's sobs wrenching her small body back and forth.

The nurse came in behind them. "Good God! What in the world is going on in here?"

"I wanted to kill them! I wanted to," Carol said through clenched teeth and tears. "And he did it! But I didn't tell him! The gunshot happened as I picked up the knife!"

The nurse shouted down the hallway and then came rushing

around the chairs. She went to the floor, and pushed her way into the position Vivian had assumed. Vivian sat hard on the floor. Other staff members rushed in, and Carol began thrashing. "I had the knife! I picked it up! To kill them!"

Jack moved to Vivian and helped her up, while Lem stood and stared.

"Get them out of here!" the nurse shouted. A couple of staff members hustled them out of the lounge and down the hallway, with curious patients appearing out of every doorway.

Carol's screams in the distance sounded like she was shrieking, "To save them!"

"Go straight down and out," one orderly said, and he closed the door behind them. The three were left standing there on the stair landing, looking at each other. Jack put his hand on Vivian's arm, and felt that she was trembling. They said nothing more, went downstairs and passed through the reception area. Staff members stared as they went by and exited via the main doors.

Lem said, "Jack."

Jack stopped, but Vivian continued on to her car.

"What do you make of all that?" Lem asked.

"I don't have the first damn idea," Jack said.

"She's heavily medicated," Lem said.

"I don't know, Lem," Jack said.

Vivian pulled up with the car. Jack said nothing more, pulled the door open, and sat inside. She pulled away, tires chirping.

* * *

Jack and Vivian settled into uneasiness. The howl of the wind seemed cooler than before. Jack wanted to know why Vivian, who had been hesitant about coming, who had at first remained silent, had suddenly thrown herself into the midst of the interview with Carol. Why had Vivian fixated on Carol's state of mind that horrible day, and then it turned out to be the seemingly most important, and yet most perplexing, thing they learned? It had been an emotional scene, but Vivian had displayed more than sympathy for Carol.

The forty miles of Interstate 95 flew by in thirty minutes. Jack did not say a word, and did not show any sign of anxiety. He sat quietly. If she needed to drive this fast to get it behind her, then he would deal with it. Leaving the toll road, Vivian slowed a bit on the state roads, but not much. In sweeping curves, she used both lanes. When Jack saw the bridge over the York River up ahead, he unconsciously slipped his hand over the door. Her head turned, looked directly at his hand holding on, and then looked out over the water at the boats. Vivian slammed both feet on the brakes and turned the wheel slightly.

The powerful little car mercifully skidded to a stop. Vivian put the car into park. Jack was amazed they hadn't hit the bridge's guardrail. The Mercedes sat at an angle, blocking both lanes on the narrow span. He turned in time to see Vivian slamming her car door as she got out. Jack got out and followed her to the guardrail. Placing his hands on her shoulders, he was about to say something, when she shrugged him off and stepped away. She looked out at the boats.

Jack watched her, but stayed back.

"I shouldn't have gone," she said, folding her arms across her chest.

"What is it, Viv?"

She snapped her head his way, as if she objected to being called that, but then her face softened, and she looked down at the river.

"God, I hate cheap commercial carpeting."

He stepped closer.

"I don't need a shoulder to cry on. I don't need a hug. Just stay back," Vivian said.

Jack stopped, and then glanced at the water.

"I'm not going to jump, you idiot."

Jack paused. "What are you going to do?"

"I'm trying to get a grip. Leave me alone for a minute."

Jack hesitated.

"Get back in the car," she said.

"You sure?" Jack asked.

Vivian looked at him. Jack said nothing, turned, and walked to the car. He opened the door and sat inside. Another car, an old station wagon, appeared at one end of the bridge, slowing as it approached.

The driver's head appeared. "Everything okay here?" He was an older man, clearly a local, with a worn fishing cap and all.

Vivian turned and walked to the car.

"You folks need help?" the local asked.

Jack said, "She needed to take a leak."

Vivian said, "Jack, you're such an ass."

The local nodded and pulled his head back in. Vivian dropped the car into gear and drove around the station wagon. The driver stared at them both, shaking his head, and Jack was sure the old man thought they were just a pair of lost Mass-holes.

They headed for Goodwin.

Ch: 13

May 13
Russia

The watcher watched. He squatted on the roof, his black coat hanging with its hem in a puddle of rainwater. The first of them was brought out into the small courtyard below. The prisoner was impossibly thin, too exhausted to resist. Two guards held the man while a third calmly raised his sidearm and shot him through the head. Blood sprayed from the wound in a fine, pulsing mist. The guards dropped him and the three went back inside. They returned with another emaciated prisoner and shot him in exactly the same way. His body collapsed onto the first. The guards went inside again. A second trio of guards came out and executed their own prisoner, and before they could get back inside a third team of guards came out, murdered a prisoner, and added his body to the growing pile. The courtyard was so small that it was only safe to execute one prisoner at a time. Soon a gruesome queue had formed as guards waited their turn to murder their next victim.

The watcher watched. Each prisoner brought out seemed healthier than the last as the guards worked their way to newer and newer arrivals. The prisoners were actively resisting now, screaming, many of them crying out. The guards, whose faces never showed any sign of emotion, struggled to control the prisoners as they climbed over the already dead.

He watched as the nine guards eventually exhausted the supply of prisoners, sat in a circle, aimed their weapons across at one another, and in a single roar of gunfire, eight of them fell dead in a crown atop their murderous handiwork. The ninth man stood, calmly accepting that he had been odd man out, put his gun to his own head and pulled the trigger.

The watcher stood, scanned his surroundings, stepped over and around the dead birds, and walked off the far edge of the roof.

Ch: 14

May 13
6:25 a.m.
Home
Goodwin, Maine

The radio was on as background noise, some morning show attempting to be amusing, while Jack layered toast, eggs, and cheese. Picking it up with both hands, he stood at the counter looking into the yard, and took a first, enormous bite. Dishes were piling up in the sink. He hadn't shaved in a couple days. On either side of where the crumbs fell to the countertop were printouts. A news story of a Sunday school teacher who murdered a little girl. Another concerning Chinese human rights abuses. An interview with a Baptist minister about the signs of the coming End Times.

The radio went to news. One of the four voices, engaged in sophomoric nonsense just moments before, began reading from the AP Wire. "In Chistopol… Shistopol?" Laughter. "In Chistopol, Russia, overnight there are reports of a mass slaughter of prisoners. Early reports describe piles of dead prisoners, each shot once in the head. Director of Chistopol Prison, Aleksander Kratsov, is reportedly under arrest."

Jack stopped chewing and listened.

"That's messed up!" one morning show host said.

"There's more!" the reader said. "Get this! Local officials also fear that the nearby temporary radioactive waste storage site may have been compromised somehow. There have been unexplained reports of dead birds. Russian and international investigators are on the way to the scene now. Chistopol is approximately five hundred miles east of Moscow."

Before the last sentence had completed, Jack was at his map. He pushed away the printouts and books on top of it, laid it out flat, and oriented himself. Russia. Moscow. East. East. There, on the Volga River. He grabbed the yardstick and the marker off of the coffee table, pulling it from beneath yet more printouts. He drew a line from Chistopol to Prévost. Jack sat back. From Brazil to eastern Canada to Russia. His brow furrowed. Jack jumped up and ran into the kitchen, to the junk drawer, and pulled it open. Scotch tape, shoe polish, twine—he found it. Running back, he dropped to his knees and laid the protractor over the angle formed by the two lines meeting in Prévost. Sixty-six degrees.

He looked at the dot on the eastern coast of Brazil. It was labeled, "Fortaleza, May 1." He followed the line through Maine, past Montreal to Prévost, and read aloud, "Prévost, May 7." His eyes went around the angle and came to rest on Chistopol. He leaned forward to label that point as well, but then stopped. The chill that children get when they first conceptualize the idea of death ran through him. Jack leaned forward again and wrote with a trembling hand, "Chistopol, May 13."

He sat up. He rose slowly and went into the kitchen. He picked up the phone.

"Hello?" she answered.

"Vivian, I need to see you."

"Actually, Jack, I've had enough. I've been meaning to call you. I can't do this anymore. I don't have the…"

"Vivian, I *need* to see you."

She said nothing.

"Please," Jack said. "It's important. I need to be sure I'm not losing it."

She paused. "I believe you. That's why I don't think I can."

Jack said. "I need your help. I've discovered something."

Nothing.

"Vivian?"

She asked, "What did you find?"

"I can't tell you on the phone. I'm not even sure it makes sense in person. I have to show you. Just come see what I've found," Jack said.

Silence. Then she hung up on him. Jack looked at the phone. He blinked a couple times. If he had been stronger, he wouldn't have called her back. If she had been stronger, he thought, she probably wouldn't have answered.

"Vivian, come look," Jack said. His voice had gone flat.

A long pause and then Jack heard a deep sigh.

"Where?" she asked.

"Please come here. It's a white farmhouse out on Sayward Road. That's a left off Main Street, about a mile up. On your left, you'll see it. The mailbox is sticking up out of a white antique lobster trap. There's no name on it."

"When?"

"Right now, Viv," Jack said. "Come right now."

"Jack, I've got a morning class..." She didn't finish. Jack knew she was coming to Maine.

"See you soon," he said and hung up.

The radio was still on. "Shut up!" said a female voice, laughing. "Shut up or we'll send you to Shistopol!" More laughter.

Jack turned it off, walked to a chair in the living room, and pushed the books off of it. He sat and he waited.

* * *

When Vivian knocked at the door, Jack did not immediately rise. The door opened slowly.

"Jack?" Vivian's voice carried into the living room. He got to his feet and made his way to the entryway. He saw her taking in the mess, her eyes sweeping the piles of paper printouts and books, the dirty dishes and half-eaten food. The open bottles of medications and the empty bottle of Crown Royal.

"Jack?" Vivian asked again. This time her voice was loaded with concern and edged with fear.

"It looks worse than it is," Jack said. "I've found something you need to see." He turned and walked back the way he came. He glanced over his shoulder and saw her hesitating, clinging to the door handle as a child might cling to the ladder on a pool's deep end.

"Come on," he said. Vivian released the door but did not close it. Jack didn't care. He led her into what had once been a spare and tidy living room—into what had become wall-to-wall maps, Wikipedia entries and news printouts. Mingled together on the floor were illustrations made for Dante's *Divine Comedy* and photos of last week's homicides. Jack lowered himself to the floor. As she approached and looked past him at the map spread out on the floor, he took her hand and gently pulled her downward until she knelt beside him.

"Vivian, there's a pattern. You remember the line from Fortaleza in Brazil to Prévost in the Montreal area," Jack said as he traced the line with one finger.

"I remember."

"Have you heard the news this morning about Chistopol, in Russia?" Jack asked.

"The prison thing? The killings?"

"I drew a line from Prévost to Chistopol," Jack said. Vivian looked at the new line, trying to find some sort of significance.

"I don't get it, Jack," Vivian said finally. She fidgeted, shifting her weight.

He placed the protractor down onto the map, moved it with two fingers, lining it up.

"The two lines form a sixty-six-degree angle," he said flatly.

"Sixty-six?" Vivian asked.

Jack waited.

"Oh, come on, Jack," she said, "you don't mean as in the biblical reference to a set of sixes being the number of the devil?"

His expression never changed. "The incident in Brazil happened on May 1, the one in Canada on May 7, the Russian one today."

She waited.

"Six days apart," he said.

Her face looked more concerned with Jack's mental state than with what he was saying. "Listen to me, Jack, the Christian devil those numbers supposedly refer to wasn't even fully realized as a character until Matthew's gospel, and the numbers don't appear until the Book of Revelation, written almost one-hundred years after the death of Jesus. Some scholars believe the number refers to Nero, the emperor, and not the devil at all, and that the author sat in a cave on Patmos writing a political document. Others even believe the number is mistranslated, and the actual number is 616. The number is a creation of a man attempting to influence other people. Thomas Jefferson referred to Revelation as the 'ravings of a maniac.' It's not a supernatural number."

"Vivian, I'm not crazy. I'm not a religious nut. I'm looking at these numbers. Look at it as if it's coincidence if you'd like, but *look*. If the numbers have no religious significance, fine, but they do have significance. There is a pattern here."

She thought for a moment and then said, "But your brother's death, here in this town, that breaks the six-day pattern."

"What if," Jack asked, "what if the six days and sixty-six degrees only apply to the major events, larger-scale occurrences? What if Keenan and the kids were simply targets of opportunity? They were struck only in passing."

"Of what?" Vivian asked. "The passing of what?"

Jack's mouth opened as if he would answer, but he said nothing.

Vivian stood. "Jack, you've taken this too far. You're out of your depth. You're an accomplished investigator, and you keep turning up clues, but you don't have the background to protect yourself. Intellectually. Psychologically."

"You're scared," Jack said.

Vivian stopped.

Jack said, "You're seeing it too, and you're scared. You're able to use your education to find places to hide from this, but I want you to think, open-mindedly. Viv, I wasn't looking for sixes. They were just there."

She said nothing. Jack stood and approached her. Vivian looked around at the mess once more and took a step back. He put his hands gently on her arms.

"Vivian, you're right, I am out of my depth, but I'm not crazy. I'm not inventing anything. I'm not clutching at straws. I'm simply paying attention."

She dropped her gaze to the floor.

"But I am in over my head. I've never pretended to know this stuff. That's what this mess is all about. It goes to show how aware I am of how little I know about the philosophy, the psychology," Jack said, and he dropped his arms.

"That's why I went to you, sought you out, in the first place. I know you're scared. I'm scared too, but I need you. We're hooked into something here, and we haven't begun to understand it, but I think you feel it too, that this is *important*."

Her eyes were wet but she held back the tears. "Jack, what you're suggesting is too big. It would mean that there is a pattern to evil. A pattern would mean that the bad things that happen to people are not random. A pattern would mean an intelligent decision-maker was behind the deaths of all those innocent people."

"But it's not simply something I'm suggesting. Vivian, it's happening."

"Jack," Vivian said, "it can't be right. There must be another explanation. If you were right, we'd be able to track that same pattern back to when? All through recorded history? What about evil that occurred before people invented the concept of a devil? What about evil that occurred that wasn't on one of your damn lines?"

"They're not my lines."

"Dammit, Jack, if you're right, we could even predict where and when the next large-scale evil will occur!"

They both stopped cold, and their eyes widened. They simultaneously dove for the map. Vivian grabbed the protractor first.

"Lay it down!"

"I am!"

With trembling hands, she laid it on the line to Chistopol. Jack laid the yardstick over the top of it. Their eyes followed the line it made. Past Volgograd. Through Turkey.

"Maybe Turkey. One of the worst genocides in history happened there. Maybe new violence, maybe against the Kurds," Vivian said.

Jack looked farther. Vivian gripped the yardstick. Through Syria, which was certainly a candidate. Into South Sudan, just east of Darfur.

"Darfur?" she asked.

He looked at her.

"It's been the site of unspeakable evil, but it's ongoing, for years now. Why would May 19 be especially important there?" Vivian asked.

He stood again, and she immediately followed.

"I'm going," Jack said.

"Where? To Darfur?" she asked. "You *are* crazy."

"I have to figure this out. I have to go. We potentially have advance knowledge of an atrocity that has yet to be committed. I have to go."

Vivian's arms swung wildly as she spoke. "Jack! You don't even know what will happen. And it's not a small place, almost impossible to get around in, spotty communication at best. You're looking for a site potentially as small as a house in a vast and savage territory! And even if you find it, what can you do?"

"I'm going. Help me figure out how to get there. Where to fly in, how to get into Darfur, do I need a visa, that sort of thing."

"I'm not a travel agent, Jack."

He paused. "Honestly, this shit scares me. Alright? All this evil shit. Why horrible things happen to seemingly innocent people, why some people die and some people live… I have to know."

"Why?" Vivian asked. "Why do you need to know so badly?"

Jack's jaw set. He wasn't going to tell her, but then he did, in spite of himself. "Because of Beth. My wife was killed. Burned, in a car wreck in New Hampshire after we were run off the road. The truck never stopped. I lived and she died."

"I'm sorry," Vivian said. "I'm so sorry."

"She was such a good person," Jack said. "Her death was inexplicable. Bad luck doesn't cover it. I can't believe it was her destiny to burn; that somehow, that was her fate."

Vivian said, "Fate can be cruel."

Jack said, "You're an expert and I need you on this."

She put her hands on her hips. Jack could see her hardening again, putting her defenses back up, and digging in.

"Call someone," she said.

"What?"

"If you really believe that you can predict these atrocities, you don't fly out there yourself, like some sort of global Lone Ranger. You call someone."

Jack said, "Who? I have no one else."

She threw her hands up. "I don't know! The FBI, the State Department, I don't know! But you don't have to go, you tell someone what you've found, and then you've done your bit. You were a detective. Don't you have any friends, any favors you could call in?"

Jack could see that she was afraid, but that her fear was for him. He stepped toward her, not sure of what he was going to do. Her face changed, ever so slightly, and she took half a step back, dropped her eyes. He reached out and took both her shoulders in his hands. Vivian pulled the left one back slightly, as if she might turn away, but she didn't. Instead, he took another step forward, closing the space between them. She looked up into his face with an expression that was part concern, part anticipation.

He bent forward slowly, his eyes open, and she closed hers as their mouths met. Jack felt her gentle exhale across his lips, soft and warm. Her arms came up around his shoulders and he folded her into him. He kissed her again, and then pulled his head back. Her eyes slowly opened.

"I've got a friend in the FBI, in Boston. I'll go see him," Jack said.

Vivian said nothing, and she placed her head on his chest. Jack closed his eyes, his nose against her hair.

She said, "I'm not even sure yet if I like you."

"You let me kiss you."

"I was just curious," she said, but didn't let him go.

Ch: 15

May 13
2:30 p.m.
FBI Field Office
Boston, Massachusetts

Assistant Special Agent in Charge James Saniqua strode directly towards Jack, hand outstretched, and said, "Jack, how have you been?"

"Hey Jim," Jack said, taking his hand. "Thanks for seeing me on such short notice."

"No problem at all. Come into my office."

Jack followed Jim into an office trimmed in dark wood, and sat in the chair offered to him, putting his messenger bag on his lap.

"So, how *have* you been?" Jim asked.

Jack took it to mean how had he been without Beth, as in how the self-exile was going. Jack had lost a wife, a brother, nieces and nephew, left his career behind, was clinically depressed, and had stumbled onto a potential pattern of global evil, but said only, "Congrats on the promotion, Jim."

"Thanks," Jim said, smiling. He was slim, a marathon runner, with that gaunt old-beyond-their-years look that many distance runners seem to eventually develop. "What do you have for me?"

Jack opened the messenger bag and pulled out the map. "Jim, I've found a pattern. It links major crime scenes, internationally."

Jim was on his feet before Jack had the map unfurled. "Over here, man, on the table."

Jack followed him and laid the map out. "Look, there was that terrorist incident, went bad in Brazil."

"Right, right, the Chilean thing."

"Right. And then there was the cult suicide outside Montreal," Jack said.

"Check. In Prévost."

"Right, now check this out. Here's the site of the prison massacre in Chistopol, in Russia. See these lines? This angle in Prévost? Sixty-six degrees, man."

Jim stared at the map, his eyes narrowing, trying to dig it out.

"Sixty-six, Jim. And these events happened six days apart. Three sixes."

A heavy pause.

"You see it, man?" Jack asked.

Jim's shoulders slumped, and he slowly straightened. "Yeah, Jack, I see it."

Jack searched Jim's face. Pity. "Wait, no, I'm not nuts here. I'm not making these numbers up."

"Jack."

"And if you take a sixty-six degree turn in Chistopol, it takes you near Darfur."

"Jack!"

"What?" Jack asked, but he knew.

"Jack, this is nothing, man. This is like a news story you'd find on page six. This is nothing," Jim said.

"It's *not* nothing. There's something to this. I feel it. This is real. It's subtle, I know, but that's why it goes unnoticed," Jack said.

"Look… this isn't subtle, this is nonexistent. You need to let this go. You and I have both seen people lose it, turning little coincidences into full-blown paranoia, and go off on crazy personal crusades. Remember that guy that pulled out all his own teeth and used them to leave a trail?"

"Fuck, Jim. I'm not fucking crazy. I'm not reaching for the pliers here. I've found a pattern. I think you should take it seriously."

"The only thing I'm taking seriously is my concern for you. You need some help. Let this go. Think small for a while."

Jack looked at the map and then back at Jim. "Have you ever known me to go off half-cocked? You know me, Jim."

"It's only because I know you that you're in here. Do you have any idea how many nutty theories are brought to the FBI on any given day? I agreed to see you because you and I go back. There is nothing on this earth more valuable than a true friendship, and as your friend, I'm telling you, let this go."

Jack looked at Jim for a moment and then rolled the map back up. "Thanks for your time."

Jim sighed. "Why don't you come to supper at my place? Hell, you can crash there tonight. We'll watch the Sox spank the Yankees."

"Thanks for your time, Jim." Jack picked up his bag and walked out of the office.

Ch: 16

May 14
4:45 a.m.
Home
Goodwin, Maine

Dream

I step out of my car and look up a hill. There's a windmill. Made of fieldstones with great canvas sails. It's spinning too quickly. I walk up the hill. The sails spin even more quickly. With each pass, they miss striking the ground by only a couple feet. A young girl appears in the arched doorway. She's wearing a green robe. She is exiting the mill, with the sails whooshing down and past in her path. I'm running. I'm shouting for her to stop. The sails are spinning faster and faster. She never looks at the coming sail. It hits her and throws her down the slope to my left. A fine mist of blood and her shoes are left behind. Then another child appears, another girl. I can't get up there. I'm slipping in the soft soil. I'm sinking in it to my ankles. She has long, blonde hair, pinned on top of her head. The mill strikes her. Her broken body is flipping feet-over-head down the slope. My little niece, Mariah, appears in the doorway. Her neck is bent. I scream to her. She smiles and waves.

She walks into the path of the next sail and is thrown like the other two. Something catches my eye. Off to the side of the mill, I see him. Keenan. He is turning a large, ridiculous crank attached to the side of the mill. He, too, smiles, as the sails kill yet another child. I hear Beth's voice. She's calling my name. I see her, atop the windmill. I stop trying to climb the hill. She is not on fire, but is badly burned, with no hair, no lips. She jumps onto a sail as it passes and rides it around as it strikes one more child, the little boy flies like the rest. The smallest child thus far exits the doorway. I try to look away, but I can't. Angelic face. He steps out and effortlessly snatches the sail with his right hand, and the entire windmill comes to an abrupt stop. Beth still clutches her sail, high above, arms and legs wrapped into it. I look at the little boy. Keenan stands watching, no longer smiling. The little boy holds the windmill still. He does not open his mouth, but I hear a deep-throated voice. It fills my brain, driving away every other thought. It says, "I am I."

The phone was ringing.

"Jack, it's me." Vivian's voice.

"What time is it?"

"Almost 5:00 a.m.," she answered.

"Are you okay?"

"I just had a dream, Jack. A bizarre dream. I dreamt of a windmill killing kids."

The fog immediately lifted, and Jack's thinking instantly focused.

"Vivian, was a man turning a crank on one side?"

Silence. Jack waited. Everything was louder. The ticking clock sounded like a hammer and anvil.

"Oh my God," Vivian said.

Jack said, "I had the same dream."

"Oh my God. Oh my God, oh God."

"What else was in your dream? Maybe you saw something different," Jack said.

"Oh my God." Her voice was soft.

"Vivian, if we're both having the same dreams, there must be a reason for it. Think," Jack said.

"A figure jumped onto one of the sails and rode it around."

Jack winced, "Describe the figure."

"Badly burned, a woman, I think."

"Beth."

"What?" Vivian asked.

"What happened next?" Jack asked.

"Another kid came out, but this time, instead of being killed, he stopped the windmill with his hand."

Jack nodded to himself. "Viv, this is important, did you hear a voice?"

"Yes."

"What did it say?" Jack asked, eyes closed. He fell back on the bed, knowing what was coming.

"It said, 'You can still save Jack.' That's why I called you."

Jack bolted upright, eyes wide. "It didn't."

"What?" Vivian asked. "It did!"

Jack fell silent and rubbed his face.

"Jack?" Vivian asked. "What did the voice say to you?"

"It said the same thing it has said in other dreams."

"What?" Vivian asked.

"The voice said, 'I am I.'"

Silence.

"Does it mean anything, Vivian? I've Googled it and found Neil Diamond lyrics."

"In the Book of Exodus, Moses, speaking for God, says it."

"He says, 'I am' or 'I am that I am' or something like that. I saw that," Jack said.

Vivian said, "It's actually recorded as Moses saying, '*Ani, ani hu*' which means 'I am I.' Isaiah also spoke for God. Using the doubled form of 'I' he said '*Anochi, Anochi*.' It's still best translated as 'I am I.'"

"You're suggesting that we're dreaming of God and windmills?"

"I'm not suggesting anything," Vivian said. "I'm telling you that 'I am I' has biblical significance."

"Why is God speaking English in our dreams?" Jack asked,

"I didn't say it is God. It was a dream. What we need to figure out is why we had virtually identical dreams on the same night. It's a psychological question. We also need to work out the significance of the difference in what the voice said." She had reverted to her professor's voice.

"This is bigger than psychology and you know it," Jack said. "I'm going to South Sudan."

Silence.

"I have to go," Jack said.

Vivian's voice grew soft. "Jack, don't go. The voice said I could still save you. You're not supposed to go."

"Didn't you just say you believe in a psychological explanation for the dreams?"

A pause, and then she said, "I'm not sure what I believe anymore, but I know I don't want you going to Africa."

Jack felt himself soften. "Vivian, what if we've stumbled upon something no one else has noticed? This pattern, what if we're the only ones who know about it?"

"But why do you have to go? So what if the FBI didn't take it seriously? Why not write a letter to the news media and walk away? Get the word out about what you've found. Write a book. You don't have to physically go anywhere."

Jack hesitated. She was right. He hadn't even considered any of this. Why hadn't he? Because he knew it wouldn't be enough. He felt incredibly drawn, he felt compelled. He wasn't supposed to be a spectator on this one. Jack knew he was already a participant. He had to go.

"I'm sorry," Jack said. "We're past that. I need to see for myself. I'll be in touch."

II

"Finally, his wit being wholly extinguished, he fell into one of the strangest conceits that ever madman stumbled on in this world; to wit, it seemed unto him very requisite and behooveful, as well for the augmentation of his honour as also for the benefit of the commonwealth, that he himself should become a knight-errant, and go throughout the world..."
—*Don Quixote*, Miguel de Cervantes Saavedra

Ch: 17

May 15
9:30 a.m.
Amsterdam Airport Schiphol
Netherlands

With a little less than an hour before his next flight, Jack walked quickly. His next connection was in a different terminal. Having flown overnight from Boston, his mouth was pasty, his hair under a hat, and it would be another nine hours before he finally made it to Nairobi. Once there, he'd have to spend a night in a local hotel, and then in the morning, try to catch a flight to Juba, in South Sudan. That was the plan, at least.

Jack wondered if Vivian was worrying about him. He glanced at his watch again. She was probably still sleeping, maybe dreaming, and hopefully not of windmills.

He shifted the weight of his canvas and leather messenger bag, and pushed the restroom door open. He stopped. A row of urinals, mounted on a wall that was itself an enormous photo of a canal in Amsterdam. The porcelain seemed to float in mid-air. The crystal-clear image seemed to invite people to urinate, through a railing, into the canal. He tried to imagine such a thing in New York—a row of men standing together, in the midst of the illusion of pissing into the Hudson.

"Europeans," Jack whispered as he walked over to the urinal.

Inside the porcelain, he noticed a fly, sitting, unmoving. The yellow stream of his urine splashed over it, but it didn't move. It was painted on. Craning his neck, he looked into the urinal to his left and saw an identical fly painted into that one as well. A target for piss? Weird. The depicted canal was lined with red-brick shops and homes. In the distance was a church steeple.

The door opened behind him. He zipped his pants and turned in time to have a fist come crashing into his face. The pain was intense, and momentarily blinding, but Jack had the sense to move out of the corner. His instincts screamed out for him to reach for the gun he no longer carried. Bent over, with an arm up to protect himself, he used the other hand to check for damage and blood, and saw the leather work boots his assailant wore. He lowered his arm. The man was taller than Jack, had thirty pounds on him, and wore a white T-shirt beneath a blue denim jacket. Black jeans were bunched up at the top of the boots. He had a beard, but was bald.

Jack asked, "What the fuck? What do you want?"

The man said nothing, and moved toward him. Jack straightened and balanced himself on the balls of his feet. The messenger bag fell limp against his hip. The man reached out with his right hand as if to grab Jack by the throat. The move, this time, was not a surprise, and was slow and telegraphed. Jack pushed the large hand past him, grabbing it firmly. His left thumb lay diagonally across the back of the man's hand and he used the man's own momentum to pull him forward and off-balance. Jack stepped back smoothly with his left foot, his hips pivoting, and turned the man's hand over. The large man came off his feet and flipped onto his back. Jack snapped a kick into the man's face, more to daze him than to injure him, and then rotated the man's extended arm. The man cried out and rolled himself onto his abdomen. Jack knelt, applying more and more pressure to the man's locked elbow and shoulder. Another three or four inches and the shoulder joint would come free. Jack was willing to go at least that far.

"Why?" Jack asked.

The man said nothing; instead he only grunted in pain. Jack knew there was a good possibility the man spoke no English. He pushed the arm another couple inches.

"Who are you?" Jack asked.

The man howled, "I was only to see that you did not make your next flight!" A local accent.

Now he was getting somewhere. "Who sent you?"

The man resisted, and Jack applied more pressure.

"I do not know him! He gave me money and said to make you miss your next flight!"

"What did he look like?" Jack asked.

He did not answer. Instead, the man lifted his own face as high as he could from the floor. Jack had seen this before. Releasing his arm, he tried to grab the man's head, but was too late. He watched helplessly as the man drove his own head into the tiled floor. With a sickening crack, the grout lines near the man's face began to turn red. Jack checked for a pulse and found one. The man was losing blood, but the cut on his forehead looked superficial.

He needed to get out of there. Checking himself for blood, his mind and heart raced. He glanced at the mirror and saw the makings of a decent shiner but nothing else. Picking up his hat, Jack smoothed his shirt, straightened his bag, and slowly opened the restroom door. He looked briefly back at the man lying on the floor, and then stepped out into the concourse. The women's restroom had a multilingual out-of-order sign hanging from the door handle. Jack moved the yellow sign to the men's door. He turned and headed for his gate. And then Jack saw him. Far in the distance, squatting atop pay-carts for luggage, was the man in the black coat. At Jack's first step toward him, the crowd doubled in density. Jack lost sight of him beyond the throng. When the crowd thinned once more, the man in the black coat had vanished.

Jack turned for the gate. He passed through the security checkpoint without incident. He looked back, past the checkpoint, and stopped. Emerging from the restroom was an old man, helping a boy, an adolescent, who might have weighed 110 pounds. The boy wore leather boots, black jeans, and a blue denim jacket over a white T-shirt. The old man and the boy walked slowly, the latter holding a bloody handkerchief to his face.

What had he done? That kid had been a large man. Hadn't he? Jack turned and quickly walked down the concourse.

When he arrived at the gate, the last of the passengers were boarding. He handed the attendant his passport and his boarding pass. She compared them and then handed back his passport. Jack looked around, scanning quickly to see if he had been followed. His heart was pounding. He was sure to be on a dozen cameras coming out of that restroom and placing the sign on the door.

"Sir?" the attendant asked, handing Jack the stub to his boarding pass.

He took the stub and walked down the gangway to the aircraft. He found his seat, slid the messenger bag under the seat in front of him, and then sat back. Jack watched the door for signs of the police or airport security, or someone else sent to stop him, perhaps even the man in black. With each passing minute he was surer someone would enter, and that there would be another confrontation. Even when the door was closed, with the plane only half full, his heart scarcely slowed. The aircraft was pushed back, and then it taxied out to the runway. The engines began howling to be set free, the aircraft was vibrating, and the pilot released the brakes.

It was only then that Jack considered what the man in black might do to an aircraft in flight. Had he gotten on the plane in the same way a fox is driven to ground, trapping itself, only to be dug out and torn to shreds by hounds?

The runway below whizzed past more and more quickly. The nose lifted and Jack watched as the ground slowly fell away. Catching only a glimpse of him, Jack spotted the man in the black coat, squatting on top of weather equipment at the far end of the pavement, watching the plane lift off. Jack checked his watch. 10:40 a.m., local time. An almost eight-hour flight. Would police be waiting for him in Nairobi?

Pulling out his messenger bag, Jack dug around the toothbrush and paste, around a shirt and some underwear, past the book by St. Augustine he had taken from the library back in Goodwin, until his hand wrapped around a small package and a novel. Removing the package, he took several chewable Dramamine. Then he pulled the novel out and left the bag on the empty seat beside him. *Sympathy for the Devil* by Kent Anderson. Jack pressed back into his seat and began to read.

"Sixth sense is only the other five senses fine-tuned to threat. A shift in the rhythm of the silence that opens your eyes. A shudder in the pattern of shadow. The hint of some smell that brings your head up. Separately they would mean nothing, but together they are enough to lift the hair on your neck, to stir little bubbles of dread deep in the back of your brain, all of them forming like a forgotten name, right on the tip of your tongue. A group of men moving through the dark with plans to kill you gives off an energy you can feel if you pay attention to what your senses tell you."

Is that what it was? Jack wondered. Maybe it wasn't a question of sanity. Perhaps it was all just a matter of being more tuned in than most people, or being more aware or sensitive. Maybe he could sense these things that others couldn't because he was simply paying attention.

* * *

The plane dropped hundreds of feet in seconds, and in the instant Jack awoke, he was virtually weightless. In the next moment, it felt as if the aircraft had hit the ground. Jack looked out the window and saw they were still high above the earth below. The cabin lights flickered off and then back on, and then they went out completely. A woman behind him screamed. The plane fell again and Jack's seatbelt strained, holding him in his seat. When the plane bottomed out in the rough air this time, overhead compartments burst open, their contents spilling out onto passengers. The lights flickered once more. The engines whined. Drinks and books and cell phones, clothes and papers and pillows flew about the cabin. The plane seemed determined to shake itself apart. Jack looked back at the wing, and the length of it flapped up and down in the turbulence like one of a panicked bird. Looking forward, he saw even the flight attendant had her eyes closed, buckled in, facing the passengers, with her fingers wrapped around the edges of her seat.

It seemed every passenger was screaming, crying, or praying. Everyone but Jack. He was staring forward, because in the flickering light, there he stood, the man in black, leaning against the bulkhead. The turbulence was tossing around everything not bolted down, but the man was unaffected. He stood there, impassively staring back. Jack felt a rage building within him. Reaching down, he unfastened his seatbelt, and fought to stand. He was shouting before he was completely on his feet. "Can you see him? Can anyone see him?"

In that instant, all was calm, the lights were on. Everyone was sitting in his or her seat, reading or sleeping. Whispering with loved ones. They all stopped and looked up at Jack. The turbulence was gone, and with it the man in black.

Jack sat back down. Those around him stared a moment longer before returning to what they had been doing before his outburst. He checked his watch, and saw that it was 5:10 p.m. There was still another hour. He looked out the window, and saw they were still six miles up. Africa was down there. And so, Jack expected, was the man in black.

Ch: 18

May 15
7:30 p.m.
Jomo Kenyatta International Airport
Nairobi, Kenya

They landed and disembarked without incident. He had, however, picked up an acute case of paranoia. As he cleared Customs, he looked downright jittery and he knew it. He was suspicious of everyone who'd so much as taken a second glance, and because of his state, many people had. Attempting to buy a ticket for the next leg wasn't any easier.

"Sir, I can sell you a ticket, but you need a visa to go to Juba." The airline clerk's face was dark, smooth, and kind. She was not even staring at his still-darkening black eye.

Jack looked up. The sign above, in bright blue letters, read, "JetLink Express." Two well-placed dots turned the "J" into the mouth of a smiley face.

"How can I get a visa?"

"You will have to go to the Government of the Republic of South Sudan office, in Nairobi, tomorrow morning. They might be able to have your visa ready by the end of the day," she said.

"But my flight to Juba is at 10:00 a.m.," Jack said.

"We have one every day at that time, sir. It appears you'll have to spend two nights in Nairobi instead of the one," she said. "The visa will cost you only forty dollars, U.S."

Tomorrow was May 16. If all went well, he'd arrive in Juba on May 17. He'd have two days to get out into the field and try to figure out what was coming, and then… and then do what?

"Sir?" she asked.

"Should I purchase my ticket now?"

"I would wait, sir, until you have a visa in hand."

Of course. "How would I find a hotel?"

She pointed across the airport. "Take a taxi. I recommend the Kestrel Court Hotel. You can exchange a bit of money right over there for the fare, but change just enough."

"Thank you," Jack said. He had checked no bags; everything was in the messenger bag. After exchanging some money, with no idea how much just enough was, he stepped out of the terminal and immediately spotted a taxi. It was an older ash-grey sedan, with a yellow stripe running down one side. Jack thought it looked like a Citroën, but he didn't know for sure.

"The Kestrel Hotel?" Jack asked as he sat inside. Without a word from the driver, the cab was in motion. The streets were wet. Eight- and ten-story buildings lined the divided road, with large palms drooping down over the roadway. The construction was reminiscent of anywhere where practicality had exceeded aesthetics in priority, with grey blocks and poured concrete walls. One squat building, faced with red brick, seemed familiar, with its blood-red, rain-soaked exterior. The street was lit by few streetlights; cars and buses were in a competition for the roadway. Pedestrians crossed anywhere and anytime they decided to test their luck.

The Kestrel Hotel had columns and arches, four of which supported a large carport. The exterior walls and the columns were painted a pale lemon yellow. The grounds were landscaped with mulch and carefully placed plants. Still, the entire scene seemed staged, and at bargain prices yet. The woman at the airport must have sensed that he had not been seeking luxury accommodations.

"How much?"

The driver didn't say anything. Instead he pointed at the meter. Jack paid him and exited the taxi. He walked into the lobby. Behind the check-in counter stood a young clerk in a jacket, scribbling something. The clerk looked up. "Checking in?"

"I don't have a reservation."

"That's fine, sir. Let us see what we have." The clerk's English was excellent and crisp, the consonants a bit overly-annunciated.

Jack looked around the lobby, which seemed clean and new, likely renovated within the last couple years.

"Ah yes, sir, we have a room on the third floor, will that do?"

"I'd prefer the first floor," Jack said.

"The view really is much better from the third floor, sir," the clerk said.

Jack just stared at him.

"Of course, sir, the first floor."

Jack didn't want to be trapped in a room from which he could not escape via the window. Things had changed. He had only been following hunches and a possible pattern, but that pattern had punched him in the face in Amsterdam.

"Ah yes, sir, your passport and credit card please?"

Jack produced his passport and credit card. He said, "Two nights please."

"Of course, sir."

Jack watched the clerk tapping away on the keyboard. He felt a sudden wave of anxiety when the credit card was swiped, because he knew he was leaving a trail. Jack signed for the room, and the clerk handed him his credit card, passport, and a key.

"Your room is right down this hallway to my right, sir. Have a nice night."

* * *

Jack pushed the door open and stepped into his room. It was very clean. The bed was a simple wooden frame with a thin mattress. The tan blanket and white sheet were already turned down for him. A wicker chair sat in one corner, a television mounted high in the opposite corner, and a small table beneath it. The table was itself a shelf, mounted to the wall alongside the window, with a small brass lamp atop it. The drapes brushed up against the table. A small armless wooden chair stood beside it. Jack walked over to the drapes and pulled them open. Fifteen feet away was another wall, another section of the Kestrel Hotel. Jack looked up and saw that it was only a couple stories high. That's why the clerk had suggested the third floor, so that he'd be able to see over that block of the hotel.

A small multilingual sign sat on the table indicating that the Internet was available in his room. He didn't have a laptop with him, but Jack wanted to check his email, so he attempted to connect using his phone. It didn't work.

He decided to go to the small business center he'd seen near the lobby. He considered leaving the messenger bag in the room, then thought better of it and kept it hanging from his shoulder.

When he found the business center, it was locked. The sign said it closed at 7:00 p.m. He spotted the lobby clerk coming his way.

"Could I get in here to check my email? I'll be quick."

"I am sorry, sir, the business center is closed," the clerk said.

From his pocket, Jack pulled two bills, 1000 Kenyan shillings each, the reddish-brown bills representing about $25. He offered them to the clerk, who slowly took them, and then opened the door.

"Thanks," Jack said. He stepped in, the door closed behind him, and through the window, Jack watched the man walk away.

The terminal was older, but not worn. It was already running. The familiar Google trademark screen was up, this time with "Kenya" pasted beneath the green and red "LE." Jack logged into his email. He found hundreds of emails, but only one worth opening, the email he had been hoping for, something from Vivian. It read:

"Hope you made it safely. I'll check my email from time to time."

Jack was relieved. He wished he had taken the time to arrange for his phone to work internationally. He typed:

"Viv, checked into a hotel in Nairobi. Need to get a visa tomorrow, expect to be in Juba the day after. I'll be careful. You be careful, too. Don't trust strangers, don't get caught alone. I'm okay, but I ran into someone who didn't want me coming down here. Be careful. Jack."

He hit "send" and logged out. Jack rose and turned for the door, and saw an older man standing on the other side of the glass, watching. He needed a shave, but his hair had been recently cut. He wore a khaki jacket and slacks, a black shirt with a priest's collar. The man turned and walked away. Jack opened the door and followed him down the hall. A drunken priest, maybe? Got lost looking for a toilet? Too much had happened already for Jack to believe in casual coincidences.

In the lounge, the priest sat at a small corner table. It seemed the few customers in the bar were white, and all of the prostitutes milling about were black. The last place one would think to find a priest. Jack walked directly toward him.

"Sit down," the priest said. "I am Father Popielsko."

Jack waited.

"Why have you come?" Popielsko asked.

"What do you want?" Jack asked.

The priest looked from Jack's face, to the empty chair, and back up. Jack sat, but did not remove the bag.

"Why have you come here, Mr. Killarney?" Popielsko asked.

"How do you know my name?" Jack asked.

"Do you think this is a game?" Popielsko had a well-worn accent, muddled probably by living in one far corner of the world after another.

Jack studied the priest for a moment. He seemed genuinely concerned, perhaps even worried. His eyes were swimmy, and his face careworn. Gin blossoms across his nose betrayed a history of hard drinking.

Jack said. "Why don't you tell me what you want? Otherwise, I'm going to go."

A hooker, probably not even 18 years old, came over. "Want to buy me a drink?" She had a tattoo on the back of her hand, a small bird.

"No, thanks," Jack said. Popielsko held up a hand, showing her his palm. Her smile fell away and she walked off to the next table.

Jack stared at Popielsko, waiting.

Loud, disingenuous laughter erupted behind the priest, who neither turned nor flinched.

"You have gotten this far, so you are after something. I want you to tell me what you think your purpose is here," Popielsko said, "What it is you intend to do?"

"About what?" Jack asked.

Popielsko frowned. "Are you an adventure-seeker? A danger junkie?"

Jack leaned across the table. "Do you have something to tell me?"

The priest came closer. "Just go home. You are not even going to the right place."

"How do you know?" Jack asked. "Does the Church know about the pattern?"

"Will you please shut up," Popielsko hissed. "You have no idea what you are dealing with."

"Are you going to tell me it's the devil or Satan?"

Popielsko winced, leaned in, and his voice dropped near a whisper. "The devil? Lucifer? Those are relatively new stories. There is an evil far older than the Gospels, older than Judaism and Zoroastrianism. The same stories, built around the same truths, have been told over the millennia. The idea of salvation delivered by an intermediary between an all-powerful god of good and an evil being goes back to the pre-Zoroastrian myth of Mithra. In pre-Zoroastrian Vedism, prophets announced Mithra would come. A savior, whose birth would be heralded by a bright star. He would be born in a cave. Sound familiar? So, you see, even the story of Jesus is recycled, so whatever you think you know..."

"Why are you telling me all this?" Jack asked.

Popielsko looked around the room. No one seemed to be paying any attention to them. "Mithra was prophesized to act as a sort of referee between Ahura Mazda, the god of good, and Ahriman, a being of ultimate evil. Twin brothers who had co-existed since time began. It was foretold that a war in Heaven would precipitate Mithra the Savior coming down to destroy the forces of evil. Pieces of these stories were transmitted directly into Judaism, Christianity, and later still, into Islam. Who knows how many times these same stories have been recast, again and again, as new religions? Even the names of some of the characters like Azaziel, Leviathan, and Lilith have been passed on."

A tired hooker walked directly toward them and placed two shots of whiskey on the table. Jack looked up at her.

"On the house," she said. She couldn't have seemed more emotionally detached. She said nothing else, and walked away.

"So, you see, your question about the devil is inadequate. Anyway, the Christian devil from the Gospels is more closely linked to the Essene devil than to Satan the adversary from the Old Testament." Popielsko drank his shot glass empty in one quick gulp. Jack considered his drink.

"They are hoping to get you drunk enough to fall under the spell of one of these young women," Popielsko said. "But I'd advise you not to."

"So, bottom line, you're trying to tell me that evil predates the devil we learned about as kids? Before Lucifer was cast out of Heaven, there was some evil force out there? How does that square with all those Sunday school lessons?" Jack drank his shot. The whiskey was rotgut, as smooth as gasoline.

"Evil has always existed," Popielsko said. "Consider this, Mr. Killarney. Lucifer was considered one of God's favorite angels. His name means the morning star, the bringer of light. Lucifer's love for God was said to be unequaled among the angels. Now, imagine what evil exists in the universe, so powerful and perverse, that it could corrupt even such a being. It was so powerful, so wicked, that it corrupted God's most beloved angel beyond mercy, redemption, and remorse. That evil, Mr. Killarney, still exists. And you are, stupidly and naively, trying to catch up with it."

Jack sat back, put the glass down, and set his mouth firm with resolve.

"Again, Mr. Killarney, why are you here?" Popielsko asked.

Jack paused a moment before asking, "Who is the man in the black coat?"

Popielsko's eyes went flat, taking on a glassy look, and not seeing anything.

"If this thing is so big, so ancient, why would he bother with me?" Jack asked. "If he's such a cosmic bad-ass, why couldn't he stop me from getting here?"

Father Popielsko's eyes snapped back into focus. "What do you mean, bother with you?"

"In Amsterdam, I'm pretty sure he sent someone in to a restroom to kick my ass. To make sure I wouldn't make the flight down here. I saw the man in black in the terminal," Jack said.

Popielsko closed his eyes. "Have you seen him anywhere else?"

"He fits the description of someone present at a murder-suicide in Maine, in the States. I've also seen him back home, in the town where I live. And I think I saw him on the plane, or dreamt about him," Jack said.

"You didn't dream him; at least, not like you think."

Jack said, "We were in mid-air, the plane was in trouble, and he disappeared. Are you suggesting he's some sort of spirit?"

"No, he's a man," Popielsko said.

"Well, if this evil is so powerful, why didn't he stop me? Why didn't he crush me like a bug? If his purpose is to stop me, he's not especially capable."

"He isn't the evil you're seeking. He's only a man."

"That doesn't answer my question," Jack said.

"Mr. Killarney, the evil you're chasing does not care about you. However, if the man in the black coat has taken notice of you, that is all the more reason to go home. You would be a curiosity to him, and you do not want to be."

"Who is he?"

"I have only seen him take personal interest once before. It ended most unpleasantly for the object of his interest," Popielsko said.

"Who is he?" Jack asked again.

Popielsko exhaled loudly and sat back. Looking around the room, he said, "Mr. Killarney, go home."

Jack said, "I didn't come this far to go home. My wife burned to death. My partner and then my brother killed themselves, his children murdered. I want some answers. I *need* some answers."

The same hooker returned with another round of whiskey shots. Jack tried to wave her away, but she left the drinks and walked off. Popielsko immediately downed his.

The priest began collecting himself as if preparing to leave, and said, "I sincerely hope you will reconsider."

"Who is the man in the black coat? What is with the dead birds? What is the pattern and why does it exist? Can it be stopped?"

Popielsko said, "Your very questions belie how unprepared you are." As he stood, Jack grabbed him by the wrist. No one in the room seemed to notice. The priest leaned over Jack, their faces inches apart.

Popielsko said, "Do you really think you can find the answers? Like the books that you carry with you? You do not even understand why you carry them, do you?" The priest tapped the messenger bag with his free hand.

Did he know which books? The messenger bag had been on him at all times. Jack released Popielsko's wrist, and the priest walked away.

After watching him go, Jack glanced at the remaining shot of whiskey, picked it up, and then realized the lounge had gone silent. Every single person, even the bartender, was quietly staring at him. The hookers stood erect, with their hands at their sides. Jack put the full shot glass down, stood, and headed for his room. Once he got there, he locked the door. Jack picked up the small chair to wedge beneath the door handle, but then realized the chair was almost completely without heft, and would do no good. He turned out the lights, remained dressed, and climbed onto the bed. He sat up, his back to the wall, his messenger bag across his lap, the book by Augustine heavy inside, leaning against his abdomen.

Ch: 19

May 15
7:30 p.m.
Winter Harbor Hospital
Westbrook, Maine

Carol sat at the desk in her small room, reading the newspaper, and sipping her water. Her iPhone was lying next to her, with Neko Case's smoky voice drifting out of it. She was more skimming than digging deep into any one story until her eyes fell upon that one headline, "Husband, wife feared lost on sailboat."

It wasn't the grammar which caught her eye, implying that the couple was lost somewhere aboard the boat, but instead the circumstance. Carol had regained her privileges, except for unmonitored internet access on her phone, and, after their ill-fated visit, she had looked up Vivian Rueil on the old computer in the common room.

Buried beneath all the results that highlighted Vivian's career and writing, Carol had found a news account about how, as a child, Vivian had found her father, below deck, where he had been working on the engine. Vivian was simply not strong enough then to lift him or drag him out of that cramped space. Her father had been a big, rugged man. Carol imagined how Vivian must have pulled and tugged, how she must have cried.

The story had gone on to explain that Vivian had had to leave him there, for fear of succumbing to the carbon monoxide herself, and how out on the deck, Vivian had passed out. She had spent days on the boat alone with her dead father.

"Carol."

She sprang from her seat, dropping the paper, spilling her water. She spun; no one was there. It had been a man's throaty voice, a voice she'd never heard before.

"Carol."

She turned toward the voice; it was coming from her phone. The voice was speaking right over the music. She approached the device, and the screen read "Middle Cyclone: Neko Case."

"Carol. Tell him to listen to the priest."

Terrified, she turned the phone off, and it went silent. She listened intently, waiting to hear the voice again, but heard only herself swallow. She sat down in the middle of the floor and waited for logic to rescue and comfort her.

"I'm together, I'm together," she whispered.

Ch: 20

May 16
9:30 a.m.
GoSS Mission Offices
6th Floor, Bishopsgate building
Nairobi, Kenya

"Thank you, Mr. Killarney. We will have your visa ready as soon as possible."

"Is there any chance it will be ready today?" Jack asked. "I'm hoping to catch a flight tomorrow morning." He was willing to pay a fee to expedite things.

"It will be ready as soon as it is ready, sir." The woman was professionally polite but clearly not interested in his dilemma.

"How will I know it is ready to be picked up?"

"When you return, sir, you can check."

Jack was about to explain how he'd just as soon not return until the visa was prepared, but held back. If there was one thing that might slow the process down, it was an ugly American who thought he could argue his way to faster service.

"Thank you," Jack said.

The woman inclined her head and might have even smiled a bit. Jack walked away. He considered going back to the hotel to catch a bite to eat, but instead decided hanging around the hotel all day would make him too easy to find. He walked outside to find his taxi waiting for him, as promised. The fares were cheap and paying for one to wait was better than attempting to find a new one each time.

"Driver, is there a decent restaurant you'd recommend?" Jack asked.

"Do you like Italian? Tortellino d'Oro?"

"How far?" Jack asked.

"Middle of Nairobi," the driver replied.

Jack looked off in the direction of the heart of Nairobi. He couldn't see much past the trees that lined the streets in this neighborhood.

"Is there someplace closer? Out that way?" Jack was pointing beyond the well-manicured grounds of a private school to a tall building not far off.

"In that one, there is La Conta Restaurant. Good?" the driver asked.

"Fine," Jack said. "Is there WiFi there?"

The driver nodded without looking back, and the taxi pulled away. It was a short drive down Bishop Road, passing between hotels, and they pulled in to a parking lot. The driver nodded to the building on the right and said, "Kenya Prisons Headquarters." The building Jack had pointed at loomed high above them on the left.

"La Conta Restaurant is in there?" Jack asked.

"Inside," the driver said.

Jack paid him and told him not to wait. He exited the cab and approached the building. It was largely covered in rectangular windows framed by off-white masonry. The main doors were sliding glass and above them, large golden letters read, "Social Security House Nairobi." A government building? He had a sinking feeling that La Conta was going to be a small café where one might buy nothing more than a scone and a paper.

It wasn't. It was a decent-sized, well-appointed restaurant. Fancier, in fact, than he wanted before lunch.

Jack decided, with the taxi gone and WiFi access somewhere in the building, that he would stay and have some brunch. He wasn't sure if he should seat himself or not. He saw only a couple tables with customers and no sign of a waiter or a maître d'. Jack waited a minute and then decided he'd find his own table. As soon as he sat, a small man came rushing in through swinging kitchen doors. He went directly to Jack.

"Good morning, sir. Would you like some tea?"

"Coffee, please. And a menu?"

"Yes sir. Here is your menu, and I will return immediately with coffee."

"You wouldn't happen to have a newspaper handy, would you?" Jack asked.

"Yes sir, of course." The waiter scurried off.

Jack suddenly felt very exposed. He studied the other diners, searching for the source of his anxiety. A couple talking to each other, sitting close, in that overly-pleasant honeymoon haze. Smiling about tea. Smiling about oatmeal.

More distant, and out of earshot, sat two men. One clearly was in sales. The kind of harmless twit, packed with hidden insecurities and a deluded sense of entitlement, who won't check luggage but will place his wheelie carry-on bag in the overhead compartment above a mother of three because she's nearer the exits. The other, older gentleman was obviously the decision maker, probably a CXO who, with a single purchase order, could make the salesman's quarter. It seemed to Jack, by both the increasingly manic disposition of the sales twit and the ever-more polite expression on the face of the mark, that the deal was not going to be closed today, if ever.

There was no one else. Jack scanned the restaurant twice more. The waiter returned with a tray. On the table, he carefully arranged a cup with saucer and spoon, a carafe of coffee, a small bowl of raw sugar cubes, and cream. Beside all this, he laid a neatly folded copy of the *Sunday Nation*. A headline announced that tensions between Kenya and a neighbor continued to be of concern, and that a young rugby star had died.

"Are you ready to order, sir?"

"I'd like some toast and eggs please, scrambled."

"Wheat bread, sir?"

"Wheat, and could I get a small glass of orange juice as well?" Jack asked.

"Yes sir." And with a smile, the waiter was gone again.

Jack opened the paper. Another headline, this time, "South Sudan primed for new round of violence," sat three-columns wide across the top of page 2:

> Khartoum, Saturday—There are signs of a new unrest brewing in South Sudan, according to the former leader of the Sudanese People's Independence Movement, Mr. Slava Waras. In a speech in Khartoum on Saturday, Mr. Waras declared, "The SPIM will not sit idly by while people starve in the shadow of rich and complacent neighbors."

"Here is your juice, sir." The waiter set the glass on the table. Jack had no idea he was there until he spoke.

"Thank you."

The waiter left without another word. Jack folded the paper and kept a sharper watch. He poured himself a cup of the coffee and dropped in a couple of the tan sugar cubes. Stirring the coffee with one hand, he lifted the juice with the other. Before he'd even taken a sip, he could tell by the smell, the near-absence of acidity, that the juice had been greatly watered down. A quick sip confirmed it.

The salesman's arms were waving about now, like a drowning man's. The couple rose and left, still smiling. Jack looked out of the restaurant and into the hallway beyond. No one. He looked over at the drowning salesman once more and found both men were staring directly at him. Jack stared back. The waiter appeared once more, this time with plates on his tray. One with eggs and fruit, a smaller one with toast, and a dish of butter and jams. The waiter obstructed his view of the two men at the other table. Once he could look that way again, both were gone.

"Who were they?" Jack asked, pointing.

"Who, sir?"

"The two men who were sitting right over there."

The waiter looked confused. "Sir, you are the only one who has come in this morning thus far. We opened minutes before you arrived. I did not know anyone was out here until I happened to come out of the kitchen."

Jack looked up at him. "What about the young couple?"

The waiter's expression shifted from confused to concerned. "Sir, you are the first customer this morning."

Jack looked around him once more. No one.

"Do you have WiFi access?" Jack asked.

"Sir, SkyWeb has a café one floor up. They have computers you can use," the waiter said.

"I want the check," Jack said.

"But you've not touched your food."

"Get me my check, please."

"Very well, sir." The waiter left in a hurry, his walk much stiffer this time. He returned within moments, placing the bill on the table. Jack glanced at it, added some for a tip, and headed for the door.

"Sir, why chase something you do not want to catch?" the waiter asked.

"What did you say?"

The waiter turned and headed for the kitchen once more. Jack followed him. The doors swung closed in front of Jack. Pushing them open, he stepped into a dark kitchen. Empty. Spotless.

What the fuck? He turned, glanced at his table. It was empty. No food, no newspaper, no coffee, no check. He scanned the restaurant. It looked like it hadn't been open in days. He stepped into the hallway, looked both ways, and walked slowly to the elevators. He really was losing it, he thought.

He went up one floor and, stepping out, immediately saw the signs for the SkyWeb Internet café. He went in.

"Hello, sir," said an attendant behind the counter. Jack wasn't sure if he was really there and he didn't really care. He hurried to a computer. It welcomed him and then prompted him to enter his credit card information in order to gain Internet access. Jack considered returning to the hotel, where access was free, but instead entered the info and logged in to his email. There were no emails from Vivian. There was one from Carol and one from Augustine. He almost opened the Augustine one first, but instead went to Carol's.

"Jack, there was a voice. I heard a voice tell me, 'Tell him to listen to the priest.' I don't know what it means, or if it means something to you. I hope you're safe. Please let me know as soon as you can that you are all right. Call if you can. Carol."

Jack replied,

"It means something to me, but not sure what yet. Having some trouble staying focused. Need to get to Juba. I'll be glad to get out of Nairobi. I'll try to call. Jack."

Jack clicked on the Augustine email.

From: Augustine@freemail.com

"Hey Jack-buddy… what men can do with real colors and substances; the demons can do by showing unreal forms… be cautious."

Whoever was writing as Augustine—or as Ben—was actually telling him to be careful now. Pulling out his phone, Jack tried to bring up his service provider's web page, hoping to set up international phone service. He couldn't log in, gave up, and put the phone away.

“If you want to make a phone call, there are public phones at the bus stall near the hotel across the road,” the attendant said.

Jack said nothing, walked out, and entered the elevator.

As the doors were closing, Jack looked out and froze. There, in the last glimpse of the hallway, at the far end, was the man in the black coat. Jack threw himself at the doors, but too late. The elevator shuddered and then began to descend. Jack checked the floors. He was one floor above the main, but there were two basements beneath that one. The elevator shuddered again. Jack pictured falling those two remaining stories in this metal box, but then the doors opened. Leaping out, Jack collided with a woman carrying a broom.

“Sorry!” Jack walked quickly through the glass doors, out of the building, and into the bright sunlight. He looked across Bishop Road and saw the bus stop. Jogging across the road, he only half-checked for cars. The phone booths were made of wood, like bathrooms stalls at a public toilet without doors. He picked up the phone and began dialing, first the number at the hospital to reach Carol, and then his credit card number. He would try to call Vivian, too. There were various recorded voices in an assortment of languages, with different levels and tones of static, until finally it was ringing on the other end, but there was no answer. How could an entire psychiatric hospital not answer?

He dialed the phone again, this time using Vivian’s number.

“Professor Rueil.” The voice wasn’t as calm as it had once been, but at hearing it, Jack pressed the phone hard against his ear.

“Hey.”

“Jack! Are you okay?”

“What do you know about Ahriman?”

Silence, and then, “Where did you hear that?”

“Things are getting more than a little weird here. I’m hallucinating, I think, or someone is playing me. I need to wait for my visa to be ready, later this afternoon. Once I have that,

I'll barricade myself in my hotel room as best I can. I'll fly out tomorrow morning."

Vivian's voice grew softer. "Just come back, Jack. This is crazy. Just come back, tonight."

Jack's eyes closed. He was tempted to go back, to simply get on a plane and go back home, and to her.

"Jack?"

"I have to see this out," Jack said. "You mentioned you heard a priest."

"Mentioned when?" Vivian asked. "I never mentioned a priest."

"In your email," Jack said. There was a strange buzzing on the phone, in the background. It made it difficult for Jack to focus.

"I didn't email you," Vivian said.

Jack paused. That's right, he thought, it was Carol who emailed. "Sorry, you're right, it was Carol. She told me to listen to the priest."

"What priest?" Vivian asked.

Should he tell her? "A priest came and found me, had a lot of questions about what I'm doing here, and said that the evil I'm chasing is ancient. Someone even older than the devil, someone called Ahriman or something like that. He also said I should go home."

"What kind of priest was this?"

"An old priest who guzzles cheap whiskey," Jack said.

"A priest who believes in ancient Vedic mythology and tells you about Ahriman, and who sought you out. Listen, these stories include Ahura Mazda, the god of good, and there is Ahriman and his arch-demons, and there is a savior who will defeat Ahriman."

"Okay?"

"Okay, so I want you to tell me, how do you fit in all this?" Vivian asked. "If you're so sure you're destined to be involved, and now you're hearing these ancient myths, are you actually thinking of yourself as a participant in this spiritual story? Have you gone messianic on me, Jack?"

"I'm not going to stop now. I'm getting closer. Whatever is going on, I never thought digging into it would be safe. No matter how many scary stories, priests, or thugs are involved, somehow, I feel like I'm supposed to be doing this. Even Ben told me…"

"Thugs?" Vivian asked.

Jack winced. "Oh yeah, some idiot in Amsterdam tried to convince me not to come down here." Jack left out the part about the thug possibly being no more than fourteen years old.

"Jesus," Vivian whispered.

"Don't you mean Mithra?" Jack said.

Silence.

"Come on, I was trying to lighten things up."

Silence.

Jack said, "Okay, so, I'm going to go."

"Be cautious—you're into stories vast and ancient here. Even if you and I don't believe all of it, there are millions of people who do. Call again when you can," Vivian said. Her voice had turned slightly harder and self-protective.

Jack hung up, and exited the booth. Children stood across the street from him, staring. The dozen or so of them, in their private school uniforms, with blazers with little crests, were watching him. Two teachers towering above them stared as well. They did not look menacing; they were simply looking at him. As a single unit, they began to move, stepping toward him with one synchronized step. Another step took them into the roadway. On the street, cars and a large truck were closing in on the children, but the kids and their teachers never looked. They took another step. Jack ran into the road.

"No! Get back!" A car nearly struck him, with its horn blaring. The kids took another step his way. An oncoming truck was lined up with the lot of them; they were walking abreast.

"Stop! Get those kids back!" Jack shouted, with arms raised, running deeper into traffic. The teachers did not give any sign of having heard him. Jack heard the truck's gears shift, picking up speed, closing fast, but just as Jack got to the first of the kids, they vanished. He looked up and saw them—frightened and huddled around the legs of their teachers. They had never left the sidewalk. The teachers looked horrified. The truck's horn sounded. Jack jumped back and the truck missed him by inches. Another car screeched to a stop, the bumper a couple feet from his legs. Father Popielsko jumped out of the driver's seat, grabbed him by the arm, and pulled him into the passenger side. The priest then climbed back into the car, put it in gear, and drove a few hundred yards before turning into a parking lot. The adjacent building was low, with an orange roof.

"What is this place?" Jack asked.

"The Israeli embassy. Let's get inside."

Ch: 21

May 16
11:00 a.m.
Israeli Embassy
Nairobi, Kenya

"So, Ahriman is trying to get me run over by a truck?" Jack asked. "Why not a bolt of lightning?"

The two men were standing inside a small library. Jack saw only one door, made of oak, with a large, bronze handle.

Popielsko said, "You mustn't mock this. As I told you before, the primary evil you are seeking takes no notice of individuals, but the 'man in black' as you call him, he has taken an interest in you."

"What do *you* call him?"

Popielsko paused. "He has been called many things by many people, but his name is Sopater."

"Why would he be interested in me?"

"Why do some predators toy with prey before killing?" Popielsko asked.

Jack asked, "So, the hallucinations I'm having, he's causing those?"

Popielsko said, "I do not have any idea what you have been seeing or not. I do not know what drugs you might be on or what your history of mental illness might be. I do know that you seeing the children in the road, and your being drawn into traffic, were most likely his doing, as was your seeing him aboard your airplane. He is working on your fear, and on your trust."

"Trust of my own senses?" Jack asked.

"Once a man doubts even his own first-hand experiences, there certainly can be no room for faith. Such a man is spiritually paralyzed. My guess is you have him curious. He is probably searching for your limit. After all, you boarded the plane after being attacked. Many people would not have. And after it landed, you pursued a visa to go on to the Republic of South Sudan. You remained undeterred. I believe he is curious, as a cat would be by a charging mouse."

"If he is a man, like me, how can he do these things? Why is it cat and mouse, instead of cat and cat?" Jack asked.

"Because he has been chosen."

"By whom?"

"There must be first-person witnesses to everything. The idea that there has ever been an event without even a single witness is simply untrue. There must always be. It has always been thus; it's part of the natural order of things. A universal requirement. That which was not perceived did not happen."

"He was chosen by the evil to be a witness?" Jack asked.

"He is human."

The oak door opened. A man, casually dressed and wearing sunglasses, slowly entered the room. He walked with the economy of a soldier.

"Ehud will take you to your hotel," Popielsko said. "You are booked on a red-eye flight tonight. He will take you safely to the airport. From there, you can return home."

"The witness for evil. How long has he been doing this?" Jack asked.

Popielsko sighed. "For this particular witness, his first witnessing was done at the Hebron massacre." He gestured with one hand and Ehud grabbed Jack by the elbow, gently but insistently pulling him toward the door.

Jack walked backwards as Ehud led. "Hebron, the bombing? Mid-1990s?"

As Jack was pulled through the door, he heard Popielsko's flat voice call after him.

"No, Mr. Killarney, not that one. The Hebron massacre in August 1929."

Jack planted his feet, but then his arm was immediately twisted behind him. Jack didn't resist. "Alright, alright, I'm going."

Ehud led him to a car and pushed Jack into the passenger seat and then got behind the wheel. They drove to the Kestrel Court Hotel. The two men went to Jack's room. Jack had nothing to pack. The messenger bag was it. Jack sat on his bed. Ehud took a chair, positioned it between Jack and the door without leaving his back exposed to either, and sat.

Jack said, "It's going to be a long evening."

Ehud said nothing.

Jack opened the messenger bag. Ehud stiffened, alert, so Jack slowed. He knew that Ehud must be armed. Jack pulled the Augustine book from the bag and opened it. He pretended to read, thinking through his options. Patience. Ehud would be all keyed up, expecting something early. How much time did he have?

Jack asked, "What time is the flight?" Jack never looked up from the book.

Ehud cocked his head, as if considering whether or not to answer. "Your flight leaves at twenty-three hundred hours, local. Through Zurich and Frankfurt. You will be back in Boston soon, Mr. Killarney."

Jack turned the page.

Ehud said, "Please Mr. Killarney, relax. Feel free to stop pretending to read."

Jack looked up, and their eyes met. The man wasn't stupid.

Jack closed the book and put it back into the bag. He had been away from his meds for too long, not to mention a bit of decent booze. With the couple days he'd had, Jack's nerves were raw.

"I have to use the bathroom," Jack said, getting up.

"Go right ahead."

Jack entered the bathroom, closed and locked the door behind him. The door wouldn't stop a determined… adolescent? He turned on the water, and let it run. Looking around the room, he saw only tile floor, wallpaper, mirror, sink, toilet, shower, and wastebasket. Shards of mirror as a knife? No. He wasn't especially in a hurry to try to kill Ehud; besides getting in a knife fight with him was probably a losing proposition. They were trying to send him home, and they could have easily killed him. In fact, they had probably saved him. Sick prisoner routine? No, he wouldn't fall for that.

"The hell with clever," Jack whispered. He pushed his hand against the light door. Flimsy and hollow. He turned off the light. The room went dark. Jack heard Ehud immediately rise to his feet. He had been watching. Jack backed against the far wall. Two shadows appeared at the bottom of the door. Jack sprinted, bringing both arms up in front of his face as he got there. Jack exploded through the door, the door Ehud had been holding his ear mere inches from. The door splintered, and Jack's forearms, and the door debris, crashed into the side of Ehud's head. Jack's body collided with Ehud's and his left knee found a soft spot. Both men went sprawling to the floor. Jack was quicker to his feet, and drove a well-placed kick to Ehud's face. The man flipped onto his back and lay still.

Jack approached cautiously. During his days as a cop, he'd seen more than one perp feign unconsciousness. Ehud was bleeding from his forehead, lip, and left ear, and Jack could see the rise and fall of the man's chest. Still breathing. Jack grabbed the brass table lamp, pulled the cord from the wall and from the lamp, and approached the motionless Ehud. Keeping the lamp well back and held high, he reached over him, grabbed his far shoulder and pulled the man over onto his chest. Blood ran from Ehud's mouth. Jack knelt on the small of Ehud's back, carefully put the lamp down, and secured Ehud's hands behind his back with the electrical cord.

Ehud began to cough, and Jack grabbed the lamp but he didn't regain consciousness, and instead, a tooth fell out of the man's mouth onto the floor.

He's going to be pissed when he wakes up, Jack thought.

Jack patted him down and found the gun he expected. A Tanfoglio Force, compact. Pocket-sized, light, high capacity magazine. Jack placed it in his own waistband and felt the reassuring pressure of it against the small of his back. Jack then tied Ehud's shoelaces tightly together.

Jack tossed the lamp onto the bed and stepped back. Even if he came to, he'd go nowhere fast. It was then that Jack tasted blood in his own mouth. He went back through the ruined doorway, turned on the bathroom light, and saw himself in the mirror. His own lip was bleeding and his eyebrow was cut. He had rake-mark scratches across one cheek. His forearms were a mess.

A knock at the hallway door.

"Mr. Killarney? Hotel staff."

Jack stepped to the side of the door, drew the gun. "Yes?"

"Sir, are you alright, sir? We had a report of a crash of some sort."

Jack moved before speaking again. "I fell, but I'm fine." Jack moved again.

Nothing. Whoever was on the other side of the door was trying to figure out what to do next.

"Very good, sir. Sorry to have troubled you."

"Not at all. Thanks for the concern," Jack said.

Jack moved away from the door and stepped back to the bed, watching. Nothing. He approached the door slowly, looked through the peephole. No one.

With a sigh of relief, Jack grabbed the messenger bag, opened the window, and climbed out. He pulled the window closed and walked quickly away. Passing a garbage can, he dropped Ehud's gun inside. He hated to let the security of it go, but a foreigner carrying a gun without a permit, one that wasn't even his, was asking for more trouble than the gun was worth. Jack surveyed the parking lot. A cab, having just dropped off a couple at the main entranceway, approached. Jack waved, and the car stopped. Climbing in behind the driver, Jack said, "Bishopsgate building, please."

The cab pulled away without a word from the driver. Jack looked down at his lacerated forearms.

"Shit," he whispered.

"Sorry, sir?" the cabby asked.

Jack checked his watch; it was almost two o'clock.

"Sir?"

"Nothing."

The cab pulled up to the building. Jack paid the driver, hurried out onto the sidewalk, and into the building. Inside, he found the same woman he'd spoken to earlier.

"Jack Killarney, I was here earlier about a visa," Jack said.

She looked up. "Ah yes, Mr. Killarney." She stopped, surprised at the fresh injuries to his face. He had a pounding headache.

She shuffled through a few pieces of paper, and then typed a few keystrokes. She looked up at Jack again. "Mr. Killarney, could you wait right there for a moment?"

Jack froze, and then nodded. She walked away and into another room. There was a problem. She was notifying a supervisor. The Israelis? Everything said run, his legs wanted to, his gut told him to, his brain was screaming it. *Run*. She returned.

"Here you are, Mr. Killarney," she said. She handed him a couple documents. "And this, you slip into your passport. Have a safe journey."

He nodded, turned, and walked away, hoping he hadn't

looked too surprised. He had a visa. Now he needed a flight, and there wasn't going to be one until morning.

Ch: 22

May 16
4:00 p.m.
Jomo Kenyatta International Airport
Nairobi, Kenya

"Your flight departs tomorrow morning at 10:00 a.m. Is there anything else I can do for you, sir?" The ticket agent seemed even younger than the one who had been there the day before. She searched his face, and handed him his travel documents. Jack turned and walked away. He had to find a way to kill eighteen hours. Walking into the restroom, he tucked his boarding pass into his messenger bag. Looking in the mirror, he was startled at what a mess he was—a black eye, swollen lip, scratched face, disheveled, wearing rumpled clothing. If he were at another airport, LAX or JFK, he'd be pulled in for questioning; he was a walking mess, with no bags, and a one-way ticket. He turned on the water and began to clean himself up. Jack attempted to groom his hair with wet fingers, and then pressed the cool, wet hand against his cheek and eye. His head still hurt.

"Aren't you the pretty one?"

Jack spun. Standing there, leaning in one corner, was Father Popielsko.

"I'm going to Juba," Jack said.

"I can see that," Popielsko said. "There comes a point when you simply can't save a man from himself."

Jack said, "That's right."

"That's right," Popielsko smiled.

"Is your guy alright?" Jack asked.

"If I were you, I would avoid any time alone with Ehud for the foreseeable future. He is less than pleased with you just now."

Jack paused and then asked, "If you're letting me go, why are you here at all?"

Popielsko's face fell. "I am here because you have no plan. What were you going to do, stay inside this piss hole until morning?"

Jack looked around. He said, "I'm going to sit out in the gate. There's no reason to hide, or even leave, right? You were going to send me back to the States. There's no sense in going home. If whatever this is, it's so bad-ass that I don't have a chance against it, and it has infinite reach across time and space, why the hell would I bother running from it? It's going to kill me, right?"

Popielsko said nothing.

"Right? So, if it's going to kill me anyway, why not be the charging mouse?"

Popielsko cleared his throat and said softly, "Your only hope was that he would become bored with you, that he would move on with his mission after you left. Just as a child soon forgets the insect that flies away. But like a true pest, you persist and you persist. His curiosity has you as an object of interest, but once you become an irritant, you will be dealt with in an entirely different manner. It might not be too late to get away."

"It *is* too late," Jack said. "Go home and do what? Go back and hide from the world? Move close to family and lay low? I tried that once before, and my family was taken from me. How can I go back? Every tragedy, every catastrophe, every act of human madness will have me running for my maps, and then inevitably looking down the next line at millions of potential victims. I can't live like that."

Popielsko looked down at the floor.

Jack said, "I think you know what I mean. When you first became involved in all this, whatever this is, you couldn't walk away either, could you?"

Popielsko suddenly stepped close, with his face mere inches from Jack's. The priest's voice became harsh but low. "I also know that, *if* you survive somehow, you might even find answers—but keep in mind that answers are not necessarily solutions."

Jack held Popielsko's gaze for a moment and then walked past him. Popielsko followed him as Jack walked to the gate and sat in one of the many empty seats. The strap of the messenger bag was around his back, the weight of it in his lap. Popielsko sat across from Jack.

"Why are you following me?" Jack asked.

Popielsko cleared his throat. "You are the first novelty in a long, long time."

Jack stared at him for a moment. "You said he first witnessed in Hebron in 1929. How long have you been at this?" Jack asked. His head really hurt.

"A long time."

"You and the Israeli government? Or the Vatican? Or just you and Ehud?"

"I do not work for the Israeli government, nor do I answer to the Pope. We have a vast network, in nearly every country, that has been working to mitigate the evil as best we can."

"Who is in this network and how long have you been doing this?" Jack asked.

"Why does it matter? Who we are or how long I have been doing this or how long the Witness has been doing this; none of this has anything to do with understanding it all. To be honest, I have already told you a great deal, more than others learned," Popielsko said.

"Others? Others have come looking for these answers?"

Popielsko rolled his eyes. "You cannot seriously ask questions like this one. Since man became self-aware, since the human who first believed in the permanence of his identity, beyond the existence of his body, people have been searching for these answers, among them, the causes of evil. From the creation of volcano gods to the invention of malicious aliens from space."

Jack said, "No, I mean, others who have recognized the pattern. Have there been others?"

Popielsko hesitated but then said, "In a manner of speaking, yes, of course. You do not think yourself some sort of super-genius, some sort of *sensitive*, do you? But it has been a very long time. Although I fear the interconnectedness of today's world, the speed at which news spreads on television and on computers, is making pieces of what you call 'the pattern' easier to see. After all, even you recognized it."

"Why do you fear people recognizing the pattern? Are you hoping the pattern continues forever? As a priest, don't you have feelings for the suffering of the people?"

Popielsko sighed. "When one goes to the seashore and sees small fish trapped in pools shrinking inward from the edges, one can feel pity even while acknowledging that there is nothing those fish can do to save themselves. In fact, it is not until well after their fate is sealed that they begin to realize something is wrong."

Jack began to say something, but Popielsko raised his hand, and continued. "Now imagine you found a pool, and in this pool, among all the other fish, was a particularly agitated fish, driving himself against the rocky edge again and again, protesting the situation they had all found themselves in. What if that one fish actually gets lucky and comes up with a theory about tidal cycles."

"I would help the fish," Jack said. "I would lift him out."

"But Jack, you are the fish. The help you describe is supernatural. Godlike. You're not claiming supernatural powers now, are you?"

"You're saying the human race is fucked," Jack said.

"I am saying the human race has always been thus," Popielsko said. "I am saying that you have recently recognized it, but that your racing headlong into the rocky edge of the pool will not change a thing. I am saying, swim back to the middle and hope to forget."

"I don't want to forget."

"Of course you do," Popielsko said. "We all do. That is what the chemicals are for, the drink and the drugs. They help us forget that the edges are drying and closing in on us."

Jack's head hurt all the more, and now there were mild waves of nausea. "Wait, the pool isn't just drying," Jack said. "There is an intelligence, seeking us out and killing us inside our pool."

Popielsko sighed again. "Yes, and you are unlucky enough to be the fish who noticed."

"Fuck the fish and fuck you," Jack said. His nausea was worsening. Maybe he needed something in his stomach; it was dinnertime. Anything but fish. Just some saltines would be nice. Jack leaned forward with his elbows on his knees. He was suddenly so tired, and his head was killing him. Opening his eyes slowly, he saw Popielsko sitting calmly back in his seat. Despite a distant voice in the back of his mind calling for resistance, Jack's eyes closed again.

"He can barely get through Nairobi."

"It won't matter in Juba."

"If he stays in Juba."

Jack looked up, and focused.

Popielsko was still sitting there, and behind him stood Ehud with his scrapes and bruises. Jack knew Ehud, showered and groomed, looked a damn sight better than he did.

"You probably have a concussion," Popielsko said.

Jack looked directly at Ehud, who only stared back, and then sat.

Long hours passed, and Jack wasn't sure for how much of that time he'd been awake. At times, Popielsko would walk away, and sometimes it was Ehud, but Jack was never left alone. The priest had been gone for some time when Jack said to Ehud, "Sorry about the… you know," and gestured to his own face.

Ehud said nothing, but did tilt his head. Popielsko returned with a cup.

"Here, ibuprofen," he said, handing Jack two pills and the water.

"What time is it?" Jack asked, and then downed the pills. He had lost track. Windows in the distance revealed only that it was still dark outside.

Popielsko said, "It is half past four."

"In the morning?" Jack asked.

Ehud walked away.

"In the morning," Popielsko said.

Jack looked at the priest. "So, you're really going to let me go? You could have sent me to the hospital, called local authorities and made up some story, taken me to the embassy…"

"Or anywhere else," Popielsko said.

"Why didn't you?"

"I told you. There comes a point when you cannot save a man from himself."

Jack suddenly clutched at his messenger bag, still hanging from around his shoulders.

Popielsko said, "No one has touched your bag. You've been awake most of the time. You most likely need to see a doctor, but I know you won't."

Jack looked around to see where Ehud had gone, and spotted him in the distance, next to the door of a small shop. Ehud nodded and Popielsko helped Jack to his feet. They approached Ehud, who turned and led them into a small café. It was dark inside, and there was no one behind the bar, but there were two cups on the table, one of tea and one of coffee, and two scones. Jack remembered the restaurant in the government building and wondered for a moment what was real. He and Popielsko sat down, while Ehud sat separately without anything to eat or drink.

"Why are you helping me now when before you were trying to stop me?" Jack asked.

"I was helping you more when I was trying to stop you."

Jack took a sip of the coffee, and asked, "You don't really care if I go to Juba, do you? I heard that."

"We are not following you to Juba. You will be on your own. Stay as safe as you can manage, and then after a couple days, please consider simply going home," Popielsko said.

Jack took a bite of the scone. He was hungrier than he had thought.

"Where are you going?" Jack asked.

Popielsko said, "We'll see you off, and that will be that."

Jack looked over at Ehud, who glanced back for a moment and then looked out at the few people milling about in the airport. "Let him know, no hard feelings, will you?"

"He doesn't care much what you have to say," Popielsko said.

Jack took another sip of coffee.

Ch: 23

May 17
10:20 a.m.
Jomo Kenyatta International Airport
Nairobi, Kenya

As the plane left the ground, Jack scanned out his window for the man in black, for Sopater. No sign of him. Why had the priest and Ehud simply let him go when before they were so bent on stopping him? What had changed? Had they learned something? What was it they had said, that he wouldn't matter, as long as he stayed in Juba? Was he going to the wrong place?

Jack reached into the messenger bag. His hand found the novel, but he released it and instead pulled out the St. Augustine volume. He looked at the cover and then flipped it open to a random page, deep within the work.

"Pessimistic choice, don't you think?"

Jack looked to his left, across the aisle. There sat a young man, sandy hair, glasses, and a khaki vest. The accent was Irish.

"Cormac O'Brien. Oxfam. Logistics."

"Jack."

"Just Jack?" Cormac asked, but he didn't wait for an answer. "There's a lot of that going 'round. I work with a Sudanese 'Elvis'."

"Elvis?" Jack asked.

"There's another named 'James Brown' and yet another who goes by 'Michael Jackson,'" Cormac said.

"Why did you say this was a pessimistic choice? Isn't Augustine all about hope?" Jack asked.

"Hope for the hereafter, for the Celestial City. 'City of God' is, in part, about how there's no hope for the earthly. Therefore, it's a pessimistic choice to carry into a place of so little hope, I say."

"How does a logistics guy for Oxfam know all about Augustine?" Jack closed the book and placed it back inside the bag.

"I'm a bit of a permanent student," Cormac said, smiling. "Who did you say you worked for?"

"I didn't. I'm on my own. Want to get out to the field, and see for myself."

"Well, you won't get far on your own. You'll have to blag about being with an NGO, but that's not difficult."

"Blag?"

"Lie."

"Ah. Can I work for Oxfam?" Jack asked.

"You might pick something fictitious and smaller. You're almost sure to bump into other Oxfam people and then you'll be in it. But you can follow along until someone stops you."

Jack paused, and then said, "I'm a bit anxious. I know things are bad, but do you think they'll be getting worse? Is there a chance of a new wave of violence? Is there potential for a new disaster?"

"You mean other than the food you'll be eating?" Cormac asked, laughing.

"I'm serious."

Cormac's face fell. "Everyday in South Sudan is a potential disaster."

* * *

The plane landed on time. Cormac stood, grabbed a backpack from the empty seat beside him, and turned to Jack. "Come on then."

Jack jumped up, grateful for the guide. Jack noticed Cormac looking around Jack's seat.

"This is it," Jack said, patting the messenger bag.

"You do travel light."

The two men walked out into an arrivals area; it was hot and dingy. They stepped into a line of other travelers. At the head of the line, Jack could see customs officials searching bags. He remembered the Dramamine and hoped no one would care. In every direction there were bored-looking police and other customs personnel. Jack could see a distant restroom; it reminded him of the incident in Amsterdam. He was also quite sure he could smell the toilets, even at this distance.

The man ahead of Cormac opened his bag, revealing four high-powered rifles. He was waved through with a smile. Cormac's bag was searched next, without fanfare, and then Jack's. It was not the Dramamine that caused the custom's officer to pause, but the dirty underwear. He waved Jack on. He and Cormac then had their visas and passports stamped and were on their way. As they passed the restrooms, Jack knew he had been right about smelling them from the line up. Cormac, apparently responding to the look on Jack's face, said, "Rotten in there. Always is."

As they stepped outside, it was steamy, and the heat was oppressive. They were on a wide sidewalk, made up of concrete squares. Men ran up to them, swarming around, trying to lure them into their cabs. Cormac held one hand up above his head and led Jack through them to a white Toyota 4X4, a Sudanese driver waiting inside and "UN" stenciled in large letters on the outside. The road surface was a reddish brown, but Jack could see a grassy field in the distance, with a few trees and, beyond those, hills. In the heat, even the green seemed an empty promise of relief. Jack and Cormac climbed into the back seats.

"Should we get a drink?" Cormac asked.

"We're not going out to the field?"

"My, but we're eager. How about a few drinks first while we're here in lovely Juba? It won't be but an hour or two." Cormac didn't wait for an answer and spoke to the driver, "Eddies."

Cormac turned to Jack. "You might want to fasten that belt."

Jack fastened his seatbelt, as did Cormac.

They drove through Juba. Everything seemed to be some shade of brown. The potholes were enormous but the driver never slowed. He swerved left and then right. Children, young children, zipped in and out of traffic on motorcycles. The driver avoided these too, along with goats, dogs, and the poverty-stricken elderly who seemed more interested in calmly committing suicide by Toyota than in crossing the roadway.

Jack shot a look at Cormac, who only smiled back.

Two cars collided in front of them. At this, finally, their driver slowed and picked his way around the accident scene as the two drivers came out of the vehicles and begin beating each other up.

Cormac laughed, and shook his head. Jack was laughing too. This land, so renowned for its suffering, was certainly alive.

They pulled up in front of a place called Fresh Eddies, and the vehicle had scarcely stopped when Cormac's door opened. He tossed a couple bills into the front seat, and he and his backpack were out before Jack had his seatbelt off. Jack hurried to catch up and reached the wooden door before it had completely closed behind Cormac.

Stepping inside, he saw Cormac sit at one of several tables with wide wooden chairs and dark green tablecloths. Jack could smell garlic, and grease, and realized how hungry he was.

"Would you like a pint?" Cormac asked as Jack sat down.

"Sure. Could we get a menu, too?"

"We'll order pizza. It's good here. All you Americans like pizza, right?"

"I'd eat just about anything right now," Jack said.

Cormac walked to the bar. Jack put his messenger bag on the floor, leaning it up against his leg. He then scanned the bar, half expecting the man in black, Sopater, to be in there. No sign of him. Cormac returned with two pints of stout. Jack was already drinking when Cormac raised his glass without a word, smiled, and took a long drink.

"Alright then," Cormac said. "What are you looking for?"

Jack paused and then decided to just come straight out. "I've come looking for a human tragedy, an impending disaster, other than the ongoing hardship these people are facing."

"What on earth for? And why here and now?"

Jack was not about to begin explaining the potentially supernatural pattern. "I believe these things happen in cycles, and I believe this place is ripe for another one."

"Why would you want to be here for it?"

"I'm writing a book," Jack said.

"Ah, go on," Cormac said. "You've not a notepad or recorder on you. You've come packed for a weekend. Not how the usual writer comes equipped."

Jack said nothing.

"It's none of my business," Cormac said. "If you don't want to tell me, then don't."

"Okay," Jack said.

Cormac seemed surprised, and a bit disappointed, at Jack's response. Jack took another sip of his beer. Cormac narrowed his eyes and said, "How long did you plan to stay?"

"I'll be done here by May 19."

"Well, that's a tight schedule for a disaster," Cormac said. "At least you don't have to register with the immigration office. If your plans change, however, be sure to register, or else it will cause you untold hassles at the airport when you do try to leave."

Jack said, "So you know of no current threat of a massacre or a mass suicide?"

"Do you know how ghoulish you sound? As if those things are on the menu? I don't go around hoping to see the worst; it happens often enough. I'm here to help, if I can, not to predict further misery," Cormac said.

Jack leaned forward over the table. "I'm here trying to understand these evils. I'm trying to help, too."

A young waitress arrived with the pizza. Jack sat back. It looked wonderful and the smell made his mouth water even more. She gave Jack a bit of an odd look, and then returned to the bar.

Cormac grabbed a slice and pulled it onto his plate, hissing at the heat of it. "Go on, it's the best pizza for a thousand miles."

Jack took his own slice, and took a bite. Cormac was right; it was delicious. When Jack next looked up, Cormac was staring at him.

"What?" Jack asked.

"I don't understand what you're doing here, but in any event, you might be in the wrong place."

"What do you mean?" Jack asked, and immediately thought of Popielsko talking about Jack staying in Juba.

"You've a better chance of finding an impending tragedy in the Democratic Republic of Congo, just across the border. We've heard that things are heating up at one of the United Nations camps for IDPs," Cormac said.

"IDPs?"

"Internally displaced people. Refugees in their own land," Cormac said, taking another bite.

Jack thought for a moment. "Is that camp roughly south-southwest of here?"

"I suppose so."

It still fit the pattern. It would be roughly on the same azimuth that brought him here. "Can I get a vehicle to take me there?" Jack asked.

"Why the hell would you want to do that?"

"You just said..."

"Yeah, but why go by land?" Cormac asked. "To go from Juba to the DRC you'd want to fly to Kampala and drive from there. Driving from Juba to DRC may seem possible when looking at the map but the roads are either poor or nonexistent. The rains wash them away all the time. Not to mention your chances of armed robbery along the way are high. Overall, it's a treacherous journey. My advice is fly."

"Fly? Like on a UN helicopter or something?" Jack asked.

"Who do you think you are?" Cormac laughed. "Go commercial. You turn around, go back to the airport, fly to Uganda. Then, much as you did with me, link up with UNHCR and get a ride to the DRC, and out to the field. The camp is north of Beni, on the Aruwimi River. Some eleven-thousand IDPs. The camp was established after some tribal disagreement over farming or fishing rights led to violence and the people fled south. Many were brutally killed, and the word is a group of armed men and boys are looking for revenge. Those in the camp will be completely unarmed."

"But the UN is there to protect them?" Jack asked, his voice uncertain.

Cormac scowled. "The UN was in Rwanda, too, and could have stopped the slaughter there in 1994. In fact, General Dallaire, commander of the U.N. Assistance Mission in Rwanda asked for permission to search for and seize the caches of machetes that would be used as the primary weapons in the genocide. Such an action probably would have prevented the entire event. However, a man named Iqbal Riza, deputy to then Undersecretary General for Peacekeeping Kofi Annan—in a letter signed by Annan, mind you—denied Dallaire permission to act. Instead, Iqbal Riza instructed Dallaire to take the information to the Rwandan government, many of whose members were actually planning the genocide. You know the rest."

"That's what I'm talking about. That's what I'm trying to understand," Jack said. "Why would men who had sworn to help the helpless, men who were leading the world's largest organization for helping to keep the peace, do nothing to confront such evil? Why did they let it happen?"

"You want to solve that riddle by entering South Sudan or going to the DRC?" Cormac asked.

"Is there another way?"

"Would you say the best way to learn the nature of fire is to thrust one's arm into the flames?"

Jack paused. Cormac took another bite of pizza without breaking eye contact.

"You're a logistics guy, can you help me get out to that camp, out at the Aroh-winni river?"

"Aruwimi."

Jack just looked at the Irishman, who put the pizza slice down, wiped his hands on a napkin, and then took a sip of his stout. "Alright, in the morning, you fly to Kampala, I'll see if I can get you out to that camp. You are probably facing at least a ten-hour ride in the back of a truck, and you won't be leaving Kampala before tomorrow afternoon," he said.

"I'd appreciate it."

"I'm not sure you'll be as grateful tomorrow night." Cormac chuckled and went back to his pizza.

"Neither am I," Jack said. "Cormac, where can I find a phone to call the U.S.?"

Cormac leaned back, reached into a pocket on his backpack, and handed a small satellite phone to Jack. It looked like any cell phone might, except for the ridiculously large antenna across the top. Thick and charcoal grey, the antenna looked like a long pistol barrel. Jack rose to step away from the table to make his call, picking up his bag in the process.

Cormac said, "Hey now, don't go far with it. People have been killed around here for those."

Jack looked at the device, realizing it wouldn't have mattered here that he hadn't bought the international plan for his phone.

Cormac took a sip of his beer. "You'll dial zero-zero-one and then the number back in the States." Jack stepped into a corner where Cormac could see him but where he might have a little privacy.

"Hello?"

A wave washed through Jack, something comforting, at hearing her voice. "It's me."

"Where are you? You sound close." Her voice was hopeful.

"I'm not, I'm in Juba," Jack said.

"You're not calling from a payphone?"

"I met a guy here, he's letting me use his phone. How are you? Are you alright?"

"I'm okay," she said.

"Did I interrupt your breakfast?" Jack was in no hurry to tell her that he was moving on, chasing a lead on a pending potential massacre, into yet another devastated country.

"What's going on? What's the matter?" she asked.

"Nothing," Jack said, but then sighed. "I think I'm in the wrong place."

"I agree."

"I mean, I think the next tragedy will be south of here, in the Democratic Republic of Congo. At a UN refugee camp just north of Beni."

There was silence, a heavy pause.

"Hello?"

"And you're going." She wasn't asking.

Jack's eyes closed. "I'll be leaving tomorrow morning. I'll be in touch as soon as I can. I just thought I should let someone know."

"Jack."

"I know. I'll be careful. Talk to you soon." Jack hung up before the call could become anything more. He walked back to the table and handed the phone back to Cormac.

"Thanks," Jack said.

"She didn't take it well?" Cormac asked.

Jack didn't respond, instead taking a long drink of his stout.

"Ah well, you'll stay with us tonight, and we'll see getting you farther along on your mad quest tomorrow."

Ch: 24

May 17
6:30 p.m.
Kenyi Staging Area
South Sudan

They hadn't driven many miles, but Cormac had been right about the condition of local roads.

Once they arrived, Cormac said, "Don't wander off. We still find the odd landmine here and there."

Jack looked out at the village. The huts were round, with conical thatched roofs, and mud walls rubbed smooth. The structures themselves were clustered in small familial compounds of four or five. Cormac slung his pack over one shoulder and headed for the center of the village, and Jack followed.

A large group of children came running, calling out, "Mister! Mister!" They encircled Jack and there was a chorus of "How are you? How are you?" Smiles all around. Cormac looked back, and Jack grinned.

"How are you? How are you?" The children were smiling broadly. All had closely cropped black hair, their skin deep, dark, and warm brown, with eyes wide. Jack could not tell the boys from the girls, with the exception of one little one. Her hair was in crude pigtails, set high, and an additional one coming straight off the back of her head. Her shirt was worn, but had frills all around, with three enormous buttons down the front. She began asking, "Camera? Camera?" The others chimed in.

"I don't have a camera," Jack said, laughing.

Their smiles never dimmed. "Itsokay, itsokay." They shifted their focus to Cormac.

"Alright, alright," Cormac said in a tone of mock irritation. He reached into his bag and pulled out a camera. A few flashes later, the kids went running off. Cormac put the camera away, and the men walked on.

Near the center of the village, Jack saw a small rectangular building constructed of blocks. Not far from the door was a large but shallow pit.

"The school," Cormac said.

"And the hole?" Jack asked.

"Protection."

Jack could picture the children he'd just seen, huddled together, lying atop one another, trying to lay flat against the bottom, seeking some sort of rudimentary cover.

Cormac suddenly called out, "Elvis!"

"Hello!" a man called back.

As the two men came together, Jack was struck by how old Elvis looked. His ebony skin was wrinkled. The whites of his eyes were anything but. He wore sky blue shorts and a light button-down shirt patterned with horizontal stripes of pale blue on white. His extremely thin legs extended from his shorts, hinged by knees that appeared bulbous between his thighs and calves. Elvis wrapped his bony arms around Cormac, who returned the embrace, and then both men turned to face Jack.

Cormac said, smiling, "Elvis, this is Jack. He's an American." Cormac stressed this last. Elvis's eyes brightened, his grin broadened, and he stepped forward and took Jack's hand. The man's skin felt like paper.

"It is a pleasure to meet you," Elvis said.

"Same here," Jack said.

"Come, we will get some dinner," Elvis said. He and Cormac led the way. They sat among the huts, in the shadow of what seemed to be a smaller hut, set off the ground on four thick poles. As Jack sat, his head was just lower than its floor.

"What's this?" Jack asked.

"A granary. Keep half an eye on it, the posts look to have been at the mercy of termites for some time."

Of all the ways Jack had considered his life might end, having a native granary collapse on top of him in South Sudan had not been one of them. His anxiety began to grow. Not simply because he was getting closer to whatever it was he was chasing but also because he had not had any medication other than Dramamine in some time. Jack missed his meds.

A short distance away, women cooked around a fire. Jack was not especially hungry, having had pizza, but he watched as they dropped small balls of some sort of dough into a heavy cast iron pan—the sizzling sound increasing each time.

"Elvis, our friend Jack here is thinking about heading over to the camp on the Aruwimi."

The man's bright smile immediately fell from his dark, lined face. "What on Earth for?"

Cormac grinned. "He's on a quest for evil."

Elvis did not. "He may find it."

"Have you heard anything more about the potential for new violence there?" Jack asked.

"There is almost sure to be. NGOs and UN are pulling out, trying to move the IDPs, but cannot move everyone. It is a bad situation." Elvis looked up as women brought each of the three men a bowl containing small, golden-brown balls. They were warm. Jack bit into one and was surprised to see the inside was green.

"Chickpeas. It's made with ground chickpeas, it's called *tamiah*."

"Not bad," Jack said.

Each of the men was given a cup of tea and Jack watched as Elvis heaped five teaspoons of sugar into his. As another woman approached, Elvis froze. She was older than the others had been. She stood in front of Jack.

"But I'm not finished," he said, looking at Elvis and Cormac.

Elvis said, "She does not want your bowl."

She stared right at Jack. Her hair was cropped very close, and if not for the skirt and the outline of ancient and flat breasts beneath her shirt, Jack would not have been sure if she were male or female.

"What does she want?" Jack asked.

The woman began to speak, quickly but quietly.

"What is she saying?"

"I don't speak Zandi," Cormac answered, holding his voice low.

"She sees *mangu*," Elvis said. "Witchcraft."

"She thinks I'm a witch?" Jack asked. The woman had not paused; she continued to speak at the same rate, in the same hushed tone.

"The Azande believe there is witchcraft in everyone. In the abdomen," Elvis said. "She is not accusing you. She is warning you."

"Ask her if I will find the evil I am searching for," Jack asked.

"Jack, this is not something to mock," Cormac said.

"I'm not mocking it. I'm serious. Ask her, Elvis."

Elvis looked hard at Jack and then spoke to the woman. His voice was hardly audible, but she stopped speaking immediately, turned and left.

Jack looked at Elvis. "Why did you tell her to leave? I was seriously asking."

"I did not tell her to leave," Elvis said. "I hope you were asking seriously because she will return, and answer seriously."

The woman returned with a bird, some sort of small fowl. It

was tan, mostly, speckled with darker colors. She sat in the dirt in front of Jack, placing her foot down upon the bird's two feet, its legs coming up between her toes. She produced a rolled leaf and began tapping one end of it on the bird's beak, all the while, speaking the same words again and again.

"What is she doing?" Jack asked.

"Quiet, Jack," Cormac said.

"She is asking your question. She is asking the Oracle," Elvis said.

"Translate for me," Jack said.

Elvis looked at the woman and then at Jack. "She is saying, 'Oracle, Oracle, look at this man, if he goes to find evil, will he find it? If he will find it, kill this chicken. Act like a buffalo and drop it dead." The woman and Elvis fell silent. Everyone stared at the bird. She picked it up by its legs and held them out horizontally. The bird flapped its wings wildly as she gently waved it a few inches up and down. It suddenly went stiff, brought its wings to its body, and its eyes closed. She laid it on the dirt. It didn't move, except for its beak. It seemed to silently mouth a couple last squawks and then was perfectly still. Dead.

"What the fuck just happened?" Jack asked.

The woman looked coolly at Jack, saying nothing.

Cormac said, "The rolled leaf. She put strychnine on the bird's beak."

"What the hell? Well then, of course it died. How is that supposed to predict anything?" Jack asked.

"The birds do not always die," Elvis said. "They only die when the Oracle kills them. The Oracle could have just as easily saved the bird."

"Bullshit."

"Look, Jack, you asked your question in this place, and you received a local answer," Cormac said.

"You believe in this shit?" Jack asked.

"You were ready to," Cormac said.

The woman sensed Jack's doubt, and spoke quickly to Elvis. Elvis answered, making a dismissive hand gesture toward Jack. The woman rose and left.

"Did he insult her, Elvis?" Cormac asked.

"She will be back," Elvis replied.

When the woman returned, she had another bird. This one had a large brown spot above its left eye. The woman, it seemed, was ready to prove the veracity of the first test by repeating it with a new chicken.

"Elvis, tell her I don't want to watch her poison another bird," Jack said.

Before Elvis could speak, the woman said something to Jack. Jack looked to Elvis for a translation, but he was looking at his feet.

"Well?" Jack asked.

"She wants you to ask another question. This time, she will apply the poison, and then allow you to pick if the Oracle should spare the bird. Then you will see," Elvis said.

Jack licked his lips. He searched Cormac's face. The joy had run out of it, and the Irishman looked weary. The woman held the bird just as she had before and began tapping the leaf on the bird's beak again.

"Will I die in the DRC?" Jack asked, his voice very soft.

Elvis said, "Do not ask this."

"Ask her!" Jack barked back.

Elvis translated the question. She looked Jack directly in the eyes and said only a few words. The setting sun was behind her. She was black against the orange horizon.

"The bird, alive or dead?" Elvis translated.

"Alive," Jack said.

She began speaking softly, but quickly, once more. Elvis, as he had before translated, "'Oracle, Oracle, look at this man, will he die at the place? If he will die, kill this chicken. Act like a buffalo and drop it dead."

The chicken flapped and squawked, but did not die. She put it down and it clumsily walked around her foot. The woman held both hands out to Jack and then clapped them together, as if she had been completely vindicated. Jack heard the air slowly rush out of Elvis; he had been holding his breath. Clearly, he was a believer. The woman picked up her bird and was gone.

Cormac put down his bowl. "I've had enough fun for one night," he said. "It will be dark in an hour. Let me show you where you will sleep."

Ch: 25

May 18
6:00 a.m.
Kenyi Staging Area
South Sudan

Dream

> *I'm in a pool, chest deep. With children. The children from the village. Children from Goodwin. Children I've never seen. On the edge, above the kids, looms Sopater. I move to save them. I rush headlong toward them. My arms are outstretched. As I rush forward, a wave forms in front of me, in front of my chest and arms. It grows. I hurry to try to reach the children before the wave does, only giving it more energy. The wave breaks over the children, the water goes crimson, the children are gone. Sopater, the Witness, looks down at me. He turns and walks away. I see Popielsko beyond. He looks at me with contempt...*

"We've got to get you back to the airport if you're to continue on your way, Ahab." It was Cormac, tapping his foot against Jack's bedding as he spoke.

Ahab. Jack didn't find it funny. His body felt different. He was losing the last residual traces of his meds. It was sort of like gradually losing the power steering while driving. He was still in control, it just took much more of a conscious effort. Jack missed more than the meds, however. He wondered what Vivian was doing that morning. He checked his watch.

"Evening for her," he said, rubbing his face.

"How's that?" Cormac asked.

"Are you driving me back?"

"Elvis will take you back," Cormac said. He seemed less friendly now, and put upon. Without another word, Cormac turned and left the hut. Jack stood, stretched, and tried to shake the last bits of the dream away.

He pulled on his shoes, picked up his bag, and stepped out into the morning sun. He didn't see any of the kids. Elvis stood off in the distance near the vehicle.

"Good luck, Jack," Cormac said, extending his hand. "From Entebbe, there will be a truck heading out to the area of the camp, near Beni. I've let them know to wait for you. The truck will not go to that camp; you'll have to walk a few miles in the middle of the night after a grueling ride. I think you're perfectly stupid for going. There will be no quick way to get you out. No one will come looking for you. You will be on your own, Jack."

"Thanks for the help."

"Don't thank me," Cormac said. "And don't blame me, either." Cormac turned and walked into a nearby hut. Jack looked back to Elvis who hadn't moved. Off to his right, he spotted the woman with the birds from the night before. He raised one hand. She did nothing; she only stood, arms across her breasts, motionless, staring back.

Jack lowered his hand. "Fuck this." He reset his resolve and strode purposefully toward Elvis, and they were soon on their way.

Elvis said nothing, and Jack was not in the mood to try to force some sort of conversation. Instead, he just looked out at the landscape. Mostly mud, with scattered trees towering above it.

When they reached the airport in Juba, Jack turned to Elvis. "Thanks for the ride."

Elvis said, "You know, you are not alone."

"You mean like God is watching me?" Jack asked.

"No," Elvis said. "I mean you have a responsibility. We all do. We are all tied together. The decisions you make carry weight."

Jack stepped out, closed the door, and looked back through the open window.

Elvis continued, saying, "The decisions a person makes affect all the people, more or less. It is as if we are all tied to one another, and bound to each other's actions, neck deep in a pool of water. Be not only cautious, but thoughtful."

Elvis pulled away with Jack's hand still on the door. A tepid tidewater pool, Jack thought. He watched Elvis drive away. He adjusted his messenger bag and walked into the airport. It seemed the same crowd was still there. The same odor certainly was, although the air was cooler than it had been.

He went to the Air Uganda counter and bought a ticket to Kampala. He walked over to the departure area. There was no line up, no orderly queue to stand in. Eventually, he pushed his way far enough forward to get his visa stamped for exit. When his flight was finally called, Jack walked forward into a curtained area, much like a changing room at a consignment shop. An impossibly thin man patted him down, less tapping than stroking really.

He checked through Jack's bag and then waved him on. Stepping out onto the runway, Jack was taken aback at how quickly the air had warmed. Here, yet another uniformed and armed officer checked Jack's passport and visa, and he took one last look through Jack's bag.

It was afternoon before Jack finally climbed the steps up into the McDonnell Douglas MD87. The fuselage was white, with simple black lettering just aft of the door. "Air Uganda." The tail was painted black, adorned with the image of two exotic birds, back-to-back, walking away from each other.

More fucking birds, Jack thought. Jack had never realized how intertwined people were with birds. In their diet, in their art, in their mythology, in their rituals. Now he was seeing birds everywhere, and his anxiety level kept climbing.

Finding his seat, he tried to calm himself. He looked out his window. There were fuelers and maintenance personnel. Jack saw security personnel milling about, and then he saw him. Jack caught sight of him, and threw his hands against the inside of the fuselage, pressing his face to the window. The man in black, Sopater, was sitting cross-legged on top of the trailer that had carried the baggage. It pulled away, taking him with it. No one else seemed to notice.

Behind Jack's seat, the door closed. He looked that way in time to see the flight attendant lock it and he felt new waves of anxiety. Maybe he should get off the plane. When he looked back out the window, he could see the tractor with its trailer in the distance, but Sopater was nowhere to be seen. He felt the aircraft begin to move. Opening his messenger bag, he took the three remaining Dramamine, and lay back.

As the engines spun up, and the brakes released, he realized he must be on the right track again. From the time he left Nairobi for Juba, he'd not seen Sopater. Once Jack decided to go to the DRC, Sopater had appeared in a dream. When Jack had boarded a plane, Sopater had appeared in the sunlight.

The flight only lasted an hour. The plane scarcely had finished climbing when it began its descent. Jack saw Lake Victoria and then the airport not far from it; the landing was a smooth one. He could still feel the Dramamine as he deplaned. The Entebbe airport was completely different than the one in Juba. It was modern, air-conditioned, and clean. Clearing Customs was quick, and the system was efficient.

He soon spotted a short, well-fed man holding a sign, "Kilarny." As Jack approached the man, he turned and led the way. There was no need to identify himself; Jack clearly stood out, even among the white tourists. He was dirty, in need of laundry, a shave, a shower, and had no luggage.

They walked out to an ancient Mercedes truck. The truck's cab upfront, as well as the sides of the undercarriage, were red. Railings above those were painted white, and an olive-drab tarpaulin was stretched over the top. The well-fed man tossed his sign into the back, pointed with a thumb for Jack to follow it, and then the man walked to the front.

Jack climbed up into the back of the truck. There he found crates, and two young boys, perhaps in their early teens, each cradling a Heckler & Koch G3. Child soldiers. He thought then of his nephew Kenny, and of the life he would have had. Jack remembered Kenny's little feet swinging above his father's body.

"Jesus," Jack whispered, and rubbed his face.

The boys looked bored; hardly interested in Jack once they saw he was unarmed. While sitting on a bench bolted to the railing, Jack looked at the crates. One with a lid pried up contained RPG-7s, a type of rocket launcher. They were old, but effective. Hadn't Cormac said that this would be a UN vehicle? Maybe he hadn't.

They were driving into the sun, leaving the inside of the back of the truck dark compared to the road behind them. As soon as the truck began rolling, the two boys lay down on bales of empty sandbags to catch some sleep. Both were on their backs, rifles across their narrow chests, arms folded over the rifles, each in contact with the other at the shoulder and hip. They fell asleep quickly, likely not knowing when they might sleep next.

It wasn't long before the road turned to orange-brown earth, and then the ruts grew deeper and wetter, until finally the truck was rocking back and forth as it made forward progress through the mud. It *can't* be like this for ten hours. Jack looked over at the boys, and saw they were still asleep despite the rough ride.

They passed a white truck, its payload area painted grey, lying over on its side in the mud. Men walked in slow circles around it, trying to decide what to do next. A large bump drove Jack hard into the railing behind him. The shadows behind the truck were lengthening.

It was only when the truck suddenly stopped that the boys sat up as one, fingers searching for triggers. Jack looked out and saw that they had stopped before a river. It was perhaps three truck-lengths wide, brown, and swift. It couldn't be very deep. The riverbanks were covered in tall grass and weeds, and the forest came to within a dozen feet on both sides.

Jack adjusted his messenger bag and jumped down. He glanced back at the boys sitting atop the bales. They weren't moving. They seemed to be listening more than looking. Jack made his way to the front of the truck. There was a bridge atop two piers made of concrete blocks. Across those piers, there were two concrete joists, and these were crossed with what looked like railroad ties for a deck. Beneath, someone had deemed it necessary to place some additional bracing; three tree trunks were wedged up between the joists and the riverbed. None of the tree trunks were plumb. The bridge was no wider than the wheelbase of the truck.

A man began guiding the driver as they attempted the truck across. He was walking backwards, giving hand signals. Watching the operation, Jack felt safer walking across than crossing in the back of that truck. He considered getting the boys out, but then realized that the boys had probably been here countless times and would be past convincing. Perhaps they were past saving.

The truck inched along and Jack followed. The deck of the bridge wasn't level and it was slick. The front tires were sliding ever so slowly toward the downstream side of the bridge. Jack watched the truck shift a fraction of an inch for every foot it traveled. He was doing the math, predicting its course. The edge of the front right tire was already beyond the lip of the bridge.

Jack searched for some concern on the face of the man leading the truck. There was none. The man calmly took step after step until he was on the other side. When the front tires finally found purchase on the far bank, Jack picked up his pace and caught the truck. He grabbed the tailgate and pulled himself up. He was still hanging onto the back when the driver shifted gears, and was nearly thrown out again. As he climbed in from the sunlight, he looked over for the boys. They were gone. Instead, sitting on the bales, was Sopater.

Jack froze. Was he really there? Would he disappear as he did on the plane?

"Be seated," Sopater said. His voice was rich, but tired. The voice of a charismatic pastor on a deathwatch. Perhaps a Greek accent, but he wasn't sure. He had expected something more like Bela Lugosi. Jack sat on the bench.

Seeing Sopater's face close up for the first time, Jack could finally make out a few features, although the lack of light cast shadows. His forehead was high, as were his cheekbones. A prominent nose and a full mouth. A thin covering of dark moustache and beard ran down his neck to his collar. With a thick thatch of hair, and his eyebrows nearly came together above his eyes. There was a scar from the corner of his left eye extending back to his ear.

"What is your purpose?" Sopater asked.

"What are you doing? Why are you going around watching this shit?" Jack asked.

"There must be a witness."

"What if there wasn't?" Jack asked.

"I cannot stop it. I am witnessing even now. You have more to do with the impending tragedy than I do. We are all responsible for the tragedy around us," Sopater said.

"I'm trying to stop it," Jack said.

"Ironic."

Jack asked, "What's that supposed to mean?"

"You could not even stop the death of your own spouse," Sopater said.

"Hey, fuck you!" Jack said.

"Think, Mr. Killarney. Had you not been in the arms of another woman that morning, you and your wife would have left earlier. You would have missed that truck by hours. Your adultery put you in the path of that truck. Your wife is dead because of you."

Jack sprang at Sopater, who moved incredibly quickly to Jack's bench. Jack was left sprawled across the bales, while Sopater was seated.

"Do not spend your anger on me. Do not behave as if you do not remember. Your partner Benjamin committed suicide because his spouse Deborah finally confessed your affair with her," Sopater said.

"That's not true! We didn't!"

"I am not here to debate. I am only a witness."

Jack scoured his memory. Flashes of Deb naked, of passion. Then of Beth burning up in the car. Ben with a hole in his head. Could it be true?

"And then you brought this to your brother's doorstep," Sopater said.

"You're fucking lying!"

"Mr. Killarney. You are at fault."

Jack rushed him again. Once more, Sopater was too quick. He went over the tailgate and out of the truck. Jack moved to the back and looked out. No sign of him in the sunset's long shadows.

Jack turned back. The two boys, rifles in hand, stared at him from their perch on the bales. Jack sat where he was, in the bed, his back to the tailgate. Beth and Ben… his fault? Did he have an affair with Deb?

The truck lurched to the left and then stopped hard. The boys were thrown forward off the bale and into the dark. Jack rolled forward into the crates of RPG's. Pain in his right wrist and ribs. There was a moment of silence. Jack stood and looked over the bales for the boys, and was greeted by the muzzle of one of the rifles. The boy behind it was clearly afraid. Jack backed away very slowly. He heard voices, speaking English. Looking out, Jack could see the front left tire had gone into a mud hole to the axle. The driver and his colleague were discussing how the situation might be fixed. Their voices had an edge of concern and urgency. Night was fast approaching. Jack jumped down and walked forward to the two men. They glanced at him and then kept talking, but now in Luganda instead of English.

"Speak English. I just heard you," Jack said.

The driver said, "We are stuck here. It is unlikely we can get out of this hole without help."

"Couldn't we just get some wood under it?" Jack asked.

The driver said, "Look." He pointed a flashlight. The front bumper of the truck had plowed into the road's surface. The truck's differential would be even worse. The hole was deeper than it looked.

Jack looked at the road ahead. Dark.

"We wait here until morning. The two soldiers in the back can stay awake on guard," the driver said.

"Those two kids?" Jack asked. He looked in the direction they'd come and then asked, "How do I get to Beni?"

The driver looked at his colleague and then back at Jack. "You mean, walk tonight?"

"Yeah, man, walk tonight. How far?" Jack asked.

The man from the airport stepped forward. "Killarney, wait for morning."

"I don't have until morning. I have to be there before tomorrow."

"This is suicide," the driver said.

His colleague agreed, "Even in a truck it is dangerous. Bandits, murderers."

"How far?" Jack said.

The men exchanged glances. "Maybe 18 kilometers and then you see a road, to the right, the Beni road. You take that one for another 7 kilometers."

Twenty-five kilometers, Jack thought. Fifteen miles. If it were a solid surface, in daylight, it would take him at least five hours. Instead, it'll be dark, tricky going, not to mention the people who'd just as soon kill him along the way. What the fuck are you doing here, Jack?

He adjusted his messenger bag, swinging it more behind him. "I'm going."

The driver threw his hands up and stepped away. The colleague hesitated and then went to the cab of the truck. He handed Jack a 9mm CZ-85 handgun and a spare magazine. He also gave Jack a flashlight.

"Thank you," Jack said. "I don't have anything to give you in exchange."

"I should just shoot you for being so stupid. I am throwing away a perfectly good gun. Cormac vouched for you, so I will see him about my losses," he said.

"And you don't need it?" Jack asked, looking around.

"We have other weapons, and the soldiers in the back. You need it far worse than we do," he said.

Jack dropped the extra mag into his bag. He slid the flashlight into his pocket, bulb-end down, and slid the CZ into the back waistband of his pants. He extended his hand, but the man refused it and rejoined the driver to plan out their night. Jack turned, looked down the dark road, and began walking.

"Pace yourself," Jack whispered to himself.

Ch: 26

9:00 p.m.
Winter Harbor Hospital
Westbrook, Maine

Carol Killarney sat working in a child's coloring book. She was exhausted. She could smell the wax of the Crayola crayon as she covered a cartoon cat with a color labeled "Fuzzy Wuzzy."

She sat quietly, but her thoughts were chaotic. She hadn't heard from Jack in some time. Beside the coloring book sat her journal and the nub of a blue-green crayon. She glanced at the journal once, and then glanced again. She stopped coloring, picked it up, and turned to the entry she had spent the last hours writing. Pages and pages filled with the same sentence, repeated again and again.

"Walk away from the bad stuff, and maybe the Devil will forget your name. Walk away from the bad stuff, and maybe the Devil will forget your name. Walk away from the bad stuff, and maybe the Devil will forget your name. Walk away from the bad stuff, and maybe the Devil will forget your name…"

Carol looked up. The man in the black coat was in the hallway, looking in through the tall, narrow, and wired window.

"Nurse!" Carol screamed.

The man in black did not move.

"Nurse! Nurse!" Carol screamed.

The man slowly turned and walked away. The door opened and the nurse came in with an orderly.

"What is it, Carol? What's the matter?"

"Did you see him?" Carol asked.

"Who?"

"The man! The man!" Carol was pointing toward her door. Neither the nurse nor the orderly went to check.

"There was no one," the nurse said calmly.

"You're safe," the orderly said.

Carol dropped the crayon, looked at the orderly, and said, "Nobody is safe."

Ch: 27

May 19
4:00 a.m.
UN Refugee Camp
North of Beni, Democratic Republic of Congo

The watcher watched. He stood across a small field, looking into the camp. He could hear them approaching from the trees. There was a heavy, sickening thud, and then another. Large vultures were falling from the sky. People in the camp began to call out as bird after bird fell from a circle of them in the sky above.

The watcher watched as men with machetes ran out of the tree line and descended upon the refugees in this corner of the camp. Many of the adults scattered but most of the children did not initially flee. Instead, they stood, fixed, and raised little arms in an attempt to fend off the falling blades. Child after child fell, and the adults who remained to defend them did as well.

He watched as the vultures fell like rain. Men ran in every direction chasing down victims. Blood sprayed into the air with the screams, until the only vertical people were the attackers. They went through the huts, taking what they wanted. There were those who were injured and not dead, but the attackers passed them without notice. None of the injured were dispatched, as if the time for violence had expired, and now was the time for looting.

Next, fires were set. Huts and tents were quickly consumed by the flames.

Without taking any large items that might have slowed their progress, and without any discernible signal, the attackers then walked out of the camp en masse.

The watcher walked toward the camp. He would wait.

Ch: 28

May 19
4:00 a.m.
Beni Road
Democratic Republic of Congo

Jack had been walking for seven hours. He had come to the realization that sunrise would come before he could get to the camp. Jack reached the Beni road, but he still had approximately four miles to walk, with perhaps two hours until sunrise. On a decent surface, it would've been an easy jog, but his legs were exhausted. With every step thus far, one foot and then the other would slide, at least doubling the work required to make progress. He had fallen twice in the mud, twisting a knee and pulling a groin muscle. He was dehydrated. More than once, he wondered if Sopater was watching him from the trees.

Jack stopped and put a hand on the signpost marking the road to Beni and the camp north of it. He adjusted the messenger bag, pushing it toward his back. He looked back the way he had come; hoping that a truck would come by at that instant, but knowing one wouldn't. The new road ahead was smaller and worse than the one he'd been on.

"But it's only a bit more than half the distance," he said aloud. More like four sevenths. Eight fourteenths. Sixteen twenty-eighths. Stop it, and get going, he thought. Jack wiped his mouth with the back of one mud-crusted hand, spit the dried earth from his mouth, and headed out.

With Jack's first step, his foot came completely out from under him. His trail foot found no traction with which to recover. He fell, but was able to hold his head out of the mud this time.

"Shit. Why are we here, Jack?" He rose carefully, began walking, and as he went, his thoughts turned to Vivian. He imagined her in her apartment, which he'd never actually seen. Its walls must be lined with bookshelves, he thought, and she was probably under a blanket, reading, with the television dark. He imagined she had a glass of wine, and maybe she was wearing flannel pajama pants, with… a tank top? A cami? Jack smiled to himself. A pink-patterned cami with flannel pajama pants, bare feet tucked under her on the sofa, under a fleece blanket. Bringing that glass of wine to her lips. Maybe a black thong instead of pajama…

His feet slid, he almost fell, and then recovered. Something moved in the trees off to the side of the road. There was nowhere to go. Jack squatted, trying to be smaller. He put his hand on the flashlight, but left it in his pocket. It would be used as a last resort. Usually all a flashlight did was pinpoint your location for others. Jack duck-walked into the tall grass, straining to see, listening intently. Movement again, this time in the grass with him. Jack slowly pulled the handgun from his pants and the flashlight from his pocket. He crossed his wrists, locking light with weapon, and rose slowly, waiting. Then he heard it again, had a best guess, and flipped on the light.

A bizarre-looking animal, like a red fox with the snout of a pig and long ears, looked back at Jack and then darted off into the tree line. Jack immediately turned off the light and squatted again. He moved back to the edge of the road and waited to see if his light had attracted anyone. He heard and saw nothing.

He didn't have time to waste, he had to get to the camp. After a few minutes of silently listening, Jack rose and began walking, and slipping, in the road again.

When the sun finally rose, it came up slowly until the last moment when it seemed to leap above the last of the trees. It was dawn, May 19. Jack figured he still had an hour of walking to go before he'd get near where the camp was supposed to be. He hadn't walked half that long before he saw the smoke rising in the distance above the forest.

Ch: 29

May 19
4:30 a.m.
UN Refugee Camp
North of Beni, DRC

The watcher waited. He knew Jack was approaching. For decades he had watched, and had seen these manifestors, like Jack, come before. Always on a quest for answers and hoping to understand. Most did not survive long enough to regret their search.

The watcher was intrigued because Jack had shown more courage and more tenacity than most. This one had been cleverer, and more stubborn. Jack had been warned time and again, and even the priest had warned him.

The watcher also knew the signs of madness. One does not witness the worst of humankind without becoming perceptive to the onset of lunacy. Not the disorganized thinking of those on psychotropic drugs, not the careening psyche of the distraught, and not the blinded senses of the enraged. Instead, madness in the purest sense.

He had stood at its center, within the circles of death, far removed from the fringes where relief and salvation might be found. Deeper still than the inner rings where animal killing animal occurs, where nature fights to live and only appears cruel to those who are afraid. He had been deeper still, at that center; that space only humans can occupy. The umbra of madness, where God's illumination seemed completely absent. He knew getting there was a frighteningly simple journey.

He wondered how far into the center of madness Jack would ultimately drift.

Ch: 30

May 19
4:30 a.m.
Beni Road
Democratic Republic of Congo

Bodies. The first thing Jack saw through the smoke as he arrived at the camp were the bodies. Many of them were children, with maybe as many as a hundred dead. Little arms in the air, faces in the mud, blood running into the brown puddles. Bodies scattered between tents of off-white canvas, straw huts, and other structures built of whatever scraps could be pulled together. The shelters were burning. A strange homemade cart was as well. There were survivors, hardly moving. Some seated, some kneeling, some walking around aimlessly with nowhere to go. Women huddled together in defensive circles, too late. A child walked by, his head bleeding from a gash on his scalp. An old man waved Jack off, as if trying to spare him the truth of it all.

And then there were the vultures. With this kind of carnage, vultures were to be expected, but here they were scattered and lifeless. The large birds lay dead among the human bodies. Some with their brown wings extended over the motionless humans around them, wingspans longer than the tallest men, thick breasts the size of Thanksgiving turkeys, with their pink and fleshy heads lying still against the ground.

Jack scanned the camp for anyone with a gun. He saw no one who appeared threatening. The only people he could see were the dead and the trauma-zombies. The smell struck him then. Not just smoke, but the odor of burning flesh. The smell of Beth's death. He felt his knees weaken, and thought he might fall, until, through pillars of smoke, he spotted Sopater walking some distance away. Jack's vision focused, as did his anger. There was a surge of adrenaline. Jack bolted forward to catch up to Sopater just as the latter disappeared behind a burning tent. The bag bounced on Jack's hip. Jack did not slow, although he was sure that once he came around the flames and smoke, Sopater would be nowhere in sight.

Instead, Sopater stood there passively. "What did you expect to find?"

"You bastard! Look at this! Look at the children!" Jack said.

"I have looked. I watched."

Jack said, "Tell me how to stop this! Tell me how to stop the pattern!"

Sopater stood, emotionless. "Go home."

Jack sprinted at Sopater, lunging with the last few steps. Sopater moved incredibly quickly to one side but Jack got one hand on him. Jack spun in mid-air, and whatever Jack was clutching tore free before he went sprawling in the mud. He slid to a stop against a dead woman clutching a motionless baby. He stared for a moment, and then Jack began to cry. Tears he'd not shed in years. Emotional scar tissue and defenses ripped away by the frustration of what he'd gone through getting here, never knowing what he had planned to do, and arriving too late to matter in any case. Tears of once again being impotent, as he was to save Beth, Ben, Keenan, the kids. They were tears of helplessness.

Then he realized something and, with tears abating, he lifted his head. Jack opened his hand, revealing a short silver chain and a small stone amulet of some kind. It was oblong, ivory in color. Set into it on one side was a pale blue disk with yet a darker blue center. It appeared as if the bottom had been exposed to a sooty flame, but the soot was fixed. It was smaller than a grape. It was also quite muddy now. Jack slipped it into his pocket.

"Get up." It was not Sopater's voice. Jack looked back, saw that Sopater was gone, and the priest, Popielsko, was there. "I said to get on your feet."

Jack's shock quickly turned to rage. He sprang out of the mud, and drove himself through the priest, grabbing two fistfuls of the older man's clothing. They both fell into the mud.

"What does this mean, priest?" Jack made a sweeping motion with his left hand, holding Popielsko down with his right. "What is all this? I felt called here! I find death, and Sopater, and you! What does this mean?"

"You need to..." Popielsko began. Jack drove his left fist into the right side of the man's face. Jack's bag swung with the punch. The priest's eyes went wild with anger and fear; blood ran from his mouth.

"This is your fault!" Popielsko shrieked. "This happened because you would not stop!"

Jack struck the man again. "Make sense! Enough of your cryptic bullshit! And enough blaming me—everything from fucking Ben's wife to this? Bullshit! Give me answers, or I swear I'll beat you to death right here!"

The priest was more stunned this time, slower to turn back to Jack. "You are causing this evil by chasing it. By expecting it to *be*."

"What the fuck are you talking about? I expected it to *be* in Darfur, not here! And the evil existed before I started chasing it! Brazil! Canada!"

"Others, before you, have done the same," Popielsko said. "They have concocted strange conspiracies out of strange coincidences.

They chased a pattern, and with the sheer certainty of their expectations, they caused the evil they sought to manifest itself."

Jack asked, "Why me?"

"You took an interest," Popielsko said. "You took an interest in evil, probably from childhood. But you looked too hard, and you were *too* interested. You were so fascinated by evil that it became interested in you."

Jack thought back to the dead girl in the pipe. He *had* been interested, poking her, and unafraid. Wincing at remembering how she had leached into the water, and after he had fallen on her, how that water had then soaked into him. Jack remembered how he had grown up reading about murders, about serial killers. Books piled high beside his bed, reading the most hideous details by flashlight, beneath a bedspread covered in cartoon characters.

He remembered becoming a cop and then a detective, and all the vile things he had seen, the evil that humans were capable of committing: the drowned, the burned, the shot, the stabbed, the electrocuted, the beaten, the defenestrated, the crushed, the suffocated, the starved, the frozen, and the poisoned. He had seen it all and had never turned away. Fascinated, interested, curious, driven, but never repulsed. He thought of Ben's suicide and of Beth's death. He thought of Keenan's kids hanging above him. Could he be to blame? His mind fought for solid logical ground from which to fight.

"That's fucking bullshit. You were warning me about Ahriman and all kinds of fucking scary shit before."

"Apparently, not scary enough," Popielsko said. He wiped his mouth with a muddy hand.

"Enough! Explain to me how my chasing after this thing can cause this shit to happen," Jack said.

Popielsko became very still. "You have become a focal point. The thin end of the funnel now. Perhaps you cannot blame the funnel for its use, but remove the funnel, and it all stops."

"I don't understand," Jack said. "Why the metaphors? Why not just fucking tell me?"

"Let me try a different way. It is like walking in a pool of water. You create a wave before you. The more rapid your movement, the less cautious you are, the bigger the wave. The longer you walk, the bigger the wave."

Jack froze. The dream he had, about the kids in the pool, with Sopater above them.

"If I'm deciding where the next evil will be, if I am the cause of these manifestations, how did you beat me here?" Jack asked. "Sopater was on the truck, he might have guessed, but you thought I was in Darfur."

Popielsko said nothing. Jack raised a fist.

"I sense the wave forming, I can predict within a day or so its direction. I was not sure it was you. It might well have been one of the others," Popielsko said, teeth clenched.

"The others?"

"The other manifestors," Popielsko said. "This is, again, larger than you think."

Jack pushed away from the priest. His head was swimming. Others? Was he really just one of many adults, grown from children preoccupied with evil, who now act as foci for some cosmic evil? Drawing malevolence down into their own personal spheres of influence? Had he been a cop one step behind the evil that men do, or had he been investigating that which he had catalyzed? Was he to blame? Jack reached into his pocket and withdrew the amulet.

"What's this?" Jack asked.

"Where did you get that?"

"You know where I got it. What is it?" Jack said. He was no longer shouting, but his tone was grave.

"Give it to me. You do not know what you have," Popielsko said. Jack saw fear in the man's eyes, and he liked it. He dropped the amulet back into his pocket.

Popielsko said, "You won't be just a curiosity now. You have taken from Sopater. You have his eye."

"His eye?"

"Give it to me, Jack, for your own good. You do not understand the powers at work."

Jack stood. "You can save that Ahriman bogeyman bullshit. I'm not buying anymore of your mystical shit anymore. Look around you."

Popielsko stared at Jack. Jack grabbed Popielsko's hair in one hand and his bruised jaw in the other. "Look around you!" Jack manipulated the man's head, giving the priest's eyes sweep of the carnage.

Jack growled, "This is the work of men! Not of a god or gods! Men!" He gave Popielsko's head a shove. "I'm going to follow the pattern. I've got nothing else to follow. I don't want to see you again, priest."

"Jack," Popielsko's said. He sat up, with his head hanging. "Everything I have told you is true. The difference is that now you know you are part of it. Please give me the eye. Before it is too late."

In the distance, Jack saw a white truck, marked UN, likely sent from the main camp.

Jack turned and walked away, leaving the carnage, the approaching truck, and the priest behind him. He walked back the way he came. He would go to where the road to Beni branched off and wait to catch a ride back to Entebbe. He reached into his pocket and pulled out the amulet, the eye. The silver clasp was broken. He tied the ends of the tiny links together in an ugly knot, and slipped the chain over his head. The stone fell against his chest. He dropped it into his shirt and felt its coolness against his skin. Sopater was flesh and blood. Jack had felt skin and bone beneath the clothing. He really was just a man. Jack would not only try to get ahead of the next disaster. If the priest's reaction was to be believed, Sopater would come after him.

"Come and get it, baby," Jack said, patting the amulet through his shirt. He set his jaw and continued the long walk back to the intersection.

Ch: 31

May 20
8:30 p.m.
Entebbe International Airport
Uganda

His walk back to the intersection in the Congo had gone surprisingly quickly. He hadn't fallen once, and despite having been awake and walking through the previous night, Jack felt refreshed when he reached the intersection late that morning. A truck had come by within an hour, and had taken him on the long ride back to the airport. Into the last of the trees, Jack threw the gun away as they drove by.

Jack spent over an hour cleaning his bag, clothes, and body in the airport bathroom. While he was still a mess, he no longer looked the part of a refugee. At a pay phone, he tried calling Vivian but there was no answer at her apartment. He left a message, "Viv, it's Jack, I'm on my way to Casablanca via Cairo. A lot has happened. It was terrible, Viv. I ran into the priest again and worse. My head's fucked up. I mean, I'm okay physically, but I'm not really sure what's real anymore. I'm so tired, Viv, so tired. I don't know."

From Entebbe, he would fly through Cairo to Casablanca. Looking at the map, Jack had decided Morocco was next. He was less sure, however, than when he had set out for Africa from Boston. Popielsko had shaken him. What if there was no pattern; that, in fact, Jack was the one causing these manifestations? Strangely, Jack was less afraid. He looked around, cautiously, for Sopater or Popielsko at the airport, but felt largely unconcerned.

He stopped at a counter to buy a bottle of water and a bit of food. The first credit card was declined. Credit limit reached. Before these travels, he hadn't used them much since Beth died. He pulled out another one.

"Here, let me buy that for you."

Jack turned, and Cormac was standing there. Jack let him buy the sandwich and the water and then he followed Cormac to a small metal table and chairs. The men sat, and Jack waited. Cormac put a small sack on the table.

"Here, it's a shirt. You've done a smart job trying to launder that shirt you've got on, but you're still a sight. A clean shirt makes all the difference." Cormac allowed a slight smile.

"What are you doing here?" Jack asked.

"I heard about the camp at Beni. A terrible shame. I came back here to wait and see if you'd come through or not, see if I could find you. I'm glad to see you don't appear any worse for the wear," Cormac said.

Jack pulled the amulet from his shirt. "Do you know what this is?"

Cormac glanced at it, his smile fell away. "No. Should I?"

"I'm led to believe it's important."

"To whom?" Cormac asked. "I think I might have seen something similar in Larnaca."

Jack slipped it back into his shirt. He took a long draw on the water and then a bite of his sandwich. With his mouth full, he asked, "You came all the way to Entebbe to see if I was okay?"

"That and to bring you a message. Elvis insisted."

"Since when do you take orders from Elvis?" Jack asked. "Aren't you the one in charge up there?"

Cormac smiled. "You still don't realize where you are, do you? The nature of things. I mean I know you're an American, but really, there must be some limit to your arrogance."

"Thanks for the shirt, but I'm not in the fucking mood, Cormac."

"He says you should return to the States immediately. I'm supposed to tell you that you are making the matter worse. That you are in deep now, and thrashing about in the pool," Cormac said. "What does that mean?"

Jack swallowed and looked hard at Cormac. "I'm supposed to believe that I am causing the evil simply by expecting it to be there, that I'm making a wave of evil in front of me. It means Elvis believes that evil itself noticed me noticing it, and that now I'm actually focusing evil by focusing *on* evil."

"Well, you certainly leave a wake."

"What's that supposed to mean?"

Cormac looked around. "The goats at the camp are no longer giving milk."

"Cormac, you can't blame me for goat lactation issues."

Cormac paused, mouth open, and then said, "Within an hour of you leaving the camp, we found the witchy woman with her throat slit."

Jack took a bite of his sandwich; he felt oddly dispassionate about the news.

"Jack? Did you hear me? Don't you find that odd?"

"It is what it is. She did what she did. I didn't have anything to do with it."

"The camp, and Elvis, certainly think you did."

"How? By creating waves? Come on. I'll be out of here soon—tell Elvis he doesn't have to worry about being in my wake again."

"He doesn't believe that it's a wake, like from a small boat. He believes the entire world, the universe, is linked. Elvis believes you are pulling on the sheet beneath all of us. That these catastrophes are signs of a sort of end times," Cormac said.

Jack was quiet for a moment. "What do you believe?"

"I'm not a religious guy, Jack," Cormac said. "I was raised going to Mass on Sundays, and I've said the occasional prayer since. Still, I've never known Elvis to be anything but genuine, and the man is afraid. It's as if he believes the whole thing is a giant sweater, that you've got a thread between your thumb and forefinger, and with one tug, you could unravel the whole of it."

Jack thought back to Goodwin, to the sweaters Dotty wore every day to the library. He looked around the terminal and was suddenly very tired, and unsure about going to Morocco. He wasn't even sure why he had picked Casablanca; there were plenty of trouble spots between the DR Congo and Morocco. Maybe it was because it was the closest place to home that was still on the line. He rubbed his eyes.

"Perhaps you should abandon this, Jack. Just give me the amulet, and head back to the States," Cormac said.

Jack froze, his eyes met Cormac's. "What do you want with the amulet?"

Cormac paused, and then said, "It's part of this mystery. Divorce yourself from it. I'll bring it back to Elvis, or throw it away, or whatever you want."

Jack felt a calm wash through him, a new resolve. "Go back to Elvis, tell him I'll hold onto it. You can tell him I'm going to Casablanca. If he and Sopater, or anyone else, want the amulet, have them come get it."

"What are you talking about?" Cormac asked. "Just go back to the States, man. By tomorrow, you can be waking up in your own bed, putting all this behind you. Just go back to your life and forget about this. Before you learn too much, go back and live like everyone else does. Go back to clucking your tongue and shaking your head at the evening news. Go back to your life, Jack."

Jack stood. "This is my life now."

"It doesn't have to be."

Jack grabbed the bagged shirt, opened his messenger bag, and stuffed it inside. "Thanks for the clean shirt."

Cormac extended his hand. "You owe me for the gun, too. That guy charged me twice what they typically go for." His voice softened, and he said, "I wish there was more I could do."

Jack took his hand, and said, "Take care, Cormac." Jack turned and walked away, heading for his gate. He'd be airborne in a little less than two hours.

Ch: 32

May 21
11:55 a.m.
Mohamed V International Airport
Casablanca, Morocco

Pale marble floors, and the ceiling and pillars were white and grey. Recessed canister lighting cast a glow straight down. The inside of the airport was as generic as one might expect. As soon as Jack cleared customs and immigration, he was set upon by locals trying to sell him SIM cards for his phone. Other people in the airport appeared to be wealthy Arabs in long robes with kufi hats, or West Africans in soccer jerseys and sneakers.

He had no luggage to claim, so he quickly walked past the local peddlers, and out to the taxi stand. The pavement was wide, and shown in the bright sun like a stretch of white beach. Boys, not yet teenagers, milled about hoping to help tourists with their bags for a bit of money.

He spotted her then; it was Vivian. She was looking right at him, walking towards him, talking on a phone. Jack was shocked, but just as he began to wave, she looked past him, and her face changed. Looking back over his left shoulder, Jack saw them coming.

Four large men, walking with purpose toward him. He looked around for a cop but saw none.

Jack left the sidewalk at a jog, crossing the taxi stand, and across the road. A horn blared as a shuttle bus nearly hit him. Jack looked over at Vivian, who was holding the phone next to her hip and who began to follow, her face twisted with fear. Looking back, Jack saw the men were jogging after him. He wanted to shout to Vivian, to tell her not to follow, but he wasn't sure if his pursuers knew anything about her. He didn't want to link Vivian to him.

The parking lot was an enormous loop. Beyond that, there was nowhere to go. There were eucalyptus trees set wide apart, nothing close to a place to hide. Jack ran to the cars and ducked low, trying to move quickly to lose his pursuers among the vehicles.

As he came around a Mercedes, one of them was right there, the largest of the four, wearing a black T-shirt with "Yaounde, Cameroon" across the chest. Jack stood up straight and saw he was surrounded. The man in the black T-shirt stepped forward and Jack, without thinking, sprang to the top of the roof of the Mercedes, landing, squatting. Jack looked more surprised than the other men did. He had leapt more than five feet into the air simply by pointing his toes.

He heard a switchblade open behind him, and when he turned, he was struck in the thigh by two prongs fired from a Taser. Jack jumped again in that moment, but in the air, he felt the electrical charge surge through him and he crashed to the ground. The men were immediately upon him. Stomping on his hands and arms, and trying to grab ahold of his legs. He felt fists striking his ribs, again and again. He kicked both feet hard, in unison, and watched a man rise up into the air and land on the windshield of a car six feet away. He felt the blade cut into his leg. A foot smashed into his face, into his eye. And then a hand ripped the amulet up, over his head, and away. His strength vanished, but at the same time, a feeling he'd not felt in many years ran through him. A flash of peace and redemption. Another foot smashed into his mouth. His eye filled with blood. Jack felt he was going to die, and that it might be all right. There would be no more bad dreams, no more meds, and no more questions. Only thoughts of Vivian.

A car screeched somewhere in the distance, and his assailants exchanged a few shouts. With a last kick to Jack's head, they ran off, with the amulet.

Through the fog, Jack heard a scream. Then, a pair of hands was pushing him up, trying to get him seated. He thought he shouldn't be moved.

"I've got a car. But you have to help me. I can't lift you."

Jack rolled onto his stomach. Worked to get to his hands and knees. He looked forward. He could only see through one eye. A grey Volkswagen Jetta.

"A Volkswagen?"

"Get up! Move!" the voice said.

Jack crawled, with someone's hands on his sides, as if they were trying to lessen his load. The pain in his sliced leg was unbearable. He looked back and saw that he was leaving a trail of blood.

"Hurry! They're coming back!" The voice sounded like it was coming from the next room. Jack rose to his feet, as best he could. The door opened for him, and he climbed up inside. Once he was in, the door closed behind him, and Jack tried to focus. He could see the four men; they were not coming back, only watching from a distance. The driver jumped into the seat beside him, put the car in gear, and accelerated right past the men who did nothing to impede their escape. He looked at the driver. Vivian. It was Vivian.

"What are you doing here?" Jack asked. "How did you know?"

Vivian said nothing, and was focused on the driving. Jack looked at the men, and then he saw it. In the hand of the man with the Cameroon T-shirt, Jack saw the amulet, swinging. Jack felt consciousness slipping away.

"Stay with me, Jack!" Vivian shouted.

He resolved to try. "Hyatt Regency."

Ch: 33

May 21
1:00 p.m.
Hyatt Regency
Casablanca, Morocco

Jack's feet felt so heavy as he walked, but was aware that Vivian was taking on more and more of his weight. He felt so tired. His ribs ached with every breath, and with every step. With his one good eye, he was still trying to sweep the lobby, with its white marble floor, striped through with black every dozen feet. The check-in was framed in cherry, the wood finished and buffed to a deep, glossy red. A row of small lamps stood across the length of the counter, each with a shade of translucent white glass on twin bars of brushed nickel. The vaulted ceiling matched the floor, and small tea tables were spaced about the lobby, each with a few empty chairs.

Behind the counter, a figure stood at a flat-screen monitor. Jack could not tell if the person had noticed them, nor even if it was a man or a woman. Calling to the figure, Vivian handed over Jack's wallet. When did she take that? Jack sat hard. He looked back the way they'd come. He was hurt, confused, scared, and he was entirely in her hands.

She was given a key and the wallet, and she helped Jack to

stand once more. They moved into the elevator, and the doors closed behind them. His right knee buckled and he fell to it, as if genuflecting before her. Vivian fell to her knees as well, and she began to cry.

She said, "I can't carry you. I need you to fight a little longer. I need you to get up."

His right eye was still sealed shut with dried blood, and Vivian's face filled what he could see.

"Please," she said.

Seeing her tears, he raised his left hand, attempting to wipe them from her cheek. When she saw his hand, she cried harder, and raised her own hand to take his. He smiled to reassure her, although the cuts inside his cheeks and the split in his lower lip made it excruciating. He couldn't fool her. She smiled at the attempt, and then more tears.

Still, when the bell sounded announcing they had reached the correct floor, she took a long draw of air, stood, and pulled Jack to his feet. He groaned in spite of himself.

"Not far now. Not far," she said.

When they got to the room, Jack leaned against the wall while she unlocked the door. It read, "904."

"Too high," Jack said. "We're too high."

The door opened and she helped him into the room. It was a large and well-appointed suite, with an entranceway of white tiles. There was a king-sized bed, its snow-white bedspread standing out against a mocha carpet, the cherry headboard, bedside tables, and credenza. On this last sat one of the two flat-screen televisions. The wall was two large banks of windows, floor to ceiling, with white sheers, and curtains that matched the carpet.

The door closed behind them. Jack took a few more steps and that same knee buckled again. This time he fell to the tiled floor and Vivian, in an attempt to at least slow his fall, went with him.

Moving to Jack's side, she rolled him to his back. She ran to the bathroom, and then Jack could hear water running. His grip on consciousness was getting steadily better, but the pain from his injuries was increasing, becoming less like pain in a body from which he was separate.

Lifting his head, he tried to survey the damage. There was more blood than he thought there would be. He gingerly lifted his right leg, the knee stayed bent. What the hell was up with that knee anyway? The jeans there were badly torn and bloody. He lowered his leg and raised his hands. Jack stared at his left hand, the fingernail on his third finger was completely missing. The knuckles were so badly torn up, he could scarcely tell where they should be. Vivian returned, and she started with the eye. Gently at first, her wiping became more insistent, as a child would when digging for something hidden she was desperate to uncover. Jack turned his head. She sat, lifted his head into her lap, and continued to wipe. The crusted blood crumbling away, sticky underneath. She passed the cloth over his eyebrow and pain shot through his face. He winced and turned.

"Sorry. Shhh. Just let me," she whispered. Jack surrendered to it until, at last, his eyelid came free. It opened and Jack could see. It was hazy, his lashes still a clotted mess, but the eye was functioning.

"Shit," Vivian said softly. The cut on his eyebrow had reopened.

She said, "Here take this, and put pressure here." Jack did as he was told. Laying his head down on the tile, she worked her way around to his side. Jack felt her open his ruined shirt.

"Oh no," she said. Jack lifted his head a bit, but then lay back down. With a second wet cloth, she wiped at his side. He flinched away, groaning again.

"Vivian," Jack said.

"Just shut up," she said. He could hear the concern, the fear, but he could also hear the determination, and the focus.

"Why did they do this? Who were they?"

"Mostly," Jack said weakly, "I fell from a car."

"Lies." She wiped again. "There are bruises here, a mass of bruises. You've been hit repeatedly."

"Vivian, I…"

"Just shut up," she said again. He tried to smile, this time for himself, with the same amount of success.

"I need ice, hon. I need ice and ibuprofen," Jack said. Vivian unbuckled his pants. She tried to pull them down, but was struggling. He lifted himself a bit and helped her. The knee was exposed. There was a deep gash above it.

"Oh, you need to go to a hospital."

"No doctors, no hospitals," he said. He'd been tasered and nearly beaten to death. He wasn't going to let himself get trapped in a hospital. She rose and went to the mini-bar. Jack could hear the tinkling of little bottles. He guessed what she was about to do.

She returned, knelt, and placed a bath towel beneath the knee. Jack knew they were lucky. If they hadn't been in a Hyatt, or some other western chain, there wouldn't have been alcohol in the room.

"Vodka, please," Jack said. He tried his best to sound like a man ordering a drink; he was trying to be funny, trying to soften her concern.

Vivian never took her eyes off his knee. "Idiot," she said, and poured the small bottle of vodka over the cut. The pain brought Jack up on his elbows, but the sudden movement was like one more body blow. Blood ran out of the cut on his leg and out of the way of the vodka, the towel beneath badly stained. She applied pressure to the cut, but the bleeding wasn't completely stopping.

"You need sutures."

Jack lay back down. "Do you have hair gel?"

"What?"

"Do you have hair gel?" he said again.

"I can look in the bath…"

"Perfect," Jack said. "Get it." His head was mercifully clearing. He could almost see his thought processes picking up steam again, memories starting to piece together.

She went into the bathroom, and then returned with a small container. Jack slowly fought his way to sitting up. The knee seemed mechanically okay, but the cut above it was probably affecting the quadricep's ability to pull and hold it straight. Jack took the gel from her. He read the label.

"Botanical? Organic?" Jack even looked like he smiled that time. "Why do you have it? Do you use this in your hair?"

"It isn't mine. I got it from the bathroom. You want it or not?" she asked.

Jack opened it. "Hopefully it's not too healthy. I really need the gelatin that is in most hair gels." He pressed down on the cut with a dry towel and then applied gel quickly to the cut. It hurt, and Jack hissed. "I just need the gelatin, if there *is* any in this shit. It's probably all mango and kiwi."

The bleeding stopped almost immediately. Jack threw the hair gel onto the floor next to her and then lay back. He exhaled.

She crawled over and looked down into his face. It was swollen, bruised. He rubbed the residual gel on his finger into his eyebrow. He winced again.

She asked, "Mango and kiwi?"

He smiled, but again it hurt terribly, and then he laughed at it hurting.

"I need to bandage that knee. Help me get my shirt off," Jack said. Once the shirt was off, it was clear that the clean shirt Cormac had given him had become unsuitable even to be a bandage. She took the shirt, tossed it in the garbage can, went to the closet and pulled out a pillow case. She brought it over.

"Wrap my knee in it, tie it, put the knot directly above the cut, make it tight," Jack said.

She did as he had said, and then took the last clean cloth and washed any remaining blood from his leg, his hands, his face and neck, his chest. As she bathed him, Jack stared at her, at how beautiful she was. The high cheekbones, the soulfulness in her eyes, the ballerina's neck, with her dark walnut hair, occasionally brushing his cheek. The soft mouth he'd kissed only a week before. She wiped at his hair, near his right ear, kneeling and leaning over him. Jack grabbed her hand, she turned, and he kissed her. His lip was badly split, the kiss hurt, and the kiss was wonderful. Jack tried to pull her down beside him, but the bruised ribs and their associated muscles would offer no help. She pulled away.

"Let's get you on the bed," she said. She helped Jack slowly to his feet and to the mattress. It was an agonizing trip. She lifted his leg into the bed and covered him with a sheet.

"I need ice, Vivian, and pain killer. Only not aspirin. I've bled enough," Jack said

"I'll get some," she said.

The bed felt wonderful to Jack. He was still in a lot of pain, and he was more aware than ever that, despite the sponge bath, he was filthy compared to the clean bed. Still, it felt good to relax, to sink into the mattress and close his eyes.

Jack felt her kiss his forehead. Opening his eyes, he was looking at her throat, and the skin looked impossibly soft.

"Be careful,"

"I'll be right back," she said.

Despite the pain, Jack knew that coming down on this side of a full-on adrenaline rush, sleep wouldn't be far off.

Ch: 34

May 22
7:00 a.m.
Hyatt Regency
Casablanca, Morocco

Dream

The people are missing. I'm walking through a medieval village and there are no people. The windows are shuttered. There is no one. No sound, just a foul breeze, the stench of shit, smoke, and death.

Ahead, a door opens and a man drags the body of a young woman into the muddy street, leaves her there, and scurries back into the house. There are dead birds everywhere. Swifts and sparrows. Crows and ravens. I walk up to the woman, look down at her. The right side of her throat is an angry, black mass. Veins spider-web out from the oozing sore. There is no life in her. Her dead eyes look back at me, her mouth open slightly.

Without moving her mouth, she says, "It has happened."

I only stare.

She says, "The trials are here."

I ask, "Who are you?"

Her mouth widens. Her voice softens. "I am I."

Jack woke. His heart was beating quickly, but the dreams, with that phrase, were becoming familiar.

Rolling over, slowly, painfully, he looked at Vivian. Her head on her pillow, her eyes were open, looking at him. She was staring, and not moving. *Oh God, no*, Jack thought, and blew a puff of breath in her face. She blinked.

"What was that for?" she asked.

Jack tried to sit up. The pain was intense, and he lay back down. He had more healing to do before he'd be able to go anywhere. Feeling trapped, he remembered they were on the ninth floor, and the sensation worsened. Looking at her once more, he knew he may be stuck, but at least it was with Vivian.

"How are you feeling?" she asked.

"I'm sore," he said. Understated, but he could tell she got it.

"Want some more ibuprofen?"

"I need water, too," Jack said, "And I need a shower and clothes."

Vivian shifted closer. "I like your smell," she said, and carefully laid a hand on his chest, closed her eyes, and smiled. Jack saw she was wearing at least a tank top. He had no memory of her coming into the bed.

"I still need a shower," Jack said.

"Okay," she said, her eyes still closed.

"Could you buy some proper bandages, too, wherever you got the ibuprofen. You'll have to be careful."

"There are stores right in the hotel. I can get everything without going outside," she said. "How long will we be here?"

"I have to heal up a bit, and then the next incident should be on the twenty-fifth."

She opened her eyes. "Incident?"

Jack turned to look at her. "You know, in the pattern."

She said nothing.

Jack thought for a moment, and then asked, "Viv, do you think there's a chance that I'm causing it all?"

"What do you mean?"

"I saw the priest, in the Congo. He was there. God, it was a nightmare. Dead people in every direction. Even the fucking vultures were dead."

She rose on one elbow, looking down at him. "Why do you think you're causing it?"

Jack looked at her. "The priest said I was. He said people like me are rushing around the world, and our expectations of finding evil cause it to happen. He called it 'manifestations.' And that I was focusing evil, and that evil had noticed me, because I had been interested instead of afraid."

She didn't respond immediately, and Jack wondered if she believed it too, but then she asked, "Should we leave, then? I will go wherever you want."

"Sopater was there, too. The beating I took yesterday, they were after an amulet I pulled off Sopater," Jack said.

She asked, "You stole something?"

"I pulled an amulet off him. I guess he wanted it back badly enough to send those guys to collect it. But did you see what I did? I jumped to the roof of a car. Without even trying."

"Adrenaline," she said.

Jack's eyes narrowed. "I was scared, true, with my heart racing, but I've been scared before. I jumped to the roof of a car without bending my knees to jump. Looking back now, I wonder if I couldn't have jumped completely out of trouble. Viv, I think it was the amulet."

She furrowed her brow. "What, it gave you super strength?"

"Stop mocking everything," Jack said. "I know you're past that now, just like me. We've seen too much, and we're beyond the point where everything can be explained away rationally."

Vivian paused. "What did the amulet look like?"

"It looked like an eye. The priest even referred to it as Sopater's eye. It was a stone, with a medium blue circular spot that contained a smaller dark blue or black spot. Like a pupil within an iris."

"Every tourist from here to Turkey has seen those. They are

in a lot of shops, in the markets. They are called 'nazars' and are supposed to ward off the evil eye. There's nothing really magical about them," she said.

"This one was different. You'll have to just believe me," Jack said, his voice growing soft, and tired.

"Where will we go?" Vivian said, cuddling up to Jack again. "We'll call whoever you want and we can go."

Jack remembered, for the first time, that when he had spotted Vivian at the airport, she had been talking on a cell phone. "Yesterday, at the airport, just before those assholes came after me, you were on the phone."

"Was I?"

Jack closed his eyes. "You were talking to Jim, weren't you? Jim Saniqua?"

She asked, "You think Jim sent those men who attacked you at the airport?"

"Did you tell Jim what time I was coming in?"

"I didn't tell Jim anything. Isn't Jim your friend? Why would he send them after you? How would Jim have known that you had the nazar?"

"Give me the cell phone," Jack said.

She looked around the room. "Where did I leave it?"

"Give me the fucking phone!"

Vivian jumped at his tone. She rose, went to the desk, and found it. The morning sun hadn't come around to the windows of this suite yet. Shadows played across her back as she walked in the tank top and underwear. Her legs were long and shapely. She returned with the cell phone and handed it to Jack. "Don't talk to me like that. Here's the phone," she said.

He clicked to the contact list, found Jim's number, and dialed it. There were a series of strange beeps and clicks, and then an automated voice. She remained beside the bed, standing. Jack looked up and then extended one hand in apology for his tone, reaching out for her to grab on, hoping to pull her back into the bed, back beside him. Instead, she turned and walked into the bathroom. Jack heard the shower start. As he was about to hang up the phone, Jim came on.

"Special Agent Saniqua."

Not an office phone. Not an administrative assistant. A phone that Jim answered personally.

"Jim, Jack Killarney."

A pause. "Jack. Where are you?"

"You know where I am. If you don't, you will in a second when you get a GPS fix on this phone. Why the goons, Jim?"

There was another pause. "What do you mean?"

"Answer me. Why the four guys at the airport?" Jack asked.

"I have no idea what you're talking about."

"Four guys beat the shit out of me for an amulet, an amulet apparently any tourist can pick up in Istanbul. You're telling me you didn't send them?" Jack said.

There was a long pause. "I'm your friend. We go way back. Listen to me. You aren't well. If you're hurt, let me get you help. Let me get you home."

Jack thought for a moment. He didn't know whom he could trust, except for Vivian. Or could he? She was on the cell phone at the airport. What if it wasn't Jim she was talking to? Fuck. The strength ran out of him. Jack knew he had to trust at least a few people. He still hurt all over, and was still injured. He was worried the knee would open up; he needed proper dressings for his wounds, and an antibiotic would be ideal.

"Jack."

"Jim, we can't leave until after the twenty-fifth. If I'm wrong, nothing will happen, and it's no big deal. If I'm right, even if the pattern makes no sense…"

"The pattern cannot make sense, Jack," Saniqua said. "You figured out your angle theory on a flat map, the Earth is a sphere."

Jack's eyes closed again, fighting the paranoia that comes with imagined conspiracy. "What do you mean?"

Jim said, "It's basically impossible to have gross measurement of angles on a flat map match up with angles determined on the planet's surface."

Jack paused. It was so simple and yet the logic was inescapable; this was high school geography. There were many ways of converting the spherical earth to the flat page of a map projection but all of them required some properties to be distorted. No flat map could match the globe.

Saniqua said, "The earth isn't even a sphere, it's flattened, oblate, and not even consistently. So, your pattern of angles over long distances simply couldn't apply."

Jack's head spun. Was this all a fool's errand based on a simple error made on a map in Maine? No, he thought, and his mind fought back. If it was true that he was the thin end of the funnel, that he was the focus, then it wouldn't matter how angles fell on the actual geoid, the actual planet. The pattern existed on the flat representation of the Earth. It existed to Jack. The pattern was no less real.

Jack said, "I'm staying until the twenty-fifth. Then, if nothing happens, I'll go home."

"And if something does happen?"

Jack didn't know the answer. "I'm staying."

"I'll meet you. I'll come get you myself."

"You'll come to Morocco?" Jack asked.

A siren sounded in the background, in the phone. A strange siren. That "mee-nah, mee-nah" sound one might hear in Europe or… and then Jack heard it coming from the ground, nine floors beneath the room he was in. He sat up, wanting to get to the windows, groaned in pain and laid back down.

Jack spoke softly into the phone. "You're here in Morocco?"

"When you're ready to meet, Jack, call this number. I'll be waiting." Saniqua hung up.

Jack was still looking at the phone when Vivian came back

into the room, her head wrapped in a towel, her body wrapped in a terrycloth robe.

"Jim Saniqua is here, in Morocco," Jack said. She didn't look his way, and she said nothing.

"I'm sorry," Jack said. "I shouldn't have spoken to you that way."

She still said nothing, pulled the towel from her head, and worked it through her short hair.

"Viv."

She stood straight and looked at him. "We should just get you to a hospital, and then when you're fit enough, we should leave."

"I told Jim that I'd go home."

She turned and took a few steps toward the bed. "You did? We can go? We can go together?"

Jack winced. "I told him I'd go home after the twenty-fifth. That's when the next incident, the next disaster is due."

Her arms fell to her sides, the towel dragging on the floor. The look of disappointment shifted to a look of resolve.

"But I want you to go," Jack said. "After you get me the stuff I need, I want you to go. You can call Jim, or we can just book it ourselves."

She walked purposefully to the bed. "I'm staying. I'll see this through. You can't manage on your own, so I'm staying. I didn't do all this just to leave now." Her voice was quiet and angry.

"I'll be fine, you just get me what I need and I…"

She backhanded his bruised ribs. He cried out in pain and curled around the injured area.

"Yeah, you're fine. If you're staying, I'm staying." She turned, and went back to working on her hair. Damn, Jack thought, that hurt.

"What do you need?" she asked. "From the store."

Jack lay back, trying to breathe regularly. "I need gauze and ace bandage to hold it in place, and a roll of medical or athletic tape. I need more ibuprofen. Also, if you can find an antibiotic, something that ends in 'cillin' or 'mycin' that would be great. You won't need a prescription here."

She said, "I know I won't need a prescription."

"Okay, sorry," Jack said.

"Is that all you want?"

"Super Glue and plastic bags," Jack said. "Small garbage bags. I want to take a shower, but I'm going to want to wrap this cut on my leg in plastic."

"You don't want to rinse it out?"

"Not yet. I'm worried the bleeding will start again."

"You're not going to attach the bags with glue?"

Jack looked at her, and said, "I'm not stupid, but I can use the Super Glue to close the wound, depending on how deep it is."

She wrinkled her nose at this and then pulled on her clothing. "So, bandages, gauze, tape, antibiotics, glue, and bags."

"When you get back, let's order some food. I'm starving," Jack said.

Ch: 35

May 23
2:30 p.m.
Hyatt Regency
Casablanca, Morocco

The next day, Jack came out of the bathroom, wearing only a towel and a plastic bag around his knee. He sat on the edge of the bed and slowly, carefully, peeled the tape away. The plastic bag came free with the last of the tape. Jack let it drop to the floor. He opened the dressing and considered the wound. It had closed nicely. There was no sign of red around the closed cut. It would undoubtedly leave a nasty scar, but it seemed the antibiotic was holding off any infection.

He sat further back on the bed and then lay down. He closed his eyes, feeling truly clean for the first time since leaving Boston. His hair was wet against the pillow, the air conditioning knocking down any of the warmth riding in on the bright sunlight. He didn't know she was there until he felt her mouth on his.

She kissed him, hard, mashing their mouths together. Jack opened his eyes. She opened his towel, and straddled him. Jack wrapped an arm around her back while his other hand was in her hair. She moaned into his mouth; her lips were so soft and warm.

As they made love, his awareness of his injuries dissipated, their singularities faded, and they lost themselves in each other. Sweat mixing, voices combining, perfectly in sync. Thrust after thrust, his hands back at her waist, pulling her down on him, until finally she cried out. His hips came up to her only twice more. Their lips touched; not conventional kissing, but just dragging their lips across the other's. Sweat dripped from her nose onto his lip, and then he kissed her passionately.

Her chest was slick against his. He held her tight, and they kissed again. Jack then cleared his throat. With his right hand, he pushed her hair back behind one ear. With a bruised smile, he asked, "Can I get some more ibuprofen?" She laughed, and gently tapped his injured ribs with her fingers. He flinched and laughed. Standing beside the bed, she pulled on a pair of underwear. She turned and went to the bathroom.

Jack lay back and closed his eyes. He took inventory of the situation, of his feelings for Vivian. Maybe they should just go back to New England and forget the outside world, hole up together, and delight in each other. He hadn't felt this way about a woman in a long while, and he knew he'd never survive losing Vivian. At the same time, he also knew that he had not come this far to stop now. He'd already lost Beth, Ben, Keenan and the kids… Double-down or quit?

Jack suddenly rose to one elbow. Her underwear had been a pair of briefs. But there was something else. Were they on backwards? The image took him back, back to childhood, and drainpipes. Those little underwear on that dead girl, on backwards. Innocence lost.

Ch: 36

May 25
8:00 a.m.
Hyatt Regency
Casablanca, Morocco

Jack went over to the counter, and the maître d' smiled broadly.

"How you doing?" Jack asked, signaling the language he'd be speaking.

"Very well, sir. And you?"

"I wonder if you can help me."

The maître d' continued to smile.

"I'm looking for a place where they might sell charms," Jack said.

The maître d's smile became forced. "You might try a market, sir."

"I know that, but I was hoping you might recommend one."

The smile fell, and the maître d' leaned a bit closer. "Why would you want to find such a place?"

"Is there one close by?"

"Sir, I recommend prayer, not charms," the maître d' said.

Jack said, "Thank you for that. Where can I find what I'm looking for?"

The maître d' lowered his voice further. "Sir, these are not things with which to trifle. There is no power and no will but from Allah. The salvation of all people is the Quran, from nowhere else. Sorcery and witchcraft exist, charms and spells, but they have no affect but by the will of Allah. There is more power in prayer and service."

Jack lowered his voice. "Then I'm praying you'll tell me where I might find a market that sells charms and magic."

A voice from Jack's right said, "Derb Soltane Market."

The maître d's eyes fluttered first, and then filled with disappointment. Both men looked to the new voice, as Jim Saniqua took the last couple steps to close the distance.

Ch: 37

May 25
Casablanca, Morocco

The watcher watched. People milled about the market outside the mosque. Sopater's face had aged by decades. He felt for the amulet, once more around his neck. Even with it reclaimed, his steps were even more painful now, and slow. The twenty-four hours he had been without it had taken their toll.

In a corner of his heart, somewhere long forgotten, he secretly wished he had not gotten the stone back in time, and had instead been restored to his natural age. That he might have been spared witnessing even one more event.

He looked up at the minaret—itself 400 years old. Towering above. With the rain that had fallen over the past couple days, the ground was soft. Worse yet, for generations the faithful had asked for the minaret to be repaired, to be strengthened. Greedy men, faithless men, had refused.

Sopater looked out at the morning crowd. Men, women, and children. Considering this fruit or that vegetable, haggling over prices. Oblivious.

Ch: 38

May 25
11:00 a.m.
Derb Soltane Market
Casablanca, Morocco

Jack, Vivian, and Jim walked through the market. There were perhaps fifty different vendors. They sold potions, herbs, and readings. They sold futures.

"What charm are you looking for Jack? What made you want to find a market like this one?" Jim asked.

Jack never looked his way. "I've recently started believing a bit more in charms and stuff like that. Not knowing where else to start in Morocco, why not here? Now, tell me why you're interested, and don't tell me it's just friendly concern for my well-being."

Jim said nothing for a few steps. "While your geographical pattern, with the angles, does not work, our analysts have also ruled out that these acts of terror are simply random. So, while what you found doesn't fit, we're trying to figure out what is going on."

"How long has the FBI been working on this? Since before I came to see you in your office?" Jack asked.

Jim stopped walking. "Jack, as best as we can tell, people have been working on this problem for centuries."

"So why wave me off? Why let me fly all over the fucking world?"

"What did you want me to do? I told you to let it go. Now I've flown to Africa to bring you back," Jim said.

"I don't understand," Vivian said.

"Why do you care if I'm here?" Jack asked.

"You're important," Vivian said.

"You're ending up on people's radar screens, Jack. You've been seen with people, you're suddenly flying around, you even beat up a kid in Amsterdam. They got you coming out of that bathroom just before the kid was found."

Jack winced. "I can explain that."

"I don't give a shit," Jim said. "I should just take you into custody and go. It *is* our friendship that brought me here, and it's only because we go back that I'm humoring you right now. I figure I can watch your back a bit, but it ends here, Jack. You can shop for your lucky charms, but then, we're all going home."

"Here Jack," Vivian said, stepping to one table. Scattered across the top were nearly identical charms, in various sizes, to Sopater's eye. Jack picked one up.

"What is it?" Jim asked.

"Just a souvenir," Jack said. He paid for the charm. The old man behind the table never smiled, nor spoke a word.

Jim asked, "Is that it? Back to the hotel?"

But then Jack saw him, sprinted over and, grabbing one shoulder, spun him around. Jack was stunned. Sopater had transformed from a middle-aged man to an elderly one. The same black coat, the shaggy hair thinner and greyer. Vivian and Jim caught up. The amulet hung around Sopater's neck. His face was absolutely impassive.

Jack took hold of both of Sopater's shoulders. "What's going to happen?"

"Um, Jack?" Jim asked.

Jack looked back, and the man from the airport, the one

who had taken the amulet from Jack, was fast approaching.

"He beat the shit out of me at the airport, he was one of them," Jack said, pointing at the approaching man.

Jim drew his handgun. He aimed the Glock 26 at the man's chest. "Stop where you are." The thug came on.

Vivian said, "Maybe we should go."

"Tell me what's going to happen!" Jack asked Sopater again.

"Jack," Jim said, firearm still leveled at the approaching man. Jack looked back again, wrapped his hand around the amulet, and yanked it over Sopater's head. Sopater did nothing to resist, but as the amulet was lifted from him, Sopater groaned and fell to one knee, head bowed.

The thug rushed at Jim who, instead of shooting him, smashed the Glock like a hammer into the side of his head, and both men fell to the ground. Jim pushed himself clear of the semi-conscious larger man. As he was getting up, a woman screamed. Tiles were falling from above.

The minaret, towering above them was visibly moving. Tiles were falling from near its top. People began running in all directions, but it was impossibly crowded. The minaret began a slow lean in Jack's direction. He dropped to his knees, looking into Sopater's face.

"I need answers! I need to know where this evil comes from!"

Sopater looked back at him and said nothing as a tile fell within a foot of them both.

"Jack!" Vivian screamed.

Jim grabbed her around the waist and pulled her away.

"Tell me! Who do you work for?" Jack was screaming, trying to be heard over the mayhem around them. Sopater still said nothing. Jack grabbed his arm, determined to haul him away, get the information he needed. A knife appeared, wrapped in Sopater's gnarled hand, and Jack released him. Tiles fell like rain now, and both Jack and Sopater were hit. When bricks began to fall, people were dropping where they were struck.

Jack looked upward; the minaret would not stay up any longer.

"Please," Jack said. "Please tell me! I have to know!"

Sopater spoke, "Seek out the priest. Popielsko. In Jerusalem. Bring him the eye. Do not keep it for yourself. Do not wear it. Bring it to the priest. Tell him that the eye is his now. Seek your answers in Jerusalem."

Something else fell, along with the tiles and the bricks. Gulls. With white bodies and pale grey wings, they fell as a paralyzed flock into the crowd.

"Jack!" Vivian's voice. Jack looked back where she stood away, Jim preventing her from coming to him. Jack turned back to Sopater, who had come to his feet.

Sopater had the slightest trace of a smile. "It is God who damns our sins."

Jack froze. It is God who damns our sins? *It's the goddamnedest thing?* Is that what Ben had actually said?

Sopater turned and walked, limping, arms outstretched wide, toward the base of the minaret. Jack took a step toward him, but a load of bricks fell at his feet. A tile struck him in the shoulder. He put an arm up to shield his head.

"Get out of there!"

Looking up at the minaret, Jack saw it was falling like a tree, slowly, almost directly toward him. He turned and ran, limping and waving with both arms for Jim to move, to get Vivian off to one side, and he did.

The screaming intensified and there was a roar as the centuries-old structure finally gave in to gravity. Jack caught up with Jim and Vivian, and helped to shield her. He turned back just in time to see Sopater, arms still outstretched, disappear beneath tons of brick and mortar.

Jim saw it too, and said only, "Jesus!"

The man Jim had struck was also buried, as best as Jack could tell, along with dozens of people.

Debris from the minaret was mixed with crushed market

stands and people. Screams of the injured echoed through the dust, which obscured all but the closest. With the cloud still hanging, men rushed to the rubble to search for survivors.

Vivian turned and clung to Jack. Jack lifted the amulet, but he did not slip it on. Her head against Jack's chest, she asked, "Now what?"

Jack said only, "Jerusalem."

She asked, "Jerusalem?"

Jack stood, watched the settling dust, the frantic men with twisted faces. "We have to go find the priest in Jerusalem," Jack said.

"We have to meet him there?"

"Sopater said so."

She considered this and then asked, "How will we find him?"

Jack looked down at the amulet. "Once we're there, we'll let him find us."

Jim said, "Let it go, Jack."

Jack turned his way. "No way, I'm going to finish this."

Jim said, "He who created us without our help will not save us without our consent."

Jack froze. "What? What did you say?"

Jim said, "I received a weird email just before coming here. It read, 'He who created us without our help will not save us without our consent.'"

"Augustine," Jack said.

"Yeah," Jim said, standing slowly. "You sent it?"

"No, I received the same email. It sounded like Ben wrote it. Called me 'Jack-buddy.'"

Jim frowned, "You received it back then?"

"No."

Jim paused, "My email addressed me as 'J.J.'"

"Like your dad used to call you," Jack said. "Are you guys working on who sent it?"

"Complete dead end. Contact at NSA says it came from

nowhere. They've never had a 'nowhere' email before, Jack. Any ideas?" Jim asked.

Jack turned and looked back at the carnage. Men pulling stones away, women beating their fists against their heads as they wailed. He stepped toward the chaos, and said, "I'm not stopping until I find out."

III

"The actual tragedies of life bear no relation to one's preconceived ideas. In the event, one is always bewildered by their simplicity, their grandeur of design, and by that element of the bizarre which seems inherent in them."

—Jean Cocteau

Ch: 39

May 28
5:00 p.m.
The Inbal Jerusalem Hotel
Jerusalem, Israel

Although he had paid for the hotel, she had chosen it. "Do you always travel like this?" Jack asked.

Walking through the handsomely decorated room, past the bed with its umber-and-mocha checkerboard bedspread, he pulled a door open, and stepped out onto the balcony. They were on the 8th floor. Too high again, Jack thought, but there was nothing available below this one.

"How's your knee?" she asked.

"It aches more than it hurts. And it itches—a good sign," he said. He looked out at the Old City, its ancient walls neither willing nor capable of defending it from tourists. "Fancy view," he said.

She stepped up behind him, leaned against him, and looked out. "Is it too fancy? Do you wonder about my money?"

Weird question, he thought. "I paid for the room," Jack said.

Vivian nodded. "I told you, my parents left me some money."

"They were wealthy then?"

"We didn't go without, but I wouldn't say we were rich or anything."

"Mansion, private jet, sailboat." Jack smiled broadly.

Jack felt Vivian go rigid, and his smile fell away. "Hey, you okay?"

"I'm fine." Vivian turned and walked into the room. Jack followed.

"Listen, the money isn't important. I won't bring it up anymore."

Vivian said, "It's not the money."

"What then?" Jack watched her struggle with something, her face a mask of pain.

"My father died on our boat."

"Oh God, Viv, I'm sorry. I had no idea."

"I found him," she said. "We were alone on the boat, a sailboat. We were off Cape Cod, far enough that we couldn't see land. I was twelve years old, and when I woke up, I couldn't find him at first. The sea was very calm. I could hear, feel, the low rumble of the engine running. So, I went down to see if he was there. When I found him, he was unconscious, maybe dead already. I tried to move him, but I just wasn't strong enough. I could barely lift one of his legs. I didn't even know how to turn off the engine." Vivian's eyes filled with tears.

Jack said, "You don't have to..."

"I became nauseated, and my head pounded. My vision was blurring. I realized I was in trouble too. I made it out to the deck, to the fresh air, but just barely"

"I'm so sorry, Viv."

"My mother and I moved to Texas," she took a deep breath and, despite the tears, spoke in an even voice. "She took a new job in a new state, and we moved. A fresh start, she said." Vivian put her hand on a dresser to steady herself.

"How did you end up back in Massachusetts?"

Vivian held up one finger, letting him know to be patient. "My mother eventually remarried. A nice enough guy, but I was a troubled kid, nightmares about my father turned into self-destructive behavior, and eventually, you know... self-loathing manifesting as eating disorders, and even suicide ideation."

Jack just listened, and she continued. "I was a complete mess. I hated myself. So much so, they had me hospitalized."

"In a mental hospital. That's why, that day with Carol, back in Maine..." Jack said.

"They're all the same. On an emotional level, anyway. The vibe in a place like that. A building containing people locked away, body and mind. I spent months in the adolescent girls' unit at Austin State Hospital. The people there were kind and genuinely wanted to help me, but I wasn't ready to heal. Furious with my mother for putting me there, I was angry when she visited, for speaking in a patronizing voice when she did come, and I hated her for leaving after her visits. Leaving me in there."

Jack asked, "What were you doing while you were in there?"

"Trying to understand," Vivian said. "I wanted to know why my father had to die. Why did he have to die that way? I was left drifting out there with his body below deck. Aware he was down there, imagining what his body was doing. What killed my father? An accident? An act of God? Why would God act in such a way? Was it an act of evil?"

"Did you come up with any answers?"

She shook her head. "The questions kept multiplying. I kept reading and the questions only grew in number and complexity, and then it dawned on me that I was looking too hard. I decided that the simplest answer was the best one. Coincidence. It's all just luck, not fate, and not God. That we make up all these myths and religions just to explain the shit we can't explain in any other way."

Jack watched her face, and saw it change.

"I used to believe that, anyway," she said.

Jack paused and then asked, "When you got out of the hospital, you went back to live with your mother?"

"I lived in my bedroom," Vivian said. "They had their new

life, and I had mine. I lived almost robotically, medicated, and doing what people expected of me. I finished high school and applied to universities."

"Including some in Massachusetts?" Jack asked.

Vivian licked her lips. "Exclusively in Massachusetts."

"Did you know anyone there?"

Vivian looked out the window, and said, "My father."

Jack understood the residual presence of dead loved ones.

"Where did you study?" Jack asked.

Vivian smiled, and said, "Boston College. Undergrad, graduate school, and now I teach there. It's home to me. Boston and a vacation property we own are the only places I feel I can truly let my guard down."

Jack asked, "You never married?"

Vivian said, "I came close once in grad school. I fell hard for a prof, and then fell harder when he ran off with another woman. So, I threw myself into my studies and began researching and writing what would become my book."

Jack approached her, and she turned to him, "The book that brought you to me and, I suppose it is because of that book that I'm standing in a room in Jerusalem, on a quest, once again finding more questions than answers."

Holding her, he felt her arms wrap behind him, and he kissed her on the forehead. She laid her cheek on his chest.

Jack said, "I'm really glad you wrote that book. It's the only reason I know you."

Ch: 40

May 29
11:30 a.m.
Christian Quarter, Old City
Jerusalem, Israel

Jack walked down the last few steps off St. Mark's Road, and crossed grey stones. A sign hung on the first archway, written in Hebrew, then Arabic, and finally in English, letting tourists know they were entering Christian Quarter Road. The narrow way was lined with shops, and the walls were draped in brightly-colored fabric. The road was so narrow that three men could scarcely walk abreast. The sky was intermittently blocked out by archways, often more like tunnels, some twenty-feet deep.

Jack had stopped at churches, but found more tourists than clerics. None of the holy men he found had even heard of Father Popielsko, or at least they claimed they hadn't. Pulling the amulet from his pocket each time he'd asked for the priest, Jack had made sure it was seen.

Each shop had their wares out on tables along the road. Old men sat, legs crossed, hands on knees, and watched. Every few shops, Jack stopped and, showing the amulet, asked if anyone had heard of a priest named Father Popielsko. Each time, the merchants would at first seem confused, and then would say they had no idea who Popielsko was, and finally they would attempt to sell him something.

Passing a set of stone steps that rose to the left through a gap in the shops, Vivian asked, “What if this is a dead end? We’re chasing a man we don’t know and we were sent here by someone who may have been evil himself.”

“I’m not sure I believe Sopater was evil,” Jack said. “The priest once told me he was only a witness. That witness told me to find the priest, and to give him the amulet.”

“Will you give him the amulet?” Vivian asked.

Jack stopped just before entering yet another archway. “I don’t know yet. I need to find him first. Whatever the secret is, we’ve come to the game late, we’re not the only ones looking for it, and the priest has the answers. It’s nagging at me, just out of reach. I feel like I could figure the whole thing out, but there’s a block, something I can’t think my way around. I need to find Popielsko.”

As it grew darker under the archway and a series of shop awnings, a noise grew in intensity. Jackhammers, unseen, behind a thin wall. The passage narrowed a bit, but it was not crowded. In fact, aside from Vivian, it seemed to Jack that he was alone. Until he felt the gun in his back. Jack stopped, and Vivian’s face filled with terror. Jack slowly raised his hands. Whoever it was had the gun against Jack’s spine, and that was good, because he knew right where it was. What was bad was that if it went off, the bullet would not only pass through Jack, but likely also hit Vivian, who stood right in front of him.

The jackhammers paused and he heard, “In there.” Vivian immediately moved off into a shop, and Jack followed. Just as they entered, the man’s hand thrust hard against Jack’s shoulder. He stumbled forward. When he turned, he stepped in front of Vivian, and screened her from Ehud and his gun, a Tanfoglio Force.

“Ehud, they gave you another one?” Jack asked. “Or did you dig that one out of the trash?”

Vivian said, "You know him?"

The jackhammers again, but not as loud in here. The shop was filled with scarves, plates, chess sets, and knickknacks.

"I have never found you amusing," Ehud said. "Give me the amulet."

"Sopater's dead," Jack said.

"Yes, we know. Give the amulet to me." Ehud leveled the gun at Vivian's head. She was behind him, but Jack knew that it would be an easy shot at this range. He couldn't protect her.

"Why do you want it? What does it do? Other than keep people young?" Jack asked.

Vivian said only, "Jack."

"It is not about youth. It is about protection," Ehud said. He stepped half a step closer. Jack saw his eyes focus, the way a shooter's eyes always focus just before the shot. "I will not ask again."

Jack pulled the amulet from his pocket. "I believe you. How do I know you won't just shoot us after I give it to you?"

Ehud said, "Because I could have simply shot you and taken it."

Jack tossed the amulet; Ehud caught it in his free hand without moving the gun, without blinking. He backed away, gun held high, stepped out of the shop, and was gone.

Jack turned to Vivian. "You okay?"

"He's got the amulet."

Jack looked over his shoulder, and said, "He didn't even thank me."

"You're taking this well. Where does this leave us?" Vivian asked.

Jack reached into his pants and pulled out the amulet. "I gave him the one I bought in Casablanca."

"God."

"Appropriate, given where we are." Jack grinned. "Let's get out of here."

"So, are we not going to look for the priest?" she asked.

"We know that he knows we're here," Jack said. "My guess is Popielsko will realize he doesn't have the real amulet. Let's go back to the hotel and wait. He'll come to us."

"Or send Ehud again," Vivian said.

Jack said. "He'll want to come himself next time. I imagine Ehud will be there too, but Popielsko will come this time."

They left the shop, and walked quickly down the road, looking over their shoulders and into every doorway.

Ch: 41

May 29
6:00 p.m.
The Inbal Jerusalem Hotel
Jerusalem, Israel

The lobby featured a series of glass-top coffee tables sitting atop wooden legs, each table surrounded on three sides by tan loveseats. Each setting included its own lamp, with a broad shade. Beyond, the exterior wall was a bank of large windows framed by stone archways. On the opposite side, a row of small tables for two, with cobalt chairs.

Waiting on one of the loveseats, Jack sat back, and watched Vivian uncross and re-cross her legs. They had been there for hours, and hadn't really spoken in a couple. There was no way Jack would wait for Popielsko on the 8th floor. The lobby was better, a public space, with many ways out and with a clear view of the entrances. An elderly couple sat in a pair of the cobalt chairs. A clutch of businessmen sat at another coffee table. People were milling about, walking at tourist-pace. Desk clerks and the maître d' were also present.

The Sofia Café provided refreshments and snacks for those in the lobby, and the waitress returned to check on them.

"Another coffee?" she asked. Her ponytail swung. Jack

remembered Jamie, the waitress back in Newton, Massachusetts. Was that really only three weeks ago?

Vivian's head snapped up, she sighed, and asked, "Instead, could we have a couple glasses of wine?"

Jack smiled. "Yes, two glasses of Pinot noir, please."

"Yes, of course." The waitress picked up their cups and saucers.

Jack said, "Actually, please bring us the bottle."

The waitress hesitated and then said, "I am sorry sir, but I can only serve it by the glass here in the lobby."

"That would be fine," Vivian said, and the waitress left.

"What's the difference? Bring us three glasses each or just leave us a couple bottles?"

Vivian asked, "You're not going to harass another waitress, are you?"

Jack chuckled.

"What if they don't come?" Vivian asked. "We can't spend the night down here."

"We won't."

The waitress returned with the glasses.

Jack smiled and said, "Thanks, Jamie."

Vivian laughed. The waitress stopped and asked, "I am sorry?"

"It's nothing," Vivian said.

They leaned forward, picked up their glasses, and raised them.

"To Montzura's," Jack said.

Vivian said, "When we get back, we'll have you go make up with Jamie."

"Well, this is certainly intimate."

Jack and Vivian looked up at Popielsko. Ehud stood off in the distance, looking more pissed off than ever.

The priest motioned to the loveseat across the table from them. "May I?"

Jack and Vivian sat back as the priest took a seat.

"Well, Jack," Popielsko said. "I must say you have been a surprise."

"How's your jaw?" Jack asked.

A phony smile flashed across Popielsko's face and was gone. "I have come for the eye. You cannot keep it. It does not belong to you."

"I don't want it."

Popielsko leaned forward, and asked, "You are not wearing it, are you?"

Jack pulled the amulet from his pocket. Popielsko held out his hand, but Jack laid it in his own lap.

"I want answers this time. In the DRC, you told me that there are many of us following patterns, and that we are manifesting the evil through our expectations," Jack said.

"That is correct," Popielsko said.

"Those pursuing the patterns—they include the American FBI."

"Entire governments," Popielsko said.

Vivian asked, "The more people expecting evil, the larger the manifestation, is that correct?"

Popielsko did not answer her, and Jack could see that Vivian was irritated by his ignoring her.

"Answer her," Jack said. "The more people that expect evil to happen, the larger the evil that actually occurs, right?"

"That is true, but without you and others like you, those expectations would not manifest as evil. Just as adding more water will not fill a jug any faster without a funnel to focus the effort," Popielsko said.

"So, should I just kill myself? What do the other funnels do?" Jack asked.

"You need only remove yourself. Suicide would surely work, but perhaps you'd be less opposed to simply going home and forgetting all about this. With some luck, if you lose interest in the evil, then it will lose interest in you," Popielsko said.

Jack considered this for a moment, but he knew he had come too far to simply abandon this now.

"You said you can sense the wave. Where is the next one going to be? Will it be here in Jerusalem?" Jack asked. "Is that why you're here?"

Popielsko shook his head sadly. "That is why I hoped you had not put the amulet on. You would not know how to use it for protection only. If worn clumsily, if worn by someone not in control of his emotions, you could greatly intensify the evil; you could single-handedly manifest an occurrence. Just as you did in Morocco." Popielsko shifted in his seat, and crossed his legs.

"Bullshit," Jack said. "Sopater was wearing it when the minaret fell."

"He was there as a witness to the destruction and death you manifested by wearing it and being emotionally out of control," Popielsko said.

Jack said, "I was attacked while I was wearing it. Sorry if that led to an emotional reaction."

"That, and by your presence and your own expectations, you attracted the expectations of members of your government and others, and funneled their expectations into a tragedy of your making. Disengage. Go home. You must come to understand that while the evil is the heat of the sun, and people are the ants, you are undoubtedly the magnifying lens. Ancient evil is using you as a focal lens, and through you and people like you, people are dying. Morocco was completely your doing."

"Jack focused their expectations, so he enabled the manifestation," Vivian said.

Popielsko said, "The enabling of much of the evil in history has been the unification, by a single charismatic individual, of expectations. We are awash in evil in every moment, but it is diffuse until someone focuses it. And as I said, your strong interest in evil has made evil interested in you. Perhaps you were born to it. Perhaps you have been, time and again, for millennia. When those expectations manifest a result, the masses only become more convinced in the mystical power of the individual leader, and the expectations are further strengthened and homogenized. Fearsome tidal waves of evil can then result. Unfortunately, every time you are present at a tragedy, you further reinforce the belief of others that you know where the next occurrence will be. That perhaps you can even control it."

"Control it?" Jack asked. "If I could control it, my brother would still be alive." The image of Keenan, with a hole in his head, flashed before his eyes.

Vivian asked, "Are people trying to harness this as a weapon?"

Jack asked, "A weapon?"

"Of course," Popielsko said. "People have tried innumerous times to harness nature in their attempts to destroy other people."

Jack lifted the amulet, and asked, "So, this can protect the wearer from evil? How did it keep Sopater young?"

"That was a function of what aging really is," Popielsko said. "People believe that aging is a natural process of a degradation in cellular replication over time, that people wear out. We worry about exposure to the sun and to certain chemicals. We worry about the food we eat and disease. However, it is exposure to *evil* which ages us."

"Interesting," Vivian said, squinting.

"Explain," Jack said.

"As a person is exposed to evil, they age. We say certain people have aged before their time. Victims of horrible abuse, combat soldiers, the neglected and abandoned, survivors of so-called natural disasters. Even world leaders, and criminals themselves," Popielsko said. "It is when a human being is in proximity to evil that they age. Rape victims with sudden onset of grey hair. Veterans who need to be medicated. They age in a direct ratio to the amount of exposure."

Jack caught the reference to meds, and he had a sudden craving for their steadying effect. "So Sopater didn't age," Jack asked. "The amulet was protecting him from evil. Why did he age so quickly without it?"

Popielsko said, "Whenever we are exposed to evil, whether as a perpetrator, a victim, or a witness, we are contaminated. The evil is stained upon us. Evil collects on us. That stain was still upon Sopater, but the eye had prevented its effect. Without it, the evil with which he was covered quickly aged him. You saw the results."

"Residue," Vivian said.

"He aged decades in days," Jack said.

The priest nodded. "And you are like a lightning rod," Popielsko said. "Evil is everywhere, like static electricity. The expectations draw it, create a wave, and you focus it, because you are being used to serve that purpose," Popielsko said.

Jack thought back to the little girl in the drainpipe. Residue. She had stained him with the evil visited upon her, it had seeped into him. His interest, his curiosity without revulsion, had allowed it in, invited it, in fact. He was stained then, by the evil, and had been repeatedly since.

Jack held up the amulet. Vivian reached for it, to pass it along, but the priest reached out past Vivian and took it. The priest slipped it into his pocket. He said, "Thank you."

"It's yours anyway," Jack said.

Popielsko slid forward, and asked, "What did you say?"

Jack said, "Sopater. He gave me the eye to give to you."

"To me? He said to give it to me?"

"He called you by name," Jack said. "He said to tell you that the eye is yours now."

The priest fell back hard, and Jack glanced at Vivian. Popielsko pulled the amulet back out from his pocket with a trembling hand.

"What is it?" Vivian asked.

"I thought he had given it to you. I thought after you, the chain was going to be broken," Popielsko said. "Instead, in my arrogance, I have taken upon myself a terrible burden."

"If you don't want it, get rid of it," Jack said.

"I cannot," Popielsko said. "Once the current witness appoints the next, the office must be accepted. Even if I do not move from this place, I will be spirited away to the next tragedy. If I do not wear the amulet, I will age and die quite quickly. I am not a young man as it is."

Jack asked, "And you thought I was chosen, and you wanted me to be without it?"

Popielsko said nothing.

Jack said, "If that's true, and you want to be free, don't wear the fucking thing."

"Jack!" Vivian said.

Instead Popielsko, with shaking hands, slipped the amulet over his head.

Jack and Vivian watched Popielsko's hands steady, his face become placid, and he sat straight.

"How long has this been going on? Since the beginning?" Vivian asked.

"Yeah, how long has this amulet been around?" Jack asked. "Where did it come from?"

"Throughout recorded time, at least," Popielsko said. "Think of all the great human tragedies. Going back to the Great Flood."

"You mean like Noah's Ark? Animals, two by two?" Jack asked.

Vivian turned to Jack. "Don't dismiss it too quickly."

"Scholars know there was a flood of enormous proportions. Various cultures passed the flood story along. In our culture, we have Noah, but in writings much older than the Bible, like the Epic of Gilgamesh, there is reference to a flood and a Noah-like character. Utnapishtim," Popielsko said.

"And older still was the Epic of Atrahasis, which was probably the source of much Gilgamesh," Vivian said.

"So, the story of the flood is old," Jack said.

"Not just old," Popielsko said. "These tellings of the flood story were separated by cultural lines, hundreds or thousands of years and miles. So, we can assume that there was a great deluge of some sort, involving the destruction of 'the world' as some knew it."

"There are, of course, others," Vivian said. "Sodom and Gomorrah, Jericho, Babylon, Edom."

"The Ad people with a 'furious wind' or Ar Rass," Popielsko said. "Shiva destroyed Tripura."

Jack asked, "What was Tripura?"

Popielsko said, "A city made of three cities, in the sky."

"So, some of this is bullshit? Your manifestations of evil, the focusing of a cosmic evil by people's expectations, some of it is just myth?" Jack asked.

"Ask the people of Machu Picchu or Angkor," Popielsko said.

"Invaders," Jack said. "Are you saying the evil can bring invaders, too?"

"The victims clearly saw others, outsiders, as evil," Popielsko said.

"But the invaders didn't think they were evil," Jack said. "That's why pure evil is a myth."

"I, too, have read the books," Popielsko said. "Here is the flaw. Pure evil is not a myth. The invaders may not think themselves evil, but they are the tools of pure evil. What the tools believe or do not believe is hardly relevant. Those who act as the tools of evil, as you have, are not pure evil themselves, but I assure you, pure evil exists. Although, once you become aware that you are an agent of evil, I suppose you then bear some responsibility."

"And natural disasters?" Jack asked. "Like the flood, and some of those cities, like Sodom and Gomorrah, wasn't that just a volcano or something?"

"Manifestations of destruction based on the expectations of people," Popielsko said. "Sinners really are punished. The reputation of Sodom had spread far and wide, and the expectation grew that someday God would smite the city. Until He did, through a focal lens named Lot."

"You're saying evil is a tool of God," Vivian said.

"You believe God uses the evil?" Jack asked.

"I am a priest," Popielsko said. "I believe in a God who set the universe on this course, and who gave mankind free will, but not carte blanche."

Vivian asked, "So, all the ancient cities and cultures destroyed, you believe they were destroyed by this evil?"

Jack asked, "Like in Vivian's book, cultures like ancient Memphis? Petra's earthquake? Mt. Vesuvius and Pompeii? Vijayangar? Persepolis?"

Popielsko said, "It is not only I who believes this. And why stop at ancient cities? What do you think destroyed Dresden? Hiroshima? Nagasaki?"

Jack said, "You said governments are following patterns, and that they want to use it as a weapon."

"They are chasing shadows, inventing patterns, causing chaos as they chase each other around," Popielsko said.

Jack said, "So maybe thousands of people are following the evil."

"At least," Popielsko said.

She asked, "What if millions, or just hypothetically everyone, believed that impending evil was going to manifest itself?"

The waitress returned, she glanced at the nearly full glasses in front of Jack and Vivian, and then turned to Popielsko. "Can I get you anything, sir?"

Popielsko waved her off. He wasn't drinking—was it the amulet? The imperative to stay in control? The waitress walked away.

"Answer the question. What would happen if everyone expected evil to happen all at once?" Jack asked.

"And it was focused by someone like you?" Popielsko leaned forward. "The end of the world."

"What?" Jack asked.

"In the west, they have even named a place," Popielsko said. "Millennia of the expectations of multitudes, building up. Even those who are not religious in anyway but are consumers of pop culture believe this to be the case."

"Armageddon," Vivian said.

"Megiddo," Popielsko said. "Armageddon."

Vivian said, "That's not far from here. Is that why you're here? Is that the site of the next occurrence?"

Popielsko leaned back.

"Where is the next one?" Jack asked.

Popielsko said nothing. Jack slid forward, to ask again, but then Vivian put her hand on his leg, so he changed course.

"Where did the amulet come from?" Jack asked. "Are there others like it? That actually work?"

"This is the original. Thousands of years ago, people began copying it, hoping to create some protection of their own. Soon, they forgot there was an original," Popielsko said.

"But what's its history?" Jack asked, wearily.

"The earliest known owner was Paul," Popielsko said. "You know, it was from Paul that Augustine derived much of his writing."

Jack only waited.

Popielsko continued. "The amulet was a gift from St. Paul of Tarsus to one of his kinsmen, a man from Berea. It has been handed down ever since."

"Where did it come from originally?" Jack asked.

Popielsko held it. "It is believed that the amulet came from the Indus River Valley. Harappa."

Jack saw Vivian's eyes widen.

Popielsko released the amulet. "Early Harappan period."

Jack asked, "Indus River? As in India?"

"In modern Pakistan," Vivian said.

Popielsko suddenly looked worried, and said, "Listen, you now have your answers. Go home."

Vivian looked at Jack.

"How are we supposed to go home?" Jack said. "How can

someone know all this and just live his life as if this doesn't exist?"

Popielsko leaned forward. "What do you think you know? You even wondered if it were possible if you had had a sexual affair with the wife of your dead partner. That was completely untrue, and yet you entertained the doubt, didn't you? I would wager you even created memories of the affair."

Jack was stunned.

"So, what is it you think you know?" Popielsko asked. "You even believe that Professor Vivian Rueil has been with you. That she's been along for part of your adventure."

Jack looked to his right. Vivian was nowhere to be seen. He leapt to his feet. "What did you do with her?"

Popielsko smiled, "She was never here, Jack. She has been back in Boston all along."

"You bastard! Where is she?" Jack sprang over the coffee table at Popielsko, and Ehud came at a run. He seized Jack, and sat him forcibly in his seat.

Popielsko said, "Listen to me."

Jack asked, "Where is she?"

Popielsko said, "What was she wearing?"

"What?" Jack asked.

"Just answer me. When you last saw her," Popielsko said, "what was she wearing?"

Ehud, holding Jack still in the chair with a fistful of shirt at Jack's chest, shook him, urging him to reply.

Jack hesitated, thought, and then said, "A white blouse, button down."

"Anything distinct about the blouse?" Popielsko asked.

"A small bit of embroidery at the cuffs," Jack said. "Why?"

"And she was in Morocco with you, correct? What was she wearing there?" Popielsko asked.

Jack remembered the underwear on backwards.

"The shirt. Was she wearing the same blouse?" Popielsko asked.

Jack suddenly felt ill. She had worn the same blouse. Exclusively. Only that blouse.

"Think back to the first time you met her," Popielsko said.

"In the restaurant. In Newtown, Mass. The same blouse. The embroidery," Jack said.

Popielsko said, "She has not been here."

"It can't be…" Jack said.

"So, what do you think you know? What is true?" Popielsko asked. "Dr. Rueil is back in Massachusetts."

Jack felt Ehud's grip loosen a bit. Jack asked, "So, was Sopater real?"

"Very," Popielsko said. "As am I and, I assure you, Ehud would love to prove how real he is. But I also assure you that you were alone in Morocco, except for a young prostitute who nursed you for a day or so."

"How do you know all this?" Jack said. "And what about Jim Saniqua?"

"We hired the young woman to look after you, although we did not task her with anything more than nurse your injuries. She seems to have been quite taken with you, since she provided so much more than first aid," Popielsko said. "And FBI Special Agent Jim Saniqua? Really, now, Mr. Killarney. Even you must have realized that the name 'Saniqua' was simply 'Aquinas' reversed. You are not especially creative in your delusions."

"But I've been calling and emailing Vivian," Jack said.

"But you haven't spoken with her. You've only left voicemails. I am afraid I must tell you that Dr. Rueil finds your messages most distressing. She is quite sure that you have gone mad," Popielsko said.

"Have you spoken with her?" Jack asked.

"At length. She also thinks you should go home, and seek medical assistance," Popielsko said.

Jack paused, and then said, "I'm crazy."

"And the focus point of an ancient evil. One does not preclude the other. In fact, it is quite safe to say that anyone who fully understands what you have become would run the risk of going mad," Popielsko said.

Jack looked at the priest, and asked, "How do I become unchosen? How do I become a normal person again?"

"You must turn your back on all of it. On all the evil in the world. End your fascination with the dark side of man. Focus on the beauty in the world, clear your mind of the poison. Show no interest in evil, and deprive yourself of those stories. In time, the evil in the world may become bored with you, and forget," Popielsko said.

"Has anyone accomplished that before?" Jack asked.

"Men have secluded themselves and lived out quiet lives," Popielsko said. "Many of the sainted monks sought solitude for exactly the same purpose. Even now, there is a man named Viktor who was a manifestor, and who has spent two decades living in peace in a makeshift wooden shack in Siberia, eating salted fish and berries."

"That's what I have to do?" Jack asked.

Popielsko said, "Go home, please." He stood and walked past Ehud, who took a moment to stare at Jack before releasing him, and then followed Popielsko.

Jack called after them. "What will you do next?"

Popielsko stopped, turned back to Jack, and his face was pained. "I will witness," he said. Popielsko, with Ehud beside him, then turned and walked away.

Ch: 42

May 29
8:00 p.m.
The Inbal Jerusalem Hotel
Jerusalem, Israel

Jack returned to his room, having no idea what he should do next. He paced, stepped out onto the balcony, and back into the room. Could he become a monk of sorts, in the woods of Maine?

And then, there, in front of him, stood Vivian.

"We can't go directly to Pakistan from here," Vivian said. "We need visas, and even though we're Americans, getting a visa to enter Pakistan isn't the easiest thing to do in Jerusalem."

She seemed so real. He wondered, was he really hallucinating? Was the priest fucking with him?

Jack grabbed her in his arms and asked, "Viv, are you really here?"

She stiffened, eyes wide, "Are you ok? Did you hit your head?"

Jack decided he could either accept he was crazy, or he could accept that he and Vivian were in love and on an important quest together. Either he was truly fucked or truly lucky. There would be time to be a monk—or a patient—later, if he was wrong.

Jack looked right at Vivian and asked, "Why are we going to Pakistan?"

"Popielsko said the amulet came from there and we have no other leads. It's either Harappa or go home," Vivian said.

"Really?" Jack asked.

"Are you sure you're okay?" she asked.

"I'm okay. So, why can't we fly directly to Pakistan?" he said.

"Well, a single ticket from Tel Aviv to Lahore is more than three-thousand dollars," Vivian said. "Plus, getting a visa to Pakistan from Israel is really tough, you know."

Jack asked, "Ok, so what's your idea?"

"Athens," she said. "We'll go to Athens, get visas there at the Pakistani embassy, and then fly from Athens to Lahore. The tickets will be much cheaper and the visas easier to get."

"How long will it take?" Jack asked.

Vivian paused. "We can be in Pakistan in a couple days."

Jack said nothing and walked into the bathroom. He placed his hands on the vanity and looked into the mirror. He had aged. Lines in his face he didn't remember. He thought of the people he'd already lost. He thought of Vivian. He stared into his own eyes, and said, "Take her home, Jack. Take yourself home."

"I'm not baggage," Vivian said.

Jack turned to see her in the doorway.

"I decide where I go and where I don't," she said.

Jack looked at her, hair in her face; she looked exhausted and yet was still so beautiful.

"What answers are you looking for?" Jack asked.

"I want to know too, Jack," Vivian said. "Did my dad die because of something we manifested? Was it my mother, always sure that the boat was dangerous—was it her expectations? Did I believe her and make it worse?"

"Viv, I'm sure…"

"On a larger scale, could most of the atrocities, both natural and man-made, have been avoided if we as a species could clear ourselves of negativity? Even with a funnel or focus present, could we, the rest of us, consciously change our world by achieving a certain state of collective inner peace? Is that the true secret? That meditation has always worked, perhaps not in the way we thought, but that it actually works?" Vivian asked. "The implications are staggering, but we need proof."

They heard sirens. Moving out onto the balcony, they saw it. A glow from beyond the walls of the Old City. Too large for a ceremony, for candles or torches. Clearly there was an enormous fire, and it seemed many structures must be involved.

"It's the Christian Quarter," Vivian said.

"I know," Jack said. "We've got to get out of here. Let's buy those tickets to Athens."

Ch: 43

May 31
8:30 a.m.
Airotel Parthenon
Athens, Greece

Dream

> *I'm walking into a field. A meadow filled with lupine and tall grasses. There are birds everywhere, little birds. I know that they are sparrows. Black-throated, House, Lincoln's, Savannah. Then, I'm aware that there are a large number of people behind me. I turn back to face them and they walk past me into the meadow. Arms at their sides. Not a word is spoken. Simultaneously, they all begin grabbing sparrows off the lupine and, with a twist, they are breaking their little necks. I am shouting for them to stop but they do not hear. I run from one to another, shouting. Their faces impassive. Snap. Snap. Snap. When all the birds are dead, lying all around us in the tall grasses and lupine, the people turn to face me, and all their mouths open wide. A voice, simultaneously singular and all of theirs, says, "I am I."*

Jack woke, and Vivian was over by the window, looking down into the street. "Jack, I said wake up!"

"I'm awake," Jack said. "What's up?"

"Come and look at this!"

Jack walked over to the window and looked down. Past the orange trees, several hundred meters from the hotel, there was a riot in progress. A car was burning. Police were there in riot gear, in a line, advancing slowly, with their shields up. Young people opposed them, and were hurling stones. Scattered about on the ground at their feet were dead birds.

"Shit," Jack said.

"What's going on?" Vivian asked.

Jack walked back to the bedside table, grabbed the remote and the channel guide, and flipped it to CNN International. The screen was filled with a scene much like the one outside the window.

"Greeks are protesting in response to Prime Minister Dimitrios Galanis announcing that he is temporarily suspending the Greek Constitution, claiming voting irregularities and calling for an investigation. Property has been damaged, windows broken, and cars set ablaze. At least four people were killed when protestors would not allow firefighters to respond to a fire in an office building in central Athens. This is the worst unrest here since the Greek government approved austerity measures in 2011. The latest round began at sunrise this morning in response to..."

Vivian said, "Do you think we can make it to the airport?"

"We'll have to swing by the Pakistani embassy on the way," Jack said.

A new story began on CNN, and Vivian gasped. The screen was filled with an NYPD service photo of Jack.

"...this man, he is identified as former New York detective Jack Killarney. According to a high-level U.S. government source, speaking on condition of anonymity, Killarney has recently been at the scene of several tragedies including a massacre at a refugee camp in the Democratic Republic of Congo, the collapse of the minaret in Casablanca, Morocco, and even the fire in Jerusalem's Old City which resulted in the death of several people. Killarney is not a suspect of any wrongdoing, and officials are referring to him only as a person of interest."

"We won't be able to leave now," Vivian said. "They won't let us go. Can we even make it home? What do they want with you?"

"Let's go now," Jack said. "Pack whatever you can into your backpack. Leave the rest." Jack opened his messenger bag and saw the book by Augustine. He began to pull it out, to leave it behind, and then thought better of it. Jack pushed the book back in. He grabbed a couple extra items and his passport.

"Let's go, Viv," Jack said.

"I'm with you," she said, and Jack stopped. He looked into her eyes, deep into them. Saw her strength, saw her love, and kissed her. At first, she only took his kiss, and then she kissed back. They embraced and kissed passionately, knowing only that they knew nothing about the future. Their mouths parted, they took a long moment with each other. She touched his cheek.

"I love you," Jack said.

"I know you do. I love you, too," Vivian said.

They made their way out the door, down the hall, and into the elevators. They walked across the lobby, and out the doors, without checking out. Jack signaled to a doorman who, in turn, signaled a taxi. Jack and Vivian climbed in.

"Pakistani embassy," Jack said.

"No, no. Too much trouble to go there today," the cab driver said. His head kept shaking until Jack pulled one hundred Euros out of a pocket on Vivian's bag, and thrust it forward.

Vivian said, "The Pakistani embassy, and then the airport." The driver hesitated but then took it.

The experience at the Pakistani embassy was much the same as Jack's at the GoSS offices in Nairobi. The visas were not stamps, but instead slips of paper to be inserted into their passports.

Jack slipped them into his shirt pocket. They returned to the street to find the taxi still waiting for them.

"Another fifty Euros," the driver said.

Vivian froze. "What?"

"Another fifty Euros, or no taxi to the airport."

Jack grabbed the driver by the shirt.

"Ah ah, Mr. Killarney, another fifty if you want to get there. They talk about you on the radio. No taxi will take you to the airport."

Jack didn't immediately release him.

"Jack," Vivian said. "Let him go. Now."

Jack looked back at her, released the driver, and stepped aside as she gave him another fifty.

The driver smiled. "Get in."

As the cab pulled away, the driver turned and said, "The radio said you were believed to be in Athens. It said that you have plane tickets to go to Pakistan. Any person that knows where you are is to call police."

"Did they say I was traveling with someone?" Jack asked.

"No," the driver said. "Nothing."

Jack reached into his pocket and pulled out the visas to enter Pakistan. He separated them, returning one to his pocket. Vivian watched as he tossed the other out the window.

"No!" Vivian screamed. She leapt at him.

Jack turned his back to Vivian. She was crying and slapping him, landing blows on his back.

Jack shouted, "Stop, Vivian! Stop it!"

"You bastard!" she screamed. "Don't do this!"

"That's enough!" Jack said.

"Stop this, or I put you out!" the driver shouted.

Jack turned to face her. She slapped him hard across the face, twice, before he managed to grab her wrists. She struggled for a moment more before dropping her head and sobbing.

She whispered, "You bastard."

"Viv, I have to go alone. Go back to Boston. I'll get in touch with you as soon as I can," Jack said softly.

"I want to come with you," she said, raising her eyes.

"You can't," Jack said. "Go home, I need you safe. I need to finish this."

There was a pause. Her body relaxed a bit. "Let go of me," Vivian said, her voice was cracking, but controlled.

"Viv, go back to Boston."

"Just shut up," Vivian said, her voice low. She took a deep breath, sat straight, and looked him in eyes. "I'm not going to Boston. My family has a house on Ambergris Caye. I'm going there."

"How can I reach you there?"

"Don't reach me, Jack," Vivian said.

"Vivian, I love you. You know that, don't you?"

Vivian dropped her eyes once more. "I know you're an asshole."

"I'll come for you," Jack said.

She looked up again.

The taxi arrived at the airport and pulled to a stop.

Jack said, "Don't get out with me. Go around the airport one time. Don't come looking for me."

They embraced, kissed only briefly.

Jack closed the door of the cab, it pulled away immediately, and Jack went into the airport.

Ch: 44

May 31
11:30 a.m.
Donade Industries chemical plant
The outskirts of the city
Lahore, Pakistan

Popielsko watched. The workers were cleaning pipes with water more than 500 feet away from the tank, and they assumed that safety valves were in place. However, because corners had been cut, the valves were carbon steel, and had been corroded away by acid.

Water from the cleaning rushed down the pipes, passed the ruined valves, and into a tank containing nearly fifty tons of methyl isocyanate, far exceeding the amount of MIC for which the tank was rated. A chemical reaction began and temperatures rose inside the tank. Material that should be stored just a bit above freezing was reaching 350°F and the pressure inside the tank was enormous.

The resulting gaseous eruption—about 35 tons worth—took only 30 minutes to escape and was massive. It contained MIC, phosgene, carbon dioxide, and hydrogen cyanide. The scrubbers designed to deal with such a disaster were offline and could not bring the necessary sodium hydroxide to bear.

Giant water cannons, another safety feature, surrounded the tank and, as designed, they fired. The cannons were installed to contain much of the deadly chemicals, in the event of a leak, within the deluge. However, the cannon did not have sufficient water pressure to reach above the cloud.

In the end, there was no stopping it.

Popielsko watched. He watched the cloud as it escaped and then dropped, creeping on the ground like a predator, stalking. The poisonous gases were heavier than air, and so they filled every hole, found every ditch, and cascaded down the slight incline toward the nearest neighborhood like a silent avalanche.

Inside the plant, unaware of how serious the situation was, operators did not sound the alarm for fear of causing a panic. People were coughing in their sleep before they understood that they had already died. They were the lucky ones.

Popielsko watched as people began to emerge from their homes. At first, only a few at a time, and then more and more. The sound of voices began to rise as well. Soon the streets were jammed with screaming and choking people, running, trampling each other. Many children were being dragged by one hand and, unbeknownst to their parents, many of them were already dead, since the dense gas was more toxic closer to the ground.

The watcher watched as a baby was torn from a mother's arms as she ran, and try as she might, she could not resist the current of panicked people to search for it.

Men, women, and children were left in the wake of the stampede either crushed or choking. Vomiting up destroyed lung tissue, eyes blinded, and faces covered in tears. As deadly as the gas was, it was still not nearly a quick enough death. The streets left behind by the crowd were filled with people drowning in their own fluids.

The new watcher sobbed as he watched. He wrapped his hand around the amulet, and bore witness. He watched. He watched. He watched.

IV

"O the sad day!
When friends shall shake their heads, and say
Of miserable me—
'Hark, how he groans!
Look, how he pants for breath!
See how he struggles with the pangs of death!'"

—"The Sad Day," Thomas Flatman

Ch: 45

May 31
10:30 a.m.
Main Terminal
Athens International Airport
Athens, Greece

His tickets were on Etihad Airways. Jack had never heard of the airline. Just as he joined a check-in line, a man in a tan suit approached. Jack took a step back and turned, only to see he was already surrounded by police.

"Will you come with me, please, Mr. Killarney?" the man said.

They walked a short distance to an office. The man in the suit motioned for Jack to sit as he closed the door. "My name is Kondylis. I have orders to put you on a flight."

"What are the charges?" Jack asked.

"I'm sorry?"

"What did I do?"

"There are no charges, Mr. Killarney," Kondylis said. "I have orders to get you out of Greece."

Jack paused. "I was on my way out of Greece already."

"Mr. Killarney, you cannot fly commercially."

Jack's brow furrowed. "Why not?"

"You will cause panic, of course. You are thought to be cursed.

Everywhere you go, tragedy occurs. People are terrified. You have heard the news," Kondylis said.

"The riots, I know," Jack said. "But you can't blame me…"

"In Pakistan, Mr. Killarney," Kondylis said. "No sooner had worldwide television media reported that you were believed to be heading to Lahore, a massive leak at a chemical plant there occurred. It is believed as many as nine thousand people have been killed."

Jack was immediately nauseated.

"We know you were here," Kondylis said. "We know you had nothing physically to do with it, but the coincidence is remarkable."

Jack mumbled, "There is no such thing as coincidence."

"I, too, believe this," Kondylis said. "So, I am instructed to get you out of Greece. I suggested simply to put a bullet in your head, but there are those that worry this might be like killing the albatross, so to speak."

The bullet sounded pretty good to Jack.

Kondylis said, "We can put you on a private jet to the United States immediately."

"To Lahore, I want to go to Lahore," Jack said.

"I doubt very much that the Pakistani government would look favorably on that."

Jack felt anger welling up within him. "Take me to Lahore. Smuggle me in, I don't care, but get me there. Or else I'll give Greece a coincidence you won't soon forget."

"Are you threatening me, Mr. Killarney?"

"I'm trying to help you," Jack said. "Put me on a private jet to Lahore, give me a new passport, and get me out to the site of the chemical leak. I'll never return to Greece again, I promise."

"Oh, I promise you, if you ever so much as buy another ticket to Greece, you will be dead before you reach our shores."

Nine thousand dead, Jack thought. Worldwide media had created the expectation in millions that catastrophe would come to Lahore, based only on his travel plans. He had focused that evil. According to the priest, Jack was doing the exact opposite of what he should. Instead of retreating to a mountain cave and living out a life imagining unicorns and rainbows, he was still pursuing evil. He did not trust the use of passivity against such an active foe. He only knew how to meet action with action, and to confront, not to ignore.

"I will pass on your request," Kondylis said. "Can I ask why you want to go to Lahore so badly? It is not the safest place to be."

"Fate," Jack said, but regretted it.

"Very well, I will see," Kondylis said. He rose and left Jack alone in the office. Jack lay his head on the desk, and when he lifted it, sitting in the seat Kondylis had just occupied was Cormac.

"Oh, no," Jack said.

"Maybe you should just go home, Jack," Cormac said.

"I imagined you, too?"

"Is that a nice thing to say?" Cormac asked. "Without me, I should think you'd still be stuck in Juba."

Jack closed his eyes, rubbed them, and reopened them. Cormac was gone.

Alone once more, Jack said aloud to himself, "You don't have a lot of time. You're losing it. Gotta hurry."

Ch: 46

May 31
11:00 p.m.
Lahore, Pakistan

Sitting in the back of a van from the Greek consulate in Lahore, Jack read his newly-minted credentials in the poor light.

"Stephanos Bezzerides," Jack said. "Jesus, I'm not even sure I'm pronouncing it correctly."

The driver said, "Not bad, but if they start speaking to you in Greek, you will be in trouble. Remember, you are a chemical engineer joining a team we already have in place."

"Where will I meet the team?" Jack asked.

The driver sniffed, and said, "There is no team, Mr. Bezzerides."

Jack paused, and said, "If they ask me about chemicals, I'll be just as fucked as if they start speaking to me in Greek."

The driver said nothing.

As they approached the suburb—a slum, really—Jack could see emergency flood lights erected on a forest of poles.

"We are arriving," the driver said. "Put your documents away. Pick up your mask. I will stop, you will get out, I will never see you again."

The van stopped abruptly and, as soon as Jack had closed the door behind him, it sped away. He stood at the edge of the light, in a chemical suit, clutching a mask and a gym bag, feeling utterly stupid. Inside the bag was his messenger bag and his papers. He could see people milling about, also in chemical suits, some with clipboards, but no masks in sight.

Many of the roofs were tin, with no more than canvas for walls. It was a neighborhood of what, in essence, were merely tents. There would have been no hiding from a chemical leak. Beside one dwelling, there was a truck, rusting and without windows. Oddly, a full-sized pool table sat out in the open next to it. There was trash everywhere, a carpet of scraps of paper and other waste.

There were also the scattered carcasses of birds. Every couple of feet, there was another muddy and feathered clump. The entire illuminated area was covered in dead birds. A couple men had begun collecting them with shovels, dumping them into plastic hazmat bags. However, there were no human bodies.

"*Tum.*"

Jack turned. A man in a chemical suit was walking past. He motioned for Jack to follow and said, "*Mere saath aaiye.*"

It was clear the man wanted Jack to follow, but if there was going to be some sort of confrontation, Jack would rather it happen here on the edge of the illuminated area and not deep inside it. The man stopped, looked at Jack for a moment, and then approached. Jack pulled out his papers and handed them to the man.

The man read, grunted, and then asked, "You speak English?"

Jack sighed with relief. "Yes."

"Good, I speak no Greek. You can join us here, where we have set up, and we will try to locate your team."

"Where are the bodies?" Jack asked.

The man frowned. "They have been moved to a field on the west side."

"I want to see," Jack said and held his breath.

The man handed Jack his papers back and pointed west. "You have only to walk to those fires."

"Fires?" Jack asked.

"They are burning the bodies. The pyres. At least until they run out of fuel to burn them."

Jack looked off toward the horizon and could see a glow in the distance. Those were pyres. It looked medieval. When he turned back, the man had already walked away. Jack walked toward the fires. Another man, also in a chemical suit, this one wearing a mask, dragged the body of a woman out of a home. He laid her in the mud, and scurried back into the tent. Her dead eyes stared up at Jack. Her mouth was open. He waited for a moment, expecting to hear the voice, expecting to hear, "I am I," but he heard nothing.

Jack looked around; no one was watching him but her. He stepped over her, straddling her momentarily, and continued on toward the fires. He did not care that she could see him, with her dead eyes, while he could not see her. He went on, he felt compelled to walk on.

When he arrived at the field, the only light was the glow of the pyres; there were more than a dozen of them. Huge blazing piles of wood and flesh. He dropped his mask and bag and stood in horrified awe. The light lit the roiling smoke from below, before it rose and disappeared into the dark. Bodies were lined up, lying side by side, in grisly queues before the pyres. Jack stood in the middle of it all.

In the distance, near the pyres furthest to the left, men were tossing bodies into the bucket of a front-end loader, loading another batch to dump into the fire. Jack looked at the bodies closest to him. An old man and a child. Their mouths were bloodstained. The light from the fires climbed and fell on the sides of their faces. The wind shifted, and the smell was intensified. The smell. The smell of burning meat and rendering fat. The sickly-sweet perfume of evaporating spinal fluid, eyes, and brain. The metallic, coppery smell of boiling blood. The stink of crisping skin. The sulfurous stench of burning hair. The smell of Beth dying.

Jack was nauseated, and he was also mesmerized. All this way he had come, and still just more death. Theories. Philosophy. Religion. Insanity. Jack fell to one knee, and wretched.

"Come now, what did you expect?"

Jack looked up into Cormac O'Brien's face. Jack's mouth fell slack.

"What did you expect?" he repeated. "You have chased evil around the world and you have found it, haven't you? But you know already, the priest told you. It is *you*, Jack. You are the evil you have been chasing."

There was a soft thud a few feet behind him. A bird, unseen and flying in the dark a moment before, had fallen dead.

Jack stood, and said, "No."

"You, Jack, you are responsible."

"No." Jack's voice was hardly audible.

The shape that was Cormac shifted, transforming itself into Father Popielsko, wearing a long black coat. "If you had listened to me, none of this would have happened."

"Who *are* you?" Jack asked.

Another bird fell with a soft thud.

The shape shifted again, this time into Ben's form. "Don't you know me, Jack-buddy?" The bullet hole in his temple looked fresh; it did not move as the figure changed into Keenan. Same hole, different face.

Jack turned his face slightly, but never took his eyes off the figure before him.

"All your fault, Jack," the Keenan-figure said. "You killed Ben for Deb, you killed me and the kids for Carol. Just conquests, Jack? You killed us just to fuck our wives?"

"That's not true," Jack said.

The shape shifted into Dr. Havel, "A clear cut case. A classic sociopath."

Two more birds fell. Thud, thud. They landed already dead, perfectly still.

The shape shifted into the girl from the culvert; the body he'd found as a child.

"You didn't find me," the girl-figure said. "You put me there. I was your first."

Jack said, "It's not true."

The girl-shape begin to shift, and Jack recognized the new form long before it was done changing.

"No," Jack said. "Please no."

Beth took shape before him. "Why Jack? You could have rescued me. You sat and watched me die. You did nothing. Why? So, you could have Deb?"

"No, Beth, no, not you, don't say that," Jack said. Tears streamed from his eyes, and Jack fell forward, clawing his fingers into the dirt.

The figure shifted again. This time, it took the form of Vivian.

"You even killed me, Jack. Even me, before you left."

Jack screamed at the soil, "No! Stop! Enough!" Had it been him all along? Had he killed all those people himself? Was he just a psychopath, hiding his sins from himself all this time?

Suddenly there was a shout from behind Jack. "Jack, do not listen to it! Do not listen!"

Jack looked up, and saw Popielsko running toward them. "Do not listen!"

The Vivian-shape swiftly changed into the form of an unknown man, beautiful and powerful. His eyes were entirely white, reflecting the glow of the fires. He wore simple cloth, natural. He raised one hand, and the priest first collided with an unseen force and then was thrown back a dozen feet. Popielsko lay, dazed, on his back.

Another bird fell dead, and then another.

Jack barely heard Popielsko say, "Do not listen to it."

The voice was different this time, directed at Popielsko, echoing within the figure's throat. "You are the witness. You cannot interfere."

"Interfere with what?" Jack asked.

Popielsko rose and, slowly, approached them both. His face now placid.

The figure looked at Jack, and said, "With your work. With that which you have wrought here."

"Who are you?" Jack asked again.

"Throughout the millennia, I have been known by many names."

"Lucifer?" Jack asked. "The fallen angel?"

The figure smiled. "No. I am what you see only because you have manifested me as such, just as you have manifested all this."

"I didn't do this."

The figure said, "Millions of people came to believe that you brought evil with you wherever you went. Once they expected this, and it was reported that you had plans to come here next, millions of people were convinced evil would befall this place. You directed evil here, with your will. With your pride. I must say, you have exceeded the others. The others like you, who still live, even began to channel the evil you channeled, causing a doubling and redoubling. What you see around you is the manifestation of the belief of millions, a belief in your wickedness, based upon your actions, intensified by your pride, willfulness, and self-importance. Bravo, bravo."

"I can't take the blame for this, for all of them," Jack said. "Please Jesus, please no."

The figure shifted again, this time assuming the standard Euro-Caucasian version of Jesus Christ. The version Jack had seen in paintings and statues throughout his childhood. "It is a bit late for that. It is entirely your fault, and you will go on spreading evil, wherever you go. Mankind will know you as the bringer of death.'"

"I can't be responsible for all this," Jack said. "I can't bear it." Jack began to rock himself, his fingers digging into his legs. "I can't live with this."

"You should have stopped in Kenya, when I told you to," the actual Popielsko, dressed now as the Watcher, said.

Jack looked at him, and hated him. "Is this it, priest?" Standing, straightening, and extending his arms, Jack pointed all around them. "Is this it? The extent of God's love?" Jack's mouth was sour with the taste of vomit, his nose filled with the odor of burning flesh.

Popielsko said nothing.

"Is this the act of a merciful and forgiving God?" Jack asked.

"Vengeful, as well," Popielsko said.

"Vengeful? *Vengeful*? Look at that kid right there! That old man behind you! Young girls clutching each other! Vengeful? What did these people do that any god would need inflict such terrible vengeance?"

Popielsko still said nothing, and the figure grinned.

Jack continued, "Drop a building on innocent people? Attack refugees? Children suffocated in plastic bags? This god of yours, Popielsko, is a monster! Beth? She had never hurt a soul in her whole life! And he didn't just kill her, he burned her alive! Slowly! Little kids hung up to die by their father? Your god is psychotic! You know that, priest?"

Popielsko's expression did not change. The figure clasped his hands together.

"You know what?" Jack was still screaming. "Your god doesn't have the right! He doesn't! For thousands of years, people have been worshiping him in one manner or another and this is what they get? He doesn't have the fucking right! He's not worthy of us! Who does he think he is?"

Then there was a sound. A sound like Jack had never heard. A rumble, a moan. It vibrated from the ground, up through his legs. He was driven to his knees. Popielsko bowed his head and genuflected, down on one knee. The figure looked in all directions. The sound grew louder; the vibration ran to Jack's gut. He vomited again and then urinated. The moan became a roar, Jack held his ears, and the pain was exquisite. He could not even hear his own screaming. And then… silence.

Jack looked up. The figure shrieked and exploded into a flock of blackbirds. The swirling flock whirled like an avian tornado around Jack, tearing at his face and clothes. He swung madly at them, he felt hot blood on his face, and all at once, they flew en masse into the nearest pyre and were gone. Blood covered Jack's face and hands.

Suddenly, every body of every single victim, as far as the eye could see, all of the dead, sat up in unison. Every face turned to Jack. Every mouth opened, the lips moved, and a thousand echoing and thunderous voices said the words, "**I am I.**"

Jack clutched his ears once more; the sound was so ferocious.

"**I am I. I have always been and always will be.**"

Jack screamed in the direction of the ground. "Are you God? Then why? Why all this? Why Beth and Ben and Keenan? Why?"

Popielsko fell prostrate. An unseen force hit Jack in the back of the head, and he was driven onto his face. He began to sob. Not tears of frustration or pain, but of guilt. He wept. He wept from, and within, his innermost spaces. His mind fought to stay in a single piece.

Popielsko said, "He does not answer to you."

"**These events come from the hearts of men. Not from any single man or woman, but from mankind.**"

Jack lay on his side. Each syllable from the voice was like having a heavy stone dropped on his head. He was sobbing. He was broken. He had nothing left. "What would you have me do?"

"**I have given you the answer. You carry it even now. Follow the message of Augustine of Hippo.**"

Jack was becoming weak. "I don't know, I don't know what to do."

Popielsko said, "Pray. Augustine said, 'Do what you can and then pray that God will give you the power and the grace to do what you alone cannot.'"

"But pray how? What are the right words?" Jack asked.

"It does not matter. Prayer is no more than finding peace. You may pray in any form or forms you wish, or you may simply take the time to be conscious of your space, your thoughts, your presence. Prayer is not begging, nor is it thanking, nor even giving praise. True prayer is a simple and deliberate effort to find inner peace. Turn your back on evil; do as my messengers have told you. Turn your back on evil, be humble, and show no further interest."

Popielsko said, "Pray, live a good life, and forget about your quest for evil."

Jack said, "I will. I turn my back on it. I will close my mind to it." Jack felt consciousness slipping away.

Ch: 47

August 4
2:00 p.m.
Winter Harbor Hospital
Westbrook, Maine

Dream

The car is on its roof. Beth is screaming inside. The flames are licking up the sides of the door. I can hear her screaming. My hands are burning. Her screams stop. I can't lift the car. My skin is sticking, and coming off on the hot metal.

"Jack."

I turn. It's Beth. She's standing up on the bank. Away from the flames. Beautiful. Unharmed. In her favorite sundress, barefoot in the snow. Smiling.

"Jack, it's alright, honey. Come away from there," she says.

My mouth hangs open. I walk up the bank to her. She reaches out to me. I try to embrace her but she disappears. The car explodes violently behind me. I fall forward into the snow. My badly burned hands are in the snow. I'm crying.

"Jack. It's alright. I'm alright."

She has reappeared and is standing a few feet away.

I say, "I tried, Beth. I tried."
"Shhh," she says. "I know. I'm alright now. Go on..."

* * *

Jack sat straight up, awake. Looking around, he saw a strange couch, coffee table, and wooden floor. It was warm. He worked to remember where he was, but he couldn't.

"Do you know who I am?"

Jack looked up, and saw a nurse's face. He read her name tag and nodded. Jack rubbed his face. He could feel the scars, but no pain. He swung his legs over the edge of the bed. With his elbows on his knees, he fought to focus.

"Here, take your meds," the nurse said, handing him a small plastic cup.

Jack's vision cleared as he remembered. He looked around, and looked out his door into the hallway. "I'm at Winter Harbor."

"Take the pills," she said.

Jack took the medication, and washed it down with a cup of water.

"Dr. Havel will be in to see you later today," she said.

"Can I see Carol?" Jack asked.

The nurse took both cups back. "Let me check and see if Carol wants to see you today."

Looking around the room, Jack searched for additional clues. His healing scars matched injuries he vaguely remembered. Had he been there, in Pakistan? Jack decided that he had, but that he would be cautious with what he claimed to know or remember. The nurse returned to the room.

"Come on, she's in the common room."

Jack rose and walked down the same hallway that he had a month before. He entered the same common room. There was Carol. She nodded to the nurse, who left them alone.

"Sit, okay, Jack?" Carol asked.

Jack did. She seemed nervous.

"I'm a bit foggy, Carol. How long have I been here?" Jack asked.

Carol tilted her head. "A month or so."

"Where did I come from?" Jack asked.

"They said you transferred from another hospital," Carol said. "From a hospital far away; they sent you here. And that you weren't traveling under your name any more, that you were calling yourself 'Steve' or something."

Someone cleared her throat behind him, and when Jack looked back the nurse had returned, and was giving Carol a stern look.

"We're okay," Jack said.

The nurse left. Carol moved back a bit.

"It's okay, I'm just relieved that my memories are matching up," Jack said.

"Oh, yeah, I know what that's like," Carol said. "They said you might not remember. I know that my memories of Keenan don't match up with what happened. Sometimes I'm not sure what happened, and what didn't happen either."

"So, why am I in a mental hospital and not just a regular hospital?"

"God," Carol said.

"What?"

"You said you believed God spoke to you. You wouldn't stop saying that," Carol said. "Do you still believe God spoke to you?"

Jack wasn't sure what to do. Then he remembered the voice. Was that really God? If so, do you deny that God spoke to you, if you believe it? Wouldn't that be denying God? Or do you play it cool?

"Did God talk to you, Jack?" Carol asked.

"No," Jack said. "Just praying, that's all."

"You were praying?" Carol said.

"That's right," Jack said. "That's all."

Carol looked past Jack, and asked, "Are you still crazy, Jack?"

Jack paused, and then asked, "Compared to what?"

"You agreed to ECT," Carol said. "You were worried that you were crazy."

"ECT?" Jack asked.

"Shock therapy," Carol said. "They warned me that you might have some short-term memory loss."

"Why would I do that?" Jack asked.

"It's supposed to give you peace. It sort of erases your old personality, when your old personality gets bogged down or stuck in its illness. You kept saying God had talked to you and that the Devil had chosen you and you couldn't stop worrying about it. So, they suggested ECT and you agreed to it, signed the papers," Carol said. "I was worried you wouldn't remember me."

Jack tried to remember the last month. He would catch glimpses of memories—of the Sudan, Morocco, Greece, and Pakistan—as if from a movie he had watched, but not clear memories. Almost as if it all had been a movie, playing on a neighbor's television, that he had seen through the windows.

Jack said, "I'm fine now. I think it's going to all be okay, Carol."

"Excuse me."

Jack and Carol looked toward the door. Dr. Havel stood there, with the nurse.

"Let's talk for a while, Jack," Havel said.

Jack looked at Carol, who placed her hand on his knee and nodded that he should go. He got up and joined Havel, and together they walked down to a small office.

* * *

Jack sat on a burnt-orange chair facing Havel, who sat in a typical swivel chair.

"Do you remember who I am?" Havel asked.

"You're Dr. Havel," Jack said.

"What else do you remember?" Havel asked.

"It's really disjointed. I remember scenes from Africa, but I'm not sure they're all in the right order," Jack said. It wasn't distressing. Jack could feel the familiar cocoon of medication knocking the edges off.

"What else? Where else do you remember going?" Havel asked, making a quick note.

Jack forced his way through the mental fog. "I remember the tower falling in Morocco, and walking in Jerusalem. I remember sending Vivian home from Greece, and I remember Pakistan." Jack was careful not to mention the figure at the disaster site in Lahore, or the voice. 'I am I.'

"Okay, Jack, try now. Think. You didn't send Professor Rueil home from Greece," Havel said.

"I didn't?"

"You didn't."

"So, when did she come back home?" Jack asked.

With a patient tone, Havel said, "Professor Vivian Rueil never left the United States."

The memory of the priest telling him that in Jerusalem came snapping back. She had never been with him. She had never called him, nor emailed him.

"So, I didn't send her home before I went to Pakistan," Jack said, stating it for himself to hear.

Havel leaned forward, and with a soft voice said, "Jack, you were never in Pakistan."

The words had zero impact. They whooshed right past Jack's ears. He blinked.

"You were never in Pakistan," Havel repeated.

All those people? The fires? The figure? The voice? "That's not possible," Jack said. "I clearly remember it."

"You came directly here from Greece, Jack. The Greek authorities in Athens put you on a plane to Boston, and you were brought home to Maine, to here," Havel said.

"It's not possible," Jack said. Was it possible? The meds were keeping him steady and talking, but he fought to focus. "I was there. The figure and the voice, the voice of God."

"Think. Think, Jack," Havel said. "Are those memories the same as the memories of Morocco? The same minute by minute detail?"

"A lot of the details are missing, from all of it," Jack said. He began rubbing his temples.

"I know. I know it's hard. We agreed, you and I, to have you try the ECT to see if, by a fresh approach to those memories, you could sort the real from the unreal," Havel said.

"The Greeks made me a fake passport," Jack said.

"That never happened," Havel said.

"They flew me to Lahore," Jack said.

"You never went. You were flown to Boston from Athens," Havel said.

"I was there, in Pakistan. I saw the horrors of the chemical leak," Jack said.

Havel leaned back in his chair, and said nothing for a moment. Then, he pulled his laptop over and opened it. He wheeled his chair over to Jack's. He laid the laptop on the arm of Jack's chair, brought up Google, and typed in "Lahore chemical leak" and hit enter.

The most recent search result was a news story from years before, when a small sulfur dioxide leak in a warehouse caused a fairly insignificant fire. There were no resultant deaths.

The room began to spin.

"It's okay, Jack, we've been here before. It's okay. You're okay. We're in Maine, and you're safe. You did go to Africa. You were in Israel and Greece. But you never went to Pakistan," Havel said. He closed his laptop and moved it away from Jack.

Jack said, "That was all in my head?"

"In a way."

"What am I? Schizophrenic?" Jack asked.

"It's called confabulation. Fabricated memories, created to fill a gap," Havel said.

"It was all a lie?" Jack asked.

"Not quite. It's different. There was no intent to deceive. You had no idea the information was false," Havel said.

"But the memories seem so real. As we talk, they are actually becoming clearer," Jack said. "How could invented memories seem so real?"

"Because your brain can't tell the difference," Havel said. "But you're going to have to convince yourself that all of the memories of Pakistan are a fabrication. It didn't happen, Jack."

"And Vivian wasn't with me?"

"Vivian was never with you," Havel said.

Jack sat back. The memories of Pakistan were false, and so were the memories of Vivian. He wondered if he could pick and choose which to keep.

Ch: 48

Years later
11:00 p.m.
Along the Allagash River
Aroostook County, Maine

The wind howled outside the small cabin. Within a few short weeks, the road would be closed and the only access would be by snowmobile.

Firewood inside the stove settled as it burned. The cabin was simple and easy to heat. The logs were old, but the chinking was good. Scattered around the cabin were maps, and half-finished paintings and drawings of birds.

Jack lay in bed and read, by the light of a hurricane lamp, from the volume by Augustine. "If we live good lives, the times are also good. As we are, such are the times."

Jack reread the words, and then closed the book. He rolled over, and lay the book on the floor beside the bed. There, lying on top of some laundry, was another book.

The cover read, *Quixotic Quests: Evil and the People Who Go in Search of It* by Vivian Rueil. It had hit bookstore shelves only the week before.

He turned down the lamp to a tiny flame, and said, "Times are good."

ACKNOWLEDGMENTS:

Anderson, Kent. *Sympathy for the Devil.* Doubleday, 1987.

Baumeister, R. F. *Evil: Inside Human Violence and Cruelty.* Henry Holt and Company, 1999.

THANKS TO:

Nylah Lyman for all her advice and support. You've perhaps had the most hope for this novel.

Jamie Carpenter who has consistently been the first to read my novels as I completed them, and provided a great deal of encouragement.

Michael Kimball, James Patrick Kelly, Richard Hoffman, Suzanne Strempek Shea—all mentors and friends.

To the entire Encircle Publications team. You've taken what I've always loved most to do and made it even more fun.

Matt Bowe and Taryn Brant Bowe for their help getting me into and out of a psychiatric hospital, and Cormac Tiernan for helping me to navigate through Kenya, South Sudan, the DR Congo, and Uganda.

Olivia Bradley, a wonderful and helpful reader of several drafts of this novel, and Karen Bailey who asked all the right questions and provided very useful feedback and advice.

Lauren Stetson Dezileau, whose feedback has always been so honest and helpful, and Will Ludwigsen for showing me that Baptism can be prologue.

Profs. Cynthia Brewer and Matthew Edney for their help in getting me around angles and great circles. Any errors here are mine, despite their best efforts.

ABOUT THE AUTHOR

Kevin St. Jarre is also the author of *Aliens, Drywall, and a Unicycle*, *Celestine*, and *The Twin*, each published by Encircle Publications. He previously penned three original thriller novels for Berkley Books, the Night Stalkers series, under a pseudonym. He's a published poet, his pedagogical essays have run in *English Journal* and thrice in *Phi Delta Kappan*, and his short fiction has appeared in journals such as *Story*.

Kevin has worked as a teacher and professor, a newspaper reporter, an international corporate consultant, and he led a combat intelligence team in the first Gulf War. Kevin is a polyglot, and he earned an MFA in Creative Writing with a concentration in Popular Fiction from University of Southern Maine's Stonecoast program. Twice awarded scholarships, he studied at the Norman Mailer Writers Center on Cape Cod,

Massachusetts, with Sigrid Nunez and David Black, and wrote in southern France at La Muse Artists & Writers Retreat.

He is a member of Maine Writers & Publishers Alliance, and International Thriller Writers. Born in Pittsfield, Massachusetts, Kevin grew up in Maine's northernmost town, Madawaska. He now lives on the Maine coast, and is always working on the next novel. Follow Kevin at www.facebook.com/kstjarre and on Twitter @kstjarre.

If you enjoyed reading this book,
please consider writing your honest review
and sharing it with other readers.

Many of our Authors are happy to participate in
Book Club and Reader Group discussions.
For more information, contact us at info@encirclepub.com.

Thank you,
Encircle Publications

For news about more exciting new fiction, join us at:

Facebook: www.facebook.com/encirclepub

Instagram: www.instagram.com/encirclepublications

Twitter: twitter.com/encirclepub

Sign up for Encircle Publications newsletter and specials:

eepurl.com/cs8taP

CPSIA information can be obtained
at www.ICGtesting.com
Printed in the USA
LVHW021835280322
714614LV00004B/52